THE BISHOP OF HELL
and Other Stories

THE BISHOP
OF HELL

and Other Stories

Marjorie Bowen

with an Introduction by
HILARY LONG

WORDSWORTH EDITIONS

In loving memory of
MICHAEL TRAYLER
the founder of Wordsworth Editions

2

Readers who are interested in other titles from
Wordsworth Editions are invited to visit our website at
www.wordsworth-editions.com

For our latest list and a full mail-order service contact
Bibliophile Books, 5 Thomas Road, London E14 7BN
Tel: +44 0207 515 9222 Fax: +44 0207 538 4115
e-mail: orders@bibliophilebooks.com

This edition published 2006 by
Wordsworth Editions Limited
8B East Street, Ware, Hertfordshire SG12 9HJ

ISBN 978-1-84022-537-2

Typeset in Great Britain by Antony Gray
Printed by Clays Ltd, St Ives plc

CONTENTS

INTRODUCTION

Reader, do you welcome an occasional escape from the harsh 'here and now'? The stories in this book will help you.

London today is certainly more magnificent than it used to be. But many of its more humble attractions have gone. Nowadays those alleyways that housed second-hand booksellers who displayed their lesser wares at bargain prices on tables set out in front of their shops are very few indeed. Charing Cross Road, for instance, was a treasure-trove for the casual browser. In 1970, as one such browser, I unearthed a small book, battered, torn, dusty but still readable. It was called *Curious Happenings*. Published in the war year of 1917, the quality of the production was poor although I knew the stories themselves to be excellent. I bought it on the spot.

The author was Marjorie Bowen. She was already well-known as a distinguished historical novelist but this was her first experiment in Tales of Terror. She went on to write many other such tales and proved herself a master of the macabre. The present volume contains a selection of some of these tales. They are short stories of rare quality. Every one is good entertainment. They defy the probing of the cynic and the cool judgment of the rationalist. They are brightly kindled by some ancient anecdote, some ruined building, a deserted landscape, a gathering of storm clouds, waterless fountains, ravaged forests, empty palaces, closed mansions, unvisited graves. They represent a desire to record the fearsome, the forbidding and the perplexing.

These narratives may remind the reader of the Gothic revival writings which chilled the blood of the British public over two hundred years ago with such classics as Walpole's *Castle of Otranto* and the tales of Ann Radcliffe. Those horrific tales were a little crude in their construction and bald in their effects. They achieved excitement by the plentiful use of the Devil in person. Marjorie Bowen's efforts in this genre strive to enthral by the use of simpler materials and to weave tales of terror and mystery out of the common-places of everyday life without the too-easy expedient of relying on the supernatural to explain everything. The author of these stories has always been most notable for her gift of description and creating atmosphere.

Here is a quotation from a private letter:

> I was born a storyteller and self-educated. Neither of these facts was conducive to clear thinking. All that I read and heard I turned instinctively into narrative, suffused with a romantic temperament and coloured by dreams and sentiment.

M.B. 1940

Perhaps the publication of this volume may do a little to restore to favour the peculiar species of romantic horror which distinguish the true Tales of Terror.

Marjorie Bowen was one of the several pen-names of Gabrielle Campbell. She also wrote under the names of George R. Preedy, Joseph Shearing, John Winch and Robert Paye. Besides being an author of repute, she was a delightful woman and, as a mother, superb. She was strikingly good-looking (there are photographs to prove it).

Unaided – by her own efforts – she maintained her entire family and brought up three sons of whom I am the youngest. I loved my mother. To me she was everything enchanting. I owe all I have to her and I like to feel that she is as near to me now as she ever was.

Finally, I must make my exit (if you have got this far) with a personal statement. I am an engineer by trade. I consider myself a worldly-wise, knockabout, matter-of-fact sort of man. I have used my hands to earn my living all my life.

I am a realist, and formal religion has little appeal to me. I fly willingly to a box of spanners or an oilcan, but a pen alarms me. Even writing this little preface has deflated my tyres a bit.

I inherited absolutely none of mother's talent for writing (Reader, you guessed?) and my knowledge of literature is slender to vanishing point. However, I hasten to put on record that I have no time for ghosts. There are no such things as ghosts. They do not exist! There are not many certainties in life, but this is one of them! Believe me.

Ghosts can be brilliantly evoked on the printed page; old men tell convincing stories about them by the fireside when the wine is flowing; children see them in their fantasies, but in real life – Nothing!

Ages ago, Sam Butler got it right:

> Some have mistaken blocks and posts,
> for spectres, apparitions, ghosts,
> with saucer-eyes and horns, and some
> have heard the Devil beat a drum.

I conclude writing these lines in a large isolated country house. I am staying here for a few days to do some repair work for the owner now on holiday. It is nearly midnight and I am alone. The electricity has been cut off by a fierce local storm. There is no living soul within three miles. I am struggling on by the uncertain light of an oil lamp. I pause in my work and am abruptly struck by the almost tangible sensation of total dead silence. It seems as if I am surrounded by a curtain of thick velvet. A rapidly swelling wave of fear mounts within me as I sense some indefinable presence.

To steady my nerves, I try to call out 'there are no such things as ghosts' but my usually strong voice is now little more than a low whistle. Yet it must have been loud enough to have been heard. For, first, I feel a gentle pressure on my shoulder. Then – close to my ear – a sigh like a cry of pain. Finally, in a whisper as soft and hissing as a snake about to strike, comes the reply: 'How do you know?'

May God – who plants his footsteps in the sea and rides the storm – have mercy on us unbelievers!

> Light thickens, and the crow
> Makes wing to the rooky wood;
> Good things of day begin to droop and drowse,
> While night's black agents to their prey do rouse.

God have mercy on us all!

HILARY LONG
Richmond, Surrey

BIOGRAPHICAL NOTE
Marjorie Bowen (1885-1952)

Margaret Gabrielle Vere Campbell Long was best known as Marjorie Bowen, but also wrote under the names of Joseph Shearing, George R. Preedy, Robert Paye, and John Winch. She may also have written under the names Evelyn Winch, E. M. Winch, and Bertha Winch. Born on the 1st November 1885 at Hayling Island, Hampshire, Long was the daughter of Vere Douglas Campbell and his wife Josephine Elizabeth Ellis Bowen Campbell. Her parents separated when she was quite young, and she lived with her mother, her sister, and a servant-nurse who was fiercely loyal to her mother.

Her autobiography, *The Debate Continues, Being the Autobiography of Marjorie Bowen*, records the difficulties she experienced in her early life because of the poverty of her family and the bohemian lifestyle of her mother, an aspiring writer whose friends were hangers-on in the theatrical world. The family's existence was nomadic, with frequent moves made to avoid paying bills. Her mother's temperament was also volatile, adding to the instability of the home environment. Long received no formal education but was taught to read and write by her mother. She taught herself to read French, Italian, and a bit of Latin. Her first novel, *The Viper of Milan*, was published in 1906, when she was just 21, and she quickly became provider for her profligate family, who remained needy yet ungrateful.

In 1912 she married Zefferino Emilio Costanzo, a Sicilian living in England. However, their first child died in infancy and her husband's health deteriorated. She left their second child in England in the care of her nurse to follow her husband to Italy and tend to his needs. With little help, little money, and at times no food, her situation became desperate. The local doctor refused to help her dying husband for fear of contagion, and when another doctor took up residence in a neighbouring villa and called on the sick man, Long fell passionately in love with him.

After her husband's death in 1916, she returned to England to care for her child. She and the doctor had planned for a future together, but he became paralysed while she was gone. He ordered her not to return, and urged her to marry again. She soon met and married Arthur L. Long, finding with him the domestic tranquillity she needed. She and her second husband had two sons.

When her mother died, her sister left and her parasitic family relationships were severed. Long continued to write until she died of a cerebral haemorrhage from a fall at her home in Kensington in 1952.

Long receives little note today. Yet she should be an important figure for those studying popular fiction and gender issues in the first half of the twentieth century. Her autobiography shows how her mother's status as a woman living apart from her husband tainted mother and child, and how constant comparison with her attractive sister caused her to withdraw inward. Her fiction often features women whose options are limited, or forceful women who flout conventional *mores*.

Her prodigious literary output testifies to her determination, her intelligence, and her creative energy.

PERSONAL NOTE

I wish to express my gratitude to Sharon Eden for gathering together the Marjorie Bowen archive. Her unfailing efforts in every aspect of this demanding work have been given over a period of years and had to be fitted in with her own busy life. I do not forget my debt to Max Eden who has helped in so many ways that they defy description.

HILARY LONG

Publisher's note

We are grateful to Hilary Long for granting us permission to use this material.

THE BISHOP OF HELL
and Other Stories

The Fair Hair of Ambrosine

Claude Boucher found himself awaiting with increasing dread the approach of the 12th of December.

He still called it December to himself; the new names of the divisions of the years of liberty had never taken root in his heart, which remained faithful to many of the old traditions.

Yet he was a good servant of the new Republic and had so far escaped peril during perilous times without sinking into servile insignificance. He was a clerk in the Chamber of Deputies, well paid and unmolested. From the safe vantage of a dignified obscurity he watched greater men come and go; and ate his supper and smoked his pipe in peace while the death-carts went to and from the prisons and the Place de la Revolution – which Boucher, in his mind, thought of as the Place du Louis XVI.

He had his ambitions, but he held them suspended till safer times: he was not the man for a brilliant, fiery career ending in the guillotine; he was not, either, pessimistic; a better epoch, he would declare, would certainly emerge from the present confusion (he refused to accept it as anything else), which could but be regarded as the birth-throes of a settled state.

Therefore, being young and calm and having lost nothing by the upheaval of society, he waited, as he felt he could afford to wait, until the order of things was once more stable and established. The horrors that had washed, like a sea of filth and blood, round his safety, had scarcely touched him; this terror he felt at looking forward to the 12th of December was the first fear that he had ever known.

A fear unreasonable and by no means to be explained.

The first and main cause of his dread was a trifle, an affair so slight that when he had first heard of it he had put it from his mind as a thing of no importance.

One of the Deputies of Lille had put his finger on a conspiracy in the Department of Béarn, involving several names that had hitherto passed as those of good friends of the Republic. The

matter did not loom large, but required some delicacy in the hand-
ling. The Deputy for the Department concerned was away; no steps
were to be taken until his return, which would be on the 12th of
December; then Boucher, as a man reliable and trustworthy, was
to carry all papers relating to the alleged conspiracy to his house
at Saint-Cloud.

At first the young clerk had thought nothing of this; then he had
been rather pleased at the slight importance the mission gave him.

That night, over his supper in the little café in the Rue Saint-
Germains, he began to think of Ambrosine, who had long been a
forbidden memory.

She was a little actress in a light theatre that existed during the days
of the Terror like a poisonous flower blooming on corruption.

She had lived in a little house on the way to Saint-Cloud, a house
on the banks of the river, an innocent and modest-looking place to
shelter Ambrosine, who was neither innocent nor modest.

Claude Boucher had loved her; and every night she had finished
her part in the wild and indecent performance, he would drive her
home in a little yellow cabriolet which had once belonged to a lady of
fashion.

They had been quite happy; she was certainly fond of Claude
and, he believed, faithful to him; he had rivals, and it flattered him
to take her away from these and make her completely his, almost
subservient to him; she was only a child of the gutters of Saint-
Antoine, but she was graceful and charming, and endearing too
in her simplicity and ardour, which she preserved despite her mani-
fold deceits and vices.

She was not beautiful, but she had dark blue eyes and kept her skin
lily pale, and her hair was wonderful, and untouched by bleach or
powder; fair and thick and uncurling, yet full with a natural ripple,
she kept it piled carelessly high with such fantastic combs as she
could afford, and from these it fell continuously on to her thin
bosom and slanting shoulders.

Claude, sitting in his café, remembered this fair hair, and how it
would fly about her when she ran from the stage, flushed, panting,
half naked from the dance by which she had amused men inflamed
with blood.

He thought: 'To take those papers I shall have to pass the house
where she lived . . . '

He checked himself; then his thought continued: 'Where she died.'

Ambrosine had been murdered three years ago.

One day in winter she had not appeared at the theatre. As there was a new topical song for her to learn, they had sent a messenger to the little house on the river.

He found her in her bed-gown on the floor of her bedchamber, stabbed through and through the fragile body. The house was in confusion and had been stripped of its few poor valuables.

No-one knew anything: the house was lonely, and Ambrosine lived alone; the old woman who worked for her came in for a portion of the day only. It was found that she had no friends or relatives and that no-one knew her real name – she was just a waif from the Faubourg Saint-Antoine.

That night Claude went to see her; they had quarrelled a little, and for two days he had kept away.

Rough care had disposed her decently on the tawdry silks of the canopied bed; she was covered to the chin, and her face, bruised and slightly distorted, had the aggrieved look of a startled child.

Her hair was smoothed and folded like a pillow beneath her head, her little peaked features looked insignificant beside this unchanged splendour of her hair.

As Claude looked at her he wondered how he could have ever loved her – a creature so thin, so charmless; his one desire was to forget her, for she now seemed something malignant.

He paid what was needful to save her from a pauper's burial and went back to Paris to forget. No-one found it difficult to forget Ambrosine; her obscure tragedy troubled no-one – there was too much else happening in France. Thieves had obviously murdered her for her few possessions: it was left at that, for no-one really cared. The Faubourg Saint-Antoine could provide plenty such as she.

For a while she held Claude at night; with the darkness would come her image, holding him off sleep.

Always he saw her dead, with the strained, half-open lips, the half-closed, fixed eyes, the thin nose, and the cheeks and chin of sharp delicacy outlined against the pillow of yellow hair.

Always dead. Again and again he tried to picture her living face, her moving form, but he could not capture them.

He could not recall the feel of her kisses or her warm caresses, but the sensation of her cold yet soft dead cheek as he had felt it beneath a furtive touch was long with him.

But after a while he escaped from Ambrosine; he forgot.

Now, as he remembered the way his route took him on the 12th of December, he remembered.

Not that he had any horror of the house or the locality – it simply had not happened that he had ever had occasion to go there since her death. Probably there were other people living there now, or the house might even be destroyed – in any case he would take a détour round the deserted park.

But it was absurd to suppose that he was afraid of that house or unwilling to pass the way he had last passed coming from her death-bed. It was all over and he had forgotten. So he assured himself; yet he began to recall Ambrosine, and always with a sensation of faint horror.

That night was the beginning of his fear.

He went home late to his lodging near the café and, on sleeping, dreamt very exactly this dream, which had the clearness and force of a vision.

He dreamt that it was the 12th of December and that he was riding towards Saint-Cloud carrying the papers he was to take to the Béarnais Deputy.

It was a cold, clear, melancholy afternoon, and the silence of dreams encompassed him as he rode.

When he reached the great iron gates of the dismantled park, his horse fell lame. He was not very far from his destination, and he decided to go on foot. Leaving his horse at a little inn, he struck out across the park.

He saw it all perfectly plainly – the great avenues of leafless trees, the stretches of greensward scattered with dead leaves, the carp ponds and fountains with their neglected statues and choked basins, the *parterres* where flowers had bloomed not so long ago, and that now looked as utterly decayed; and to his right, as he walked, always the pale glimpse of the river, shining between the trees.

Now, as he proceeded and the dusk began to fill the great park with shadows, he was aware of a companion walking at his side, step for step with him. He could not discern the head and face of this man, which seemed inextricably blended with the shadows, but he saw that he wore a green coat with dark blue frogs.

And he at once began to conceive of this companion a horror and dread unspeakable. He hastened his steps; but the other, with the silent precision of dreams, was ever beside him. The day had now faded to that fixed, colourless light which is the proper atmosphere of visions, and the trees and grass were still, the water without a ripple.

They came now, Claude and the figure that dogged him, to a flat carp-basin, dried and lined with green moss. A group of trees overshadowed it with bare branches; a straight stone figure rose behind, faceless and ominous. Claude could not remember this place, well known as was Saint-Cloud to him.

His companion stopped and bent down to adjust the buckles of his shoe. Claude longed to hasten on, but could not move; the other rose, took his hand, and led him hurriedly across the dry grass.

They approached the bank of a river and a house that stood there, on the confines of the park.

Claude knew the house. It was shuttered as when he had seen it on his last visit to Ambrosine. The garden was a mass of tangled weeds – he noticed a bramble that barred the door across and across.

'They did not find the place so easy to let,' he found himself saying.

His companion released him, and, wrenching off the rotting shutter of one of the lower windows, climbed into the house. Claude, impelled against his will, followed.

He saw, very distinctly (as, indeed, he had seen everything very distinctly in his dream), the dreadful, bare, disordered room of Ambrosine.

Then a deeper and more utter horror descended on him. He knew, suddenly, and with utter conviction, that he was with the murderer of Ambrosine.

And while he formed a shriek, the creature came at him with raised knife and had him by the throat, and he knew that he was being killed as she had been killed, that their two fates were bound together; and that her destiny, from which he had tried to free himself, had closed on him also.

This being the culmination of the dream, he woke; he slept no more till morning, and even in the daylight hours the dream haunted him with a great and invincible dread.

It was the more horrible that reality mingled with it – remembrance of days that had really existed were blended with remembrance of that dreadful day of the dream, recollections of Ambrosine were blended with that vision of her deserted home.

The past and the dream became one, rendering the dead woman an object of horror, hateful and repellent. He could not without a shudder recall her gayest moments or think of the little theatre where she used to act.

So three days passed, and then he dreamt the dream again.

In every detail he went through it as he had been through it before, and by no effort could he awake until the dream was accomplished and he was in the grip of the murderer of Ambrosine, with the steel descending into his side.

And the day of his journey was now only a week off; he hardly thought of trying to evade it, of pleading illness or asking another to take his place; it was part of the horror of the thing that he felt that it was inevitable that he should go – that his journey was not to be evaded by any effort, however frantic, that he might make.

Besides, he had his sane, reasonable moments when he was able to see the folly of being troubled by a dream which had recalled a little dancer with whom he had once been in love, and involved her with a certain journey near her dwelling that he was bound to make.

That was what it came to – just a dream and a recollection.

He argued in these quiet moments that it was not strange that his proposed journey to Saint-Cloud should arouse memories of Ambrosine and that the two should combine in a dream.

He distracted himself by taking a deeper interest in the wild, fierce life of Paris, by listening to all the tragedies daily recounted, by visiting all the quarters most lawless and most distressed. One day he even went, for the first time, to watch the executions. The real horror would check, he thought, the fanciful horror that haunted him.

But the first victim he saw was a young girl with hands red from the cold, a strained mouth and fair hair turned up on her small head; her eyes, over which the dullness of death seemed to have already passed, stared in the direction of Claude. He turned away with a movement so rough that the crowd, pressing round him, protested fiercely.

Claude strode through the chill and windy streets of Paris and thought of the approaching 12th of December as of the day of his death. So intense became his agitation that he turned instinctively towards his one friend, as one being enclosed in darkness will turn towards the one light.

René Legarais was his fellow clerk and his first confidant and counsellor – a man a few years older than himself, and, like himself, sober, quiet, industrious, and well balanced.

Claude found his lodging near the Pre-aux-Clercs empty; René was yet at the Chamber.

Claude waited; he found himself encouraged even by the sight of the cheerful, familiar room, with books, and lamp, and fire, and the coffee-service waiting for his friend's return.

He now tried hard to reason himself out of his folly.

He would tell René, and with the telling he would see the absurdity of the whole thing and they would laugh it away together over a glass of wine.

René, he remembered, had also been in love with Ambrosine, but in a foolish, sentimental fashion – Claude smiled to think of it, but he believed that René had been ready to marry the little creature. She had even favoured his respectful wooing (so gossip said) until Claude had appeared, with bolder methods and his vivid good looks and his lavish purse.

René had retired with the best of grace, and that was all long ago and forgotten by both; Claude wondered why he thought of it now, sitting here in the warmth and light. Only because he was unnerved and unstrung and obsessed by that weird dream.

René came home at his usual hour, flushed by the sharp wind and shaking the raindrops from his frieze coat. He was a pale young man with heavy brown hair, insignificant features, and a mole on his upper lip. He looked unhealthy and pensive, and wore horn-rimmed glasses when he worked.

'Where were you this afternoon?' he asked. 'Your desk was empty.'

'I was not well,' said Claude.

René gave him a quick glance.

Claude looked well enough now, a colour from the fire in his handsome brown face, his slim figure stretched at ease in the deep-armed leather chair and a half-mocking smile on his lips.

'I went to see the executions,' he added.

'Bah!' said René.

He came to the fire and warmed his hands, which were stiff and red with cold; they reminded Claude of the hands of the girl whom he had seen on the platform of the guillotine.

'It is the first time,' replied Claude, 'and I shall not go again.'

'I have never been,' said René.

'There was a girl there.' Claude could not keep it off his tongue.

'There always are girls, I believe.'

'She was quite young.' 'Yes?' René looked up, aware that interest was expected of him.

'And then – like Ambrosine.'

'Ambrosine?'

'You remember,' said Claude impatiently, 'the little dancer . . . at Saint-Cloud.'

'Oh, whatever made you think of her?' René looked relieved, as if he had expected something more portentous and terrible.

'That is what I wish to know – what has made me think of her? I believed that I had forgotten.'

'I had, certainly.'

'So had I.'

'What has reminded you?'

Claude struggled with his trouble, which now seemed to him ridiculous.

'I have to go to Saint-Cloud,' he said at last.

'When?'

'The 12th.'

'On business of the Chamber?'

'Yes.'

'And this reminded you?'

'Yes – you see,' explained Claude slowly, 'I have not been there since.'

'Not since?' René pondered, and seemed to understand.

'And lately I have had a dream.'

'Oh, dreams,' said René; he lifted his shoulders lightly and turned to the fire.

'Do you dream?' asked Claude, reluctant to enter on the subject, yet driven to seek the relief of speech.

'Who does not dream – now – in Paris?'

Claude thought of the thin girl on the steps of the guillotine. 'There is good matter for dreams in Paris,' he admitted, adding gloomily; 'I wish that I had not been to the executions.'

René was making the coffee; he laughed good-naturedly.

'Come, Claude, what is the matter with you? What have you on your conscience?'

'Ambrosine.'

René lifted his brows. 'Have you not found, in Paris, in three years, a woman to make you forget Ambrosine, poor little fool?'

'I had forgotten,' said Claude fiercely, 'but this cursed journey – and this cursed dream – made me remember.'

'You are nervous, overworked,' replied his friend; it was quite true that in these few weeks Claude had been working with a desperate energy; he snatched eagerly at the excuse.

'Yes, yes, that is it . . . but the times . . . enough to unnerve any man – death and ruin on either side and the toils closing on so many one knew.'

René poured out the coffee, took his cup, and settled himself comfortably in the armchair opposite Claude. He drank and stretched his limbs with the satisfaction of a man pleasantly tired.

'After all, you need not take this journey,' he said thoughtfully; 'there are a dozen would do it for you.'

'That is just it – I feel *impelled* to go, as if no effort of mine would release me.' He hesitated a moment, then added: 'That is part of the horror of it.'

'The horror?'

'Of the whole thing – do you not see the horror?' asked Claude impatiently.

'My dear fellow, how can I, when you have not told me what this wonderful dream is about?'

Claude flushed, and looked into the fire; after all, he thought, René was too commonplace to understand his ghostly terrors – and the thing did seem ridiculous when he was sitting there warm and comfortable and safe.

Yet it could not be dismissed from his mind – he had to speak, even if to a listener probably unsympathetic.

'It is like a vision,' he said. 'I have had it three times – it is a prevision of the journey to Saint-Cloud.'

René, attentive, waited.

'It is so very exact,' continued Claude, 'and each time the same.'

'Tell me.'

'Oh, it is only that – the ride to the gate, the leaving of the lame horse, the walk through the park, and then – '

'Well?'

'The appearance of a man walking beside me.'

'You know him?'

'I hardly saw the face.'

'Well?' René continued to urge Claude's manifest reluctance.

'We went, finally, to the house of Ambrosine.'

'Ah yes, she lived there on the banks of the river – '

'Surely you remember – '

'We were never intimate,' smiled René. 'I do not believe that I ever went to her house. Of course, it was familiar to you?'

'I saw it again exactly – it was shut up; deserted and in decay. My companion broke the window shutters and stepped in. I followed. The room was in disrepair, unfurnished. As I looked round the place – '

He shuddered, in spite of his strong control.

'The fiend with me revealed himself. I knew that he was the murderer of Ambrosine, and he fell on me as he had fallen on her.'

René was silent a moment.

'Why should the murderer of Ambrosine wish to murder you?' he asked at length.

'How do I know? I tell you my dream.'

'An extraordinary dream.'

'Would you take it as a warning?'

'A warning?'

'Of what will happen?'

'It is obviously absurd,' said René quietly.

'Yes, absurd – yet I feel as if the 12th of December would be the day of my death.'

'You have brooded over it – you must put it out of your mind.'

'I cannot,' said Claude wildly. 'I cannot!'

'Then don't go.'

'I tell you it is out of my power to stay away.'

René looked at him keenly. 'Then how can I help you?'

Claude took this glance to mean that he doubted his wits. 'Only by listening to my fool's talk,' he said, smiling.

'Does that help?'

'I hope it may. You see, the whole thing – that wretched girl – has become an obsession, waking and sleeping.'

'Strange.'

'Strange indeed.'

'After you had forgotten.'

'Yes, I had forgotten,' said Claude.

'So had I, to tell the truth.'

'Why should one remember? It was a curious affair.'

'Her death?'

'Her murder, yes.'

'I do not see that it was so curious. A little wanton, living alone with some spoils foolishly displayed – she courted her fate.'

'But she had so little – a few bits of imitation jewellery, a few coins; and who should have known of them?'

René shrugged and put down his empty coffee-cup.

'And they said she was liked by the few poor folk about – '

'There are always ruffians on the tramp on the watch for these chances.'

'Yes; yet it was strange – '

René interrupted with an expression of distaste. 'Why go back to this?'

Claude stared, as if amazed at himself. 'Why, indeed?'

'You become morbid, unreasonable, Claude; rouse yourself, forget this thing.'

The other laughed; it did not have a pleasant sound.

'I suppose I am haunted.'

'Why should you be? You did not do her any wrong.'

'She cared for me.'

René laughed now.

'By God!' said Claude fiercely. 'She cared for me – I believe she still cares. That is why she will not let me go . . . '

René rose and took a step or two away from him.

'What are you talking of?' he asked.

'I say, she cares – that is why she is trying to warn me.'

'You think it is she?'

'Ambrosine – yes.'

'You must not allow yourself these fancies, my poor fellow.'

'You may well pity me. *I* never cared for her; I think I hated her when she was dead. I hate her now. Why won't she keep quiet in her grave and leave me alone?'

He rose and walked across the room with a lurching step.

René, leaning against the table, watched him.

'What was the house like – in your dreams?'

'I told you.'

'Decayed – deserted?'

'And tainted.''It had a taint of death – like a smell of stale blood.'

'It is not likely,' said René, 'that the place is empty. Now, if it was inhabited, would not that shake your faith in your vision?'

Claude stopped short in his walk; he had not thought of that.

'Now,' smiled René, 'send someone to look at the place.'

'Who could live there – after that?'

'Bah! Do you think people stop for that nowadays? If they did, half the city would be uninhabited. The place is cheap, I presume, and someone's property. I do not suppose it has been allowed to fall into disrepair. That was your fancy.'

'I might send someone to see,' reflected Claude.

'That is what I suggest – find out before the 12th, and if the house is inhabited, as I am sure it is, all this moonshine will clear away from your brain and you will undertake your journey with a good heart.'

'I will do that,' answered Claude gratefully. 'I knew that you would help me – forgive me for having wearied you, René.'

His friend smiled.

'I want you to be reasonable – nothing is going to happen. After all, these papers to the Béarnais are not of such importance; no-one would murder you to get *them*.'

'Oh, it had nothing to do with the Béarnais, but with Ambrosine.'

'You must forget Ambrosine,' said René decidedly. 'She has ceased to exist and there are no such things as ghosts.'

Claude smiled; he was thinking that once René had been quite sentimental over Ambrosine; certainly he was cured of that fancy. Why could not he too completely put the little dancer from his mind?

He also had long ceased to care.

But he was ashamed to refer further to his fears and imaginings.

'You have done me good,' he declared. 'I shall think no more of the matter. After all, the 12th will soon come and go, and then the thing will cease to have any meaning.'

René smiled, seemingly relieved by his returned cheerfulness.

'Still, send someone to look at the house,' he said; 'that will send you on your journey with a lighter heart.'

'At once – tomorrow.' They parted, and Claude went home through the cold streets.

As soon as he had left the lighted room and the company of his friend, the old dreary terror returned.

He hastened to his chamber, hoping to gain relief amid his own surroundings, and lit every candle he could find.

He would not go to bed, as he dreaded the return of the dream, yet he was sleepy and had nothing to do.

Presently, he went to a bottom drawer in the modest bureau that served him as a wardrobe and took out a small parcel wrapped in silver paper. He unfolded it and brought forth a chicken-skin fan, wreathed with figures of flying loves in rose and silver tones that surrounded a delicate pastoral river scene, the banks trailing with eglantine, the azure sky veiled in soft clouds, and a blue, satin-lined boat fastened by a gold cord to an alabaster pillar in readiness for amorous passengers.

The fan was not new: there were the marks of some spots that had been cleaned away, spots of blood perhaps, and the fine ivory sticks were stained in places.

Claude had bought it at a bric-à-brac shop filled with the plunder of château and hôtel; it had been cheap and valuable, and at the time

he had not cared that it had probably been stolen from some scene
of murder and violence and that its one-time owner had almost
certainly bowed her neck to a bitter fate – no, it had rather amused
him to buy for the little dancer of the Faubourg Saint-Antoine the
property of some great lady.

Now it seemed a sinister and horrid omen, this toy with the blood-
spots scarcely erased. It had been meant as a peace-offering for
Ambrosine – after their little quarrel, which was never to be mended
this side of the grave.

He had had it in his pocket when he had gone to look at her for the
last time.

Since then it had lain in the drawer forgotten, it had never occurred
to him to give it to another woman – it was doubly the property of the
dead. Now he handled it carefully, opening and shutting it in the
candlelight and staring at those cupids who brought no thoughts of
love and that faery scene that brought no thoughts of peace.

And as he looked he seemed to see the delicate thing in the small
hands of Ambrosine as she sat up in the big bed with the gaudy
draperies, and her fair hair fell down and obscured the fan.

Her fair hair . . .

How plainly he could see her fair hair as he had last seen it, folded
into a neat pillow for her head.

He put the fan away and built up a big fire, feeding it with pine
knots; he was possessed by the certainty that if he slept he would
again dream of the journey to Saint-Cloud.

It seemed as if Ambrosine was in the room, trying to speak to him,
to tell him something; but he would not let her, he would not put
himself in her power; he would not sleep.

Among the neglected books on the little shelf by his bed was an old
copy of Pascal. Claude took this down and began reading it with
painful exactitude and attention. With this and strong coffee he kept
himself awake till morning.

Before he left for the Chamber, he paid his landlord's son to go to
Saint-Cloud and look at the house of Ambrosine, which he very
carefully described, adding the excuse that he had been told of the
place as a desirable house for the summer heat; above all things, the
boy must notice whether it was inhabited or not.

All that day he was languid and heavy-eyed, weary from lack of
sleep, with his nerves on the rack.

Through the dreary, monotonous hours he was picturing his
messenger, treading unconsciously the way that had become so

terrible to him, approaching the fatal house and finding it, as he had found it, three times in his dreams, deserted and decayed.

René made no reference to their conversation of the previous night, but he was more than ever friendly and pleasant.

When the intolerable day was at last over, he asked Claude to dine with him, but the other declined; his reason, which he did not give, was that he was desperately anxious to hear the news the boy had brought from Saint-Cloud.

When he reached home the fellow had returned; a boat had given him a lift each way.

Claude was foolishly relieved to see his calm cheerfulness.

'Well?' he asked, with the best indifference he could assume.

'Well, Citizen Boucher, I should not take that house at Saint-Cloud.'

'Why?' The words came mechanically.

'First of all, there has been a bad murder there.'

'How did you find that out?'

'The people on the boat told me – they go past every day.'

So the thing was known – remembered.

'Never mind that, boy. What of the house?'

'It is in ruins, decay – '

'Ruins – decay?'

'Well, all shuttered up – '

'Shuttered?'

'Yes, citizen,' he began, staring at Claude, whose manner was certainly startling, 'and the garden full of weeds.'

Claude made an effort to speak rationally.

'So you did not see the house inside, eh?' he asked.

'No-one knew who had the key – the landlord lived in Paris, they said, and never came there. The place had a bad reputation because of the horrid murder done there.'

'In these times,' muttered Claude, 'are they so sensitive?'

'They are just ignorant people, citizen – those on the boat and those I met in the forest.'

'And the house was impossible?'

'It would need a good deal of repairing.'

'Ah – '

'And the weeds in the garden were monstrous – there was one great bramble across and across the door.'

Claude gave him a terrible look and dismissed him.

So it was all there, exactly like his dream.

There were only three days to the 12th – only three days perhaps to live.

When he reached his room he looked at the calendar, hoping he had made some mistake in the date.

No; in three days it would be the 12th.

He could not go to bed, but no coffee could keep him awake.

As soon as he was asleep he dreamed his dream of the journey to Saint-Cloud, nor could he rouse himself until the horrid sequence of events was complete.

He awoke shivering, unnerved and cold with sweat. He had to take brandy before he could fit himself to make his toilet and go to the Chamber.

As he hurried along the street fresh with the transient morning freshness of the city, the burden of his misery was lightened by a sudden thought. He would take a companion with him, he would take René.

That would defeat the dream.

The warning would have saved him; no-one would attack two of them and they could go armed; they need not go near the house, and they could proceed by water and not walk through the Park.

Claude felt almost himself again as he thought out this plan.

No sooner had he reached the Chamber than he found his friend and broached the scheme to him. René was agreeable, and readily accorded his company.

'I thought of it myself,' he said. 'I can easily get permission to come with you, and we will lay this ghost once and for ever.'

Claude was so relieved that he almost lost his old foreboding.

But the night before the journey he again dreamed that he was being murdered by the murderer of Ambrosine, who wore a green coat with dark blue frogs.

At the appointed hour they set out, René endeavouring to cheer Claude, who was gloomy and taciturn, but as the journey proceeded, his spirits rose; the charm had been proved wrong in the first instance, he was not going on horseback to Saint-Cloud.

But when they reached the gates of the park, he was disappointed to find the boat stopped at the little quay and began unloading.

René had arranged with the captain; and René, it seemed, had misunderstood.

The boat went no farther.

But it was only a short walk across the park to Saint-Cloud and the Deputy's house – the captain could not understand Claude's discomfiture.

Well, they must walk – here again the dream was wrong.

He had a companion. René laughed at him; the walk would do them good this cold evening, and they would be at their destination long before dusk – as for the return, if they were not offered hospitality, well, there were good inns at Saint-Cloud.

They entered the magnificent iron gates, now always open, and started briskly across the grass.

Here it was, exactly as he had seen it in his dreams, the huge bare trees, the dead leaves underfoot, the pallid gleam of the river to the right, the expanse of forest to the left, through which now and then a fountain or a statue showed.

It was bitterly cold, the sky veiled, and presently a thin mist rose off the river, dimming everything with fog. Like the dim light of his dream.

'We shall lose our way,' he said.

'No; I know this way well.'

'You know it?'

'When I was a boy I used to live at Saint-Cloud,' said René.

They proceeded more slowly, muffled to the throats in their greatcoats, which they had worn all the journey, for it had been cold on the river also.

Claude thought of Ambrosine till his senses reeled round that one image.

Here she had walked, he with her, often enough – near was her house, near her grave.

He seemed to see her in every dimness between the trees – Ambrosine, with her fair hair mingling with the mist.

Suddenly before him a huge fountain arose with a dried basin and a featureless statue behind. And René stopped to latch up his shoe.

He was not thinking of his dream now, but he had the sensation that this had all happened before. As he looked at René, he muttered to himself, half stupidly: 'What an extraordinary coincidence!'

Then René straightened himself and slipped his hand through his friend's arm.

His mantle had fallen back a little, and Claude saw that he wore a new suit, dark green, frogged with dark blue, and again he muttered: 'What an extraordinary coincidence!'

'I know the way,' said René, and led him, as if he had been a blind man, through the shifting mist.

In a few moments they stood on the outskirts of the park and before the decayed and deserted house of Ambrosine – as he had seen it, with the weeds in the garden and the bramble across the door.

They entered the little patch of ground.

'Now we are here,' said René, 'we may as well look inside.'

So saying, he wrenched off one of the rotting shutters and climbed into the room.

Claude followed him, like a creature deprived of wits.

They stood together in the damp, dull, bare room – as they had stood together in the dream.

Claude looked at René's face, which had quite changed.

'So you murdered her?' he said in a sick voice.

'You never guessed?' asked René. 'I *loved* her, you see, and she loved me till you came. And then I hated both of you. I was mad from then, I think, as mad as you with your infernal dreams.'

'You murdered Ambrosine!' whimpered Claude.

'And your dream showed me the way to murder you. I have been waiting so long to find how to do it.'

Claude began laughing.

'Her fair hair – if one could open her grave one might see it again – like a pillow for her head. . . .' He looked at René, whose pale and distorted face seemed to grow larger, until it bore down on him like an evil thing blotting out hope.

Claude did not put a hand to any of the weapons he had brought; he fell on his knees and held up his hands in an attitude of prayer, while he began to gabble senseless words.

And René fell on him with the knife that had killed Ambrosine.

The Crown Derby Plate

Martha Pym said that she had never seen a ghost and that she would very much like to do so, 'particularly at Christmas, for, you can laugh as you like, that is the correct time to see a ghost.'

'I don't suppose you ever will,' replied her cousin Mabel comfortably; while her cousin Clara shuddered and said that she hoped they would change the subject, for she disliked even to think of such things.

The three elderly, cheerful women sat round a big fire, cosy and content after a day of pleasant activities. Martha was the guest of the other two, who owned the handsome, convenient country house; she always came to spend her Christmas with the Wyntons, and found the leisurely country life delightful after the bustling round of London, for Martha managed an antique shop of the better sort and worked extremely hard. She was, however, still full of zest for work or pleasure, though sixty years old, and looked backwards and forwards to a succession of delightful days.

The other two, Mabel and Clara, led quieter but none the less agreeable lives; they had more money and fewer interests, but nevertheless enjoyed themselves very well.

'Talking of ghosts,' said Mabel, 'I wonder how that old woman at Hartleys is getting on – for Hartleys, you know, is supposed to be haunted.'

'Yes, I know,' smiled Miss Pym; 'but all the years we have known of the place we have never heard anything definite, have we?'

'No,' put in Clara; 'but there *is* that persistent rumour that the house is uncanny, and for myself, *nothing* would induce me to live there.'

'It is certainly very lonely and dreary down there on the marshes,' conceded Mabel. 'But as for the ghost – you never hear *what* it is supposed to be, even.'

'Who has taken it?' asked Miss Pym, remembering Hartleys as very desolate indeed and long shut up.

'A Miss Lefain, an eccentric old creature – I think you met her here once two years ago – '

'I believe that I did, but I don't recall her at all.'

'We have not seen her since. Hartleys is so ungetatable and she didn't seem to want visitors. She collects china, Martha, so really you ought to go and see her and talk shop.'

With the word 'china' some curious associations came into the mind of Martha Pym; she was silent while she strove to put them together, and after a second or two they all fitted together into a very clear picture.

She remembered that thirty years ago – yes, it must be thirty years ago, when, as a young woman, she had put all her capital into the antique business and had been staying with her cousins (her aunt had then been alive) – she had driven across the marsh to Hartleys, where there was an auction sale; all the details of this she had completely forgotten, but she could recall quite clearly purchasing a set of gorgeous china which was still one of her proud delights, a perfect set of Crown Derby save that one plate was missing.

'How odd,' she remarked, 'that this Miss Lefain should collect china too, for it was at Hartleys that I purchased my dear old Derby service – I've never been able to match that plate.'

'A plate was missing? I seem to remember,' said Clara. 'Didn't they say that it must be in the house somewhere and that it should be looked for?'

'I believe they did; but of course I never heard any more, and that missing plate has annoyed me ever since. Who had Hartleys?'

'An old connoisseur, Sir James Sewell. I believe he was some relation to this Miss Lefain, but I don't know – '

'I wonder if she has found the plate,' mused Miss Pym. 'I expect she has turned out and ransacked the whole place.'

'Why not trot over and ask?' suggested Mabel. 'It's not much use to her if she has found it, one odd plate.'

'Don't be silly,' said Clara. 'Fancy going over the marshes this weather to ask about a plate missed all those years ago. I'm sure Martha wouldn't think of it.'

But Martha did think of it; she was rather fascinated by the idea. How queer and pleasant it would be if, after all these years, nearly a lifetime, she should find the Crown Derby plate, the loss of which had always irked her! And this hope did not seem so altogether fantastical; it was quite likely that old Miss Lefain, poking about in the ancient house, had found the missing piece.

And, of course, if she had, being a fellow-collector, she would be quite willing to part with it to complete the set.

Her cousin endeavoured to dissuade her; Miss Lefain, she declared, was a recluse, an odd creature who might greatly resent such a visit and such a request.

'Well, if she does I can but come away again,' smiled Miss Pym. 'I suppose she can't bite my head off, and I rather like meeting these curious types – we've got a love for old china in common, anyhow.'

'It seems so silly to think of it after all these years – a plate!'

'A Crown Derby plate,' corrected Miss Pym. 'It is certainly strange that I did not think of it before, but now that I have got it into my head I can't get it out. Besides,' she added hopefully, 'I might see the ghost.'

So full, however, were the days with pleasant local engagements that Miss Pym had no immediate chance of putting her scheme into practice; but she did not relinquish it; and she asked several different people what they knew about Hartleys and Miss Lefain.

And no-one knew anything except that the house was supposed to be haunted and the owner 'cracky'.

'Is there a story?' asked Miss Pym, who associated ghosts with neat tales into which they fitted as exactly as nuts into shells.

But she was always told – 'Oh no, there isn't a story; no-one knows anything about the place, don't know how the idea got about; old Sewell was half-crazy, I believe. He was buried in the garden and that gives a house a nasty name.'

'Very unpleasant,' said Martha Pym, undisturbed.

This ghost seemed too elusive for her to track down; she would have to be content if she could recover the Crown Derby plate; for that at least she was determined to make a try and also to satisfy that faint tingling of curiosity roused in her by this talk about Hartleys and the remembrance of that day, so long ago, when she had gone to the auction sale at the lonely old house.

So the first free afternoon, while Mabel and Clara were comfortably taking their afternoon repose, Martha Pym, who was of a more lively habit, got out her little governess cart and dashed away across the Essex flats.

She had taken minute directions with her, but she soon lost her way.

Under the wintry sky, which looked as grey and hard as metal, the marshes stretched bleakly to the horizon, the olive-brown broken reeds were harsh as scars on the saffron-tinted bogs, where the sluggish waters that rose so high in winter were filmed over with the first stillness of a frost. The air was cold, but not keen; everything was damp. Faintest of mists blurred the black outlines of trees that rose stark from the ridges above the stagnant dykes; the flooded fields were haunted by black birds and white birds, gulls and crows, whining above the high ditch grass and wintry wastes.

Miss Pym stopped the little horse and surveyed this spectral scene, which had a certain relish about it to one sure to return to a homely village, a cheerful house, and good company.

A withered and bleached old man, in colour like the dun landscape, came along the road between the spare alders.

Miss Pym, buttoning up her coat, asked the way to Hartleys as he passed her; he told her, straight on; and she proceeded, straight indeed along the road that went with undeviating length across the marshes.

'Of course,' thought Miss Pym, 'if you live in a place like this you are bound to invent ghosts.'

The house sprang up suddenly on a knoll ringed with rotting trees, encompassed by an old brick wall that the perpetual damp had overrun with lichen, blue, green, white, colours of decay.

Hartleys, no doubt; there was no other residence or human being in sight in all the wide expanse; besides, she could remember it, surely, after all this time – the sharp rising out of the marsh, the colony of tall trees; but then fields and trees had been green and bright – there had been no water on the flats, it had been summertime.

'She certainly,' thought Miss Pym, 'must be crazy to live here. And I rather doubt if I shall get my plate.'

She fastened up the good little horse by the garden gate, which stood negligently ajar, and entered. The garden itself was so neglected that it was quite surprising to see a trim appearance in the house – curtains at the windows and a polish on the brass door-knocker, which must have been recently rubbed there, considering the taint in the sea damp which rusted and rotted everything.

It was a square-built, substantial house with 'nothing wrong with it but the situation,' Miss Pym decided, though it was not very attractive, being built of that drab, plastered stone so popular a hundred years ago, with flat windows and door; while one side was gloomily shaded by a large evergreen tree of the cypress variety which gave a blackish tinge to that portion of the garden. There was no pretence at flower beds nor any manner of cultivation in this garden, where a few rank weeds and straggling bushes matted together above the dead grass. On the enclosing wall, which appeared to have been built high as protection against the ceaseless winds that swung along the flats, were the remains of fruit trees; their crucified branches, rotting under the great nails that held them up, looked like the skeletons of those who had died in torment.

Miss Pym took in these noxious details as she knocked firmly at the door; they did not depress her; she merely felt extremely sorry for anyone who could live in such a place.

She noticed at the far end of the garden, in the corner of the wall, a headstone showing above the sodden, colourless grass, and remembered what she had been told about the old antiquary being buried there, in the grounds of Hartleys.

As the knock had no effect, she stepped back and looked at the house: it was certainly inhabited – with those neat windows, white curtains, and drab blinds all pulled to precisely the same level. And when she brought her glance back to the door she saw that it had been opened and that someone, considerably obscured by the darkness of the passage, was looking at her intently.

'Good afternoon,' said Miss Pym cheerfully. 'I just thought I would call and see Miss Lefain – it is Miss Lefain, isn't it?'

'It's my house,' was the querulous reply.

Martha Pym had hardly expected to find any servants here, though the old lady must, she thought, work pretty hard to keep the house so clean and tidy as it appeared to be.

'Of course,' she replied. 'May I come in? I'm Martha Pym, staying with the Wyntons. I met you there – '

'Do come in,' was the faint reply. 'I get so few people to visit me, I'm really very lonely.'

'I don't wonder,' thought Miss Pym; but she had resolved to take no notice of any eccentricity on the part of her hostess, and so she entered the house with her usual agreeable candour and courtesy.

The passage was badly lit, but she was able to get a fair idea of Miss Lefain. Her first impression was that this poor creature was most dreadfully old, older than any human being had the right to be; why, she felt young in comparison – so faded, feeble, and pallid was Miss Lefain.

She was also monstrously fat; her gross, flaccid figure was shapeless and she wore a badly cut, full dress of no colour at all, but stained with earth and damp where, Miss Pym supposed, she had been doing futile gardening; this gown was doubtless designed to disguise her stoutness, but had been so carelessly pulled about that it only added to it, being rucked and rolled 'all over the place', as Miss Pym put it to herself.

Another ridiculous touch about the appearance of the poor old lady was her short hair; decrepit as she was and lonely as she lived, she had actually had her scanty relics of white hair cropped round her shaking head.

'Dear me, dear me,' she said in her thin, treble voice. 'How very kind of you to come. I suppose you prefer the parlour? I generally sit in the garden.'

'The garden? But not in this weather?'

'I get used to the weather. You've no idea how used one gets to the weather.'

'I suppose so,' conceded Miss Pym doubtfully. 'You don't live here quite alone, do you?'

'Quite alone, lately. I had a little company, but she was taken away – I'm sure I don't know where. I haven't been able to find a trace of her anywhere,' replied the old lady peevishly.

'Some wretched companion that couldn't stick it, I suppose,' thought Miss Pym. 'Well, I don't wonder – but someone ought to be here to look after her.'

They went into the parlour, which, the visitor was dismayed to see, was without a fire, but otherwise well kept.

And there, on dozens of shelves, was a choice array of china, at which Martha Pym's eyes glistened.

'Aha!' cried Miss Lefain. 'I see you've noticed my treasures. Don't you envy me? Don't you wish that you had some of those pieces?'

Martha Pym certainly did, and she looked eagerly and greedily round the walls, tables, and cabinets, while the old woman followed her with little thin squeals of pleasure.

It was a beautiful little collection, most choicely and elegantly arranged, and Martha thought it marvellous that this feeble, ancient creature should be able to keep it in such precise order as well as doing her own housework.

'Do you really do everything yourself here and live quite alone?' she asked, and she shivered even in her thick coat and wished that Miss Lefain's energy had risen to a fire, but then probably she lived in the kitchen, as these lonely eccentrics often did.

'There was someone,' answered Miss Lefain cunningly, 'but I had to send her away. I told you she's gone; I can't find her and I am so glad. Of course,' she added wistfully, 'it leaves me very lonely, but then I couldn't stand her impertinence any longer. She used to say that it was *her* house and her collection of china! Would you believe it? She used to try and chase me away from looking at my own things!'

'How very disagreeable,' said Miss Pym, wondering which of the two women had been crazy. 'But hadn't you better get someone else?'

'Oh no,' was the jealous answer. 'I would rather be alone with my things. I daren't leave the house for fear someone takes them away – there was a dreadful time once when an auction sale was held here – '

'Were you here then?' asked Miss Pym; but indeed she looked old enough to have been anywhere.

'Yes, of course,' Miss Lefain replied rather peevishly, and Miss Pym decided that she must be a relation of old Sir James Sewell. Clara and Mabel had been very foggy about it all. 'I was very busy hiding all the china – but one set they got – a Crown Derby tea service . . .'

'With one plate missing!' cried Martha Pym. 'I bought it, and do you know, I was wondering if you'd found it – '

'I hid it,' piped Miss Lefain.

'Oh, you did, did you? Well, that's rather funny behaviour. Why did you hide the stuff away instead of buying it?'

'How could I buy what was mine?'

'Old Sir James left it to you, then?' asked Martha Pym, feeling very muddled.

'*She* bought a lot more,' squeaked Miss Lefain, but Martha Pym tried to keep her to the point.

'If you've got the plate,' she insisted, 'you might let me have it – I'll pay quite handsomely. It would be so pleasant to have it after all these years.'

'Money is no use to me,' said Miss Lefain mournfully. 'Not a bit of use. I can't leave the house or the garden.'

'Well, you have to live, I suppose,' said Martha Pym cheerfully. 'And, do you know, I'm afraid you are getting rather morbid and dull, living here all alone – you really ought to have a fire – why, it's just on Christmas and very damp.'

'I haven't felt the cold for a long time,' replied the other; she seated herself with a sigh on one of the horsehair chairs, and Miss Pym noticed with a start that her feet were covered only by a pair of white stockings. 'One of those nasty health fiends,' thought Miss Pym; 'but she doesn't look too well for all that.'

'So you don't think that you could let me have the plate?' she asked briskly, walking up and down, for the dark, clean, neat parlour was very cold indeed, and she thought that she couldn't stand this much longer; as there seemed no sign of tea or anything pleasant and comfortable, she had really better go.

'I might let you have it,' sighed Miss Lefain, 'since you've been so kind as to pay me a visit. After all, one plate isn't much use, is it?'

'Of course not, I wonder you troubled to hide it.'

'I couldn't *bear*,' wailed the other, 'to see the things going out of the house!'

Martha Pym couldn't stop to go into all this; it was quite clear that the old lady was very eccentric indeed and that nothing very much could be done with her; no wonder that she had 'dropped out' of everything and that no-one ever saw her or knew anything about her; though Miss Pym felt that some effort ought really to be made to save her from herself.

'Wouldn't you like a run in my little governess cart?' she suggested. 'We might go to tea with the Wyntons on the way back, they'd be delighted to see you; and I really think that you do want taking out of yourself.'

'I was taken out of myself some time ago,' replied Miss Lefain. 'I really was; and I couldn't leave my things – though,' she added with pathetic gratitude, 'it is very, very kind of you – '

'Your things would be quite safe, I'm sure,' said Martha Pym, humouring her. 'Who ever would come up here this hour of a winter's day?'

'They do, oh, they do! And *she* might come back, prying and nosing and saying it was all hers, all my beautiful china here!'

Miss Lefain squealed in her agitation, and rising up ran round the wall fingering with flaccid, yellow hands the brilliant glossy pieces on the shelves.

'Well, then, I'm afraid that I must go. They'll be expecting me, and it's quite a long ride; perhaps some other time you'll come and see us?'

'Oh, must you go?' quavered Miss Lefain dolefully. 'I do like a little company now and then, and I trusted you from the first – the others, when they do come, are always after my things and I have to frighten them away.'

'Frighten them away!' replied Martha Pym. 'However do you do that?'

'It doesn't seem difficult. People are so easily frightened, aren't they?'

Miss Pym suddenly remembered that Hartleys had the reputation of being haunted – perhaps the queer old thing played on that; the lonely house with the grave in the garden was dreary enough to create a legend.

'I suppose you've never seen a ghost?' she asked pleasantly. 'I'd rather like to see one, you know – '

'There is no-one here but myself,' said Miss Lefain.

'So you've never seen anything? I thought it must be all non-sense. Still, I do think it rather melancholy for you to live here all alone.'

Miss Lefain sighed. 'Yes, it's very lonely. Do stay and talk to me a little longer.' Her whistling voice dropped cunningly. 'And I'll give you the Crown Derby plate!'

'Are you sure you've really got it?' Miss Pym asked.

'I'll show you.'

Fat and waddling as she was, she seemed to move lightly as she slipped in front of Miss Pym and conducted her from the room, going slowly up the stairs – such a gross, odd figure in that clumsy dress with the fringe of white hair hanging on to her shoulders.

The upstairs of the house was as neat as the parlour – everything well in its place; but there was no sign of occupancy; the beds were covered with dust sheets. There were no lamps or fires set ready. 'I suppose,' said Miss Pym to herself, 'she doesn't care to show me where she really lives.'

But as they passed from one room to another, she could not help saying: 'Where do you live, Miss Lefain?'

'Mostly in the garden,' said the other.

Miss Pym thought of those horrible health huts that some people indulged in.

'Well, sooner you than I,' she replied cheerfully.

In the most distant room of all, a dark, tiny closet, Miss Lefain opened a deep cupboard and brought out a Crown Derby plate, which her guest received with a spasm of joy, for it was actually that missing from her cherished set.

'It's very good of you,' she said in delight. 'Won't you take some-thing for it or let me do something for you?'

'You might come and see me again,' replied Miss Lefain wistfully.

'Oh yes, of course I should like to come and see you again.'

But now that she had got what she had really come for – the plate – Martha Pym wanted to be gone; it was really very dismal and de-pressing in the house, and she began to notice a fearful smell – the place had been shut up too long, there was something damp rotting somewhere – in this horrid little dark closet no doubt.

'I really must be going,' she said hurriedly.

Miss Lefain turned as if to cling to her, but Martha Pym moved quickly away.

'Dear me,' wailed the old lady. 'Why are you in such haste?'

'There's – a smell,' murmured Miss Pym rather faintly.

She found herself hastening down the stairs, with Miss Lefain complaining behind her.

'How peculiar people are! *She* used to talk of a smell – '

'Well, you must notice it yourself.'

Miss Pym was in the hall; the old woman had not followed her but stood in the semi-darkness at the head of the stairs, a pale, shapeless figure.

Martha Pym hated to be rude and ungrateful, but she could not stay another moment; she hurried away and was in her cart in a moment – really, that smell . . .

'Goodbye!' she called out with false cheerfulness. 'And thank you *so* much!'

There was no answer from the house.

Miss Pym drove on; she was rather upset and took another way than that by which she had come – a way that led past a little house raised above the marsh. She was glad to think that the poor old creature at Hartleys had such near neighbours, and she reined up the horse, dubious as to whether she should call someone and tell them that poor old Miss Lefain really wanted a little looking after, alone in a house like that and plainly not quite right in her head.

A young woman, attracted by the sound of the governess cart, came to the door of the house and, seeing Miss Pym, called out, asking if she wanted the keys of the house.

'What house?'

'Hartleys, mum. They don't put a board out, as no-one is likely to pass, but it's to be sold. Miss Lefain wants to sell or let it – '

'I've just been up to see her – '

'Oh no, mum; she's been away a year, abroad somewhere – couldn't stand the place. It's been empty since then; I just run in every day and keep things tidy.'

Loquacious and curious, the young woman had come to the fence; Miss Pym had stopped her horse.

'Miss Lefain is there now,' she said. 'She must have just come back – '

'She wasn't there this morning, mum.' 'Tisn't likely she'd come, either – fair scared she was, mum, fair chased away, didn't dare move her china. Can't say I've noticed anything myself, but I never stay long; and there's a smell – '

'Yes,' murmured Martha Pym faintly, 'there's a smell. What – what – chased her away?'

The young woman, even in that lonely place, lowered her voice.

'Well, as you aren't thinking of taking the place, she got an idea in her head that old Sir James . . . well, he couldn't bear to leave Hartleys, mum. He's buried in the garden, and she thought he was after her, chasing round them bits of china – '

'Oh!' cried Miss Pym.

'Some of it used to be his, she found a lot stuffed away; he said they were to be left in Hartleys, but Miss Lefain would have the things sold, I believe – that's years ago.'

'Yes, yes,' said Miss Pym with a sick look. 'You don't know what he was like, do you?'

'No, mum; but I've heard tell he was very stout and very old – I wonder who it was you saw up at Hartleys?'

Miss Pym took a Crown Derby plate from her bag.

'You might take that back when you go,' she whispered. 'I shan't want it, after all.'

Before the astonished young woman could answer, Miss Pym had darted off across the marsh; that short hair, that earth-stained robe, the white socks, 'I generally live in the garden . . . .'

Miss Pym drove away, breakneck speed, frantically resolving to mention to no-one that she had paid a visit to Hartleys, nor lightly again to bring up the subject of ghosts.

She shook and shuddered in the damp, trying to get out of her clothes and her nostrils that indescribable smell.

The Housekeeper

Mr Robert Sekforde, a rather damaged man of fashion, entered with a lurching step his mansion near the tavern of the 'Black Bull', High Holborn. He was still known as 'Beau Sekforde' and was still dressed in the extreme of the fashion of this year 1710, with wide brocade skirts, an immense peruke, and a quantity of lace and paste ornaments that were nearly as brilliant as diamonds.

About Mr Sekforde himself was a good deal of this spurious gorgeousness; from a little distance he still looked the magnificent man he once had been, but a closer view showed him ruddled with powder and rouge like a woman, heavy about the eyes and jaw, livid in the cheeks – a handsome man yet, but one deeply marked by years of idleness, good living, and the cheap dissipations of a nature at once brutal and effeminate. In the well-shaped features and dark eyes there was not a contour or a shadow that did not help towards the presentment of a type vicious and worthless; yet he had an air of breeding, of gallantry and grace that had hitherto never failed to win him facile admiration and help him over awkward places in his career. This air was also spurious – spurious as the diamonds at his throat and in his shoe-buckles; he was not even of gentle birth; the obscurity that hung round his origin was proof of the shame he felt at the dismal beginning of a career that had been so brilliant.

He entered his mansion that was modest but elegant, and called for candles to be brought into his study.

Taking off slowly his white, scented gloves, he stared thoughtfully at his plump, smooth hands and then at the walnut desk, scattered with silver and ebony stand dishes, pens and taper-holders, and a great number of little notes on gilt-edged and perfumed papers.

There were a great many others, neither gilt-edged nor perfumed; Mr Sekforde knew that these last were bills as surely as he knew the first were insipid invitations to rather third-rate balls and routs.

Everything in Mr Sekforde's world was becoming rather third-rate now.

He looked round the room desperately, with that ugly glance of defiance which is not courage but cowardice brought to bay.

Nothing in the house was paid for and his credit would not last much longer; this had been a last venture to float his shaky raft on the waters of London society; he could foresee himself going very comfortably to the bottom.

Unless . . .

Unless he could again carry off some successful 'coup' at cards; and this was unlikely; he was too well known now.

Every resource that could, at any pinch, afford means of livelihood to an unscrupulous rogue and yet permit him to move among the people on whom he preyed, had already been played by Mr Sekforde.

The sound of the opening door caused him to look up; he dreaded duns and was not sure of the unpaid servants.

But it was his wife who entered; at sight of her, Beau Sekforde cursed in a fashion that would have surprised his genteel admirers, over whose tea-tables he languished so prettily.

'Oh, pray keep civil,' said the lady, in a mincing tone.

She trailed to the fireplace and looked discontentedly at the logs that were falling into ashes.

'The upholsterer came,' she added, 'with a bill for near a thousand guineas – I had difficulty in sending him away. Is nothing in the house paid for?'

'Nothing.'

She looked at him with a contempt that was more for herself than for him; she was quite callous and heartless; a sense of humour, a nice appreciation of men and things alone prevented her from being odious.

'Lord!' she smiled. 'To live to be fooled by Beau Sekforde!'

She was a Countess in her own right; her patent was from Charles II and explained her career; she still had the air of a beauty and wore the gowns usually affected by loveliness, but she was old with the terrible old age of a wanton, soulless woman.

Her reputation was bad even for her type; she had cheated at everything from love to cards, and no tenderness or regret had ever softened her ugly actions. At the end of her career as presiding goddess of a gambling saloon she had married Robert Sekforde, thinking he had money or at least the wits to get it, and a little betrayed by his glib tongue, that had flattered her into thinking her beauty not lost, her charm not dead; only to find him an adventurer worse off than herself, who had not even paid for the clothes in which he had come to woo her. Her sole satisfaction was that he had also been deceived.

He had thought her the prudent guardian of the spoils of a lifetime; instead, selfishness had caused her to scatter what greed had gained, and for her too this marriage had been seized as a chance to avert ruin.

Haggard and painted, a dark wig on her head, false pearls round her throat, and a dirty satin gown hanging gracefully round a figure still upright and elegant, she stared at the fire.

'We shall have to disappear,' she remarked drily.

He looked at her with eyes of hate.

'You must have some money,' he said bluntly.

Avarice, the vice of old age, flashed in her glance as jealousy would have gleamed in that of a younger woman.

'What little I have I need,' she retorted. 'The man has turned simple.' She grinned at her reflection in the glass above the fireplace.

'Well, leave me, then,' he said bitterly; could he be rid of her, he felt it would gild his misfortune.

But my lady had come to the end of all her admirers; she could not even any longer dazzle boys with the wicked glory of her past; she had no-one save Mr Sekforde, and she meant to cling to him; he was a man and twenty years younger than herself – he ought, she thought, to be useful.

Besides, this woman who had never had a friend of her own sex shuddered to think of the utter loneliness it would be to live without a man attached to her – better the grave; and of that she had all the horror of the true atheist.

'You talk folly,' she said with a dreadful ogle. 'I shall remain.'

'Then you will starve, my lady!' he flung out violently.

'Oh, fie, sir; one does not starve.'

He could not endure to look at her, but staring at the desk began to tear up the notes before him.

'Will you not go to a mask tonight?' she asked querulously.

'I have no money to pay for a chair,' he sneered.

'We might win something at cards.'

'People are very wary.'

'You were very clever at tricking me,' remarked the Countess, 'cannot you trick someone else, Mr Sekforde?'

He wheeled round on her with concentrated venom.

'Ah, madam, if I were a bachelor – '

She quailed a little before his wrath, but rallied to reply with the spirit of a woman who had been spoilt by a king: 'You think you are so charming? *Wealthy matches are particular. Look in the glass, sir; your face is as ruined as your reputation!*'

He advanced on her and she began to shriek in a dreadful fashion; the town woman showed through the airs of a great lady.

'I'll call the watch!' she shrilled.

He fell back with a heavy step and stood glaring at her.

'A pair of fools,' said my lady bitterly. Then her cynical humour triumphed over her disgust. 'Your first wife would smile to see us now,' she remarked.

Beau Sekforde turned to her a face suddenly livid.

'What do you know about my first wife?' he demanded fiercely.

'Nothing at all,' replied my lady. 'You kept her rather in the background, did you not? But one can guess.'

Mr Sekforde raged; he loathed any reference to the woman whom he had married in his obscurity, and who had been his drudge in the background through all his shifting fortunes – her worn face, her wagging tongue, her rude manners had combined to make the thorn in the rose bed of his softest days.

He had hated her and believed that she had hated him; she was a Scotswoman, a shrew, thrifty, honest, plain, and a good housekeeper; she had always made him very comfortable at home, though she had shamed him on the rare occasions when she had forced him to take her abroad.

She had died only a few months before his present marriage.

'One can guess,' repeated the Countess, showing teeth dark behind her rouged lips in a ghastly grin, 'that you made her life very pleasant.'

He sprang up and faced her, a big, heavy bully for all his satins and French peruke.

'Oh,' she shrilled, frightened but defiant, 'you look like murder.'

He turned away sharply and muttered some hideous words under his breath.

'What are you going to do?' asked my lady, with a quizzical glance round the tawdry splendour that had been hired to lure her into marriage and that now would so shortly be rent away.

Beau Sekforde controlled his wrath against the terrible woman who had deceived him into losing his last chance of retrieving ruin.

'Where are the servants?' he asked.

'All gone. I think they have taken some of the plate and all of the wine. There is some food downstairs.'

Mr Sekforde had seen it as he came up – a hacked piece of fat ham on a dirty dish, a stained cloth, and a jagged loaf had been laid out on the dining-room table.

'I have had my dinner,' remarked the Countess.

Her husband rudely left the room; he was hungry and forced to search for food, but the remembrance of the meal waiting nauseated him. He was delicate in his habits, and as he descended the stairs he thought of his late wife – she had been a wonderful housekeeper – even in poverty she had never failed to secure comfort.

As he opened the door of the dining-room he was agreeably surprised. Evidently one of the servants had remained after all.

The hearth had been swept and a neat fire burnt pleasantly; a clean cloth was on the table, and the service was set out exactly; a fresh loaf, butter, wine, fruit, a dish of hot meat, of cheese, of eggs stood ready; there was wine and brightly polished glasses.

'I did not know,' Mr Sekforde muttered, 'that any of the hussies in the house could work like this.'

He admired the spotless linen, the brilliant china, the gleaming glasses, the fresh and appetising food; and ate and drank with a pleasure that made him forget for the moment his troubles.

One thing only slightly disturbed his meal: among the dishes was a plate of goblin scones; they were of a peculiar shape and taste, and he had never known anyone make them but the late Jane Sekforde.

When he had finished he rang the bell for candles, for the short November day was closing in.

There was no answer. Surprised and slightly curious to see the servant who had been so deft, Mr Sekforde went to the head of the basement stairs and shouted lustily; still there was no reply.

He returned to the dining-room; the candles were lit and set precisely on the table.

Mr Sekforde ran upstairs to his wife. 'Who is in this house?' he asked in a tone of some agitation. The Countess was by the fire, seated on a low chair; before her on the floor was a wheel of playing cards from which she was telling her fortune.

'Who is in the house?' she sneered. 'A drunken ruffian.'

Misery was wearing thin the courtier-like manner from both of them.

'You old, wicked jade,' he replied, 'there is someone hiding in this house.'

She rose, scattering the cards with the worn toe of her little satin shoe. 'There is no-one in the house,' she said, 'not a baggage of them all would stay. I am going out. I want lights and amusement. Your house is too dull, Mr Sekforde.'

With this speech and an air that was a caricature of the graces of a young and beautiful woman, she swept out of the room.

Even her own maid, a disreputable Frenchwoman, had left her, having moved out of the impending crash; but my lady had never lacked spirit; she attired herself, put all the money she had in her bosom, and left the house to pass the evening with one of her cronies, who kept an establishment similar to that which she had been forced to abandon.

Even the departure of her vindictive presence did not sweeten for Beau Sekforde the house that was the temple of his failure.

He glared at the furniture that should have been paid for by bills on his wife's fortune, and went to his chamber.

He too knew haunts, dark and gleaming, where health and money, wits and time might be steadily consumed, and where one who was bankrupt in all these things might be for the time tolerated if he had a flattering and servile tongue and an appearance that lent some dignity to mean vices and ignoble sins.

He found a fire in his bedchamber, the curtains drawn, his cloak, evening rapier, and gloves put ready for him, the candles lit on his dressing-table. He dressed himself rather soberly and went downstairs.

The meal was cleared away in the dining-room, the fire covered, the chairs put back in their places.

Beau Sekforde swore. 'If I had not seen her fastened down in her coffin I should have sworn that Jane was in this house,' he muttered, and his bloodshot eyes winced a little from the gloom of the empty house.

Again he went to the head of the basement stairs and listened. He could hear faintly yet distinctly the sound of someone moving about – the sound of dishes, of brisk footsteps, of clattering irons.

'Some wench *has* remained,' he said uneasily, but he did not offer to investigate those concealed kitchen premises.

That evening his companions found him changed – a quiet, sullen, dangerous mood was on him; they could easily understand this, as tales of the disaster of his marriage had already leaked abroad.

But something deeper and more terrible even than his almost accomplished ruin was troubling Robert Sekforde.

He returned very late to the mansion in High Holborn; he had drunk as much wine as his friends would pay for, and there was little of the elegant gallant about the heavy figure in the stained coat, with wig awry and the flushed, sullen face, who stumbled into the wretched place he named home with unconscious sarcasm.

A light stood ready for him in the hall; he took this up and staggered upstairs, spilling the candle-grease over his lace ruffles.

Halfway up he paused, suddenly wondering who had thought to leave the light.

'Not my lady wife – not my royal Countess,' he grinned.

Then a sudden pang of horror almost sobered him. Jane had never forgotten to put a candle in the hall.

He paused, as if expecting to hear her shrill, nagging voice.

'You're drunk,' he said to himself fiercely; 'she is dead, dead, *dead*.' He went upstairs.

The fire in his room was bright, the bed stood ready, his slippers and bed-gown were warming, a cup of posset stood steaming on the side table.

Mr Sekforde snatched up his candle and hurried to the room of the Countess. He violently entered and stood confronting her great bed with the red damask hangings.

With a shriek she sat up; her cheeks were still rouged, the false pearls dangled in her ears, the laced gown was open on her skinny throat; a cap with pink ribbons concealed her scant grey hair.

She flung herself, with claw-like hands, on an embroidered purse on the quilt and thrust it under her pillow; it contained her night's winnings at cards.

'Have you come to rob me?' she screamed.

Terror robbed her of all dignity; she crouched in the shadows of the huge bed, away from the red light cast on her dreadful face by the candle her husband held.

Beau Sekforde was not thinking of money now, and her words passed unheeded.

'Who is in this house?' he demanded.

'You are mad,' she said, a little recovering her composure, but keeping her hands very firmly on the purse beneath the pillow. 'There is no-one in this house.'

'Did *you* put a candle for me, and prepare my room and light the fire and place the posset?'

He spoke thickly and leant against the bedpost; the candle, now almost guttered away, sent a spill of grease on the heavy quilt.

'You are drunk, you monstrous man!' screamed my lady. 'If you are not away instantly I'll put my head out of the window and screech the neighbourhood up.'

Beau Sekforde, regarding her with dull eyes, remained at his original point.

'There was someone in the kitchen this afternoon,' he insisted. 'I heard sounds – '

'Rats,' said my lady; 'the house is full of 'em.'

A look of relief passed over the man's sodden features.

'Of course, rats,' he muttered.

'What else could it be?' asked the Countess, sufficiently impressed by his strange manner momentarily to forget her grievance against him.

'What else?' he repeated; then suddenly turned on her with fury, lurching the candle into her face.

'Could rats have set *this* for me?' he shouted.

The Countess shrank back; when agitated her head trembled with incipient palsy, and now it trembled so that the false pearls rattled hollow against her bony neck.

'You will fire the bed-curtains!' she shrilled desperately.

He trembled with a loathing of her that was like a panic fear of fury. 'You time-foundered creature!' he cried. 'You bitter horror! And 'twas for *you* I did it!'

She sprang to her knees in the bed, her hands crooked as if ready for his face; there was nothing left now of the fine dame nurtured in courts, the beauty nursed in the laps of princes. She had reverted to the wench of Drury Lane, screaming abuse from alley to alley.

'If you are disappointed, what about me?' she shrieked. 'Have I not tied myself to a low, ugly fool?'

He stepped back from her as if he did not understand her, and, muttering, staggered back into his own room.

There he lit all the candles, piled up the fire with more fuel, glanced with horror at the bed, flung off his coat and wig, and settled himself in the chair with arms before the fire to sleep.

The Countess, roused and angered, could sleep no more.

She rose, flung on a chamber-robe, of yellow satin lined with marten's fur, that was a relic of her court days, and threadbare and moth-eaten in places though giving the effect of much splendour.

Without striking a light she went cautiously out into the corridor, saw the door of her husband's room ajar, a bright glow from it falling across the darkness, and crept steadily in.

He was, as she had supposed, in an intoxicated stupor of sleep by the fire.

His head had sunk forward on the stained and untied lace cravat on his breast; his wigless head showed fat and shaven and grey over the temples, his face was a dull purple and his mouth hung open. His great frame was almost as loose as that of a man newly dead, his hands hung slack and his chest heaved with his noisy breathing. My lady was herself a horrid object, but that did not prevent her from giving him a glance of genuine disgust.

'Beau Sekforde indeed!' she muttered.

She put out all the candles save two on the dressing-table, found the coat her husband had flung off, and began going swiftly through the pockets.

He had been, as she had hoped, fortunate at cards that night; he was indeed, like herself, of a type who seldom was unfortunate, since he only played with fools or honest men, neither of whom had any chance against the peculiar talents of the sharper.

The Countess found sundry pieces of gold and silver, which she knotted up in her handkerchief with much satisfaction. She knew that nothing but money would ever be able to be of any service to her in this world.

Pleased with her success, she looked round to see if there were anything else of which she could despoil her husband.

Keeping her cunning old eyes constantly on him, she crept to the dressing-table and went over the drawers and boxes. Most of the ornaments that she turned out glittered and gleamed heavily in the candlelight. But she knew that they were as false as the pearls trembling in her own ears; one or two things, however, she added to the money in the handkerchief, and she was about to investigate further when a little sound, like a cough, caused her to look sharply round.

The room was full of warm shadows, the fire was sinking low and only cast a dim light on the heavy, sleeping figure on the hearth, while the candlesticks on the dressing-table served only to illuminate the bent figure of the Countess in her brilliant wrap.

As she looked round she found herself staring straight at the figure of a woman, who was observing her from the other side of the bed.

This woman was dressed in a grey tabinet fashioned like the dress of an upper servant. Her hair was smoothly banded and her features were pale and sharp; her hands, that she held rather awkwardly in front of her, were rough and workworn.

Across one cheek was a long scratch.

The Countess dropped her spoils; she remembered her husband's words that she had taken for the babbling of a drunkard.

So there *was* someone in the house.

'How dare you?' she quavered, in a low voice, for she did not wish to rouse her husband. 'How dare you come here?'

Without replying the woman moved across to the sleeping man and looked down at him with an extraordinary expression of mingled malice and protection, as if she would defend him from any evil save that she chose to deal herself.

So sinister was this expression and the woman's whole attitude that the Countess was frightened as she never had been in the course of her wicked life.

She stood staring; the handkerchief, full of money and ornaments, dropped on the dressing-table unheeded.

Beau Sekforde moved in his sleep and fetched a deep groan.

'You impertinent creature!' whispered the Countess, taking courage. 'Will you not go before I wake my husband?'

At these last words the woman raised her head; she did not seem to speak, yet, as if there were an echo in the room, the Countess distinctly heard the words 'My husband!' repeated after her in a tone of bitter mockery.

A sense of unreality such as she had never known before touched the Countess; she felt as if her sight were growing dim and her hearing failing her; she made a movement as if to brush something from before her eyes.

When she looked again at Beau Sekforde he was alone; no-one was beside him.

In dreaming, tortured sleep he groaned and tossed.

'The baggage has slipped off,' muttered the Countess; 'belike it is some ancient dear of his own. I will send her away in the morning.'

She crept back to her own room, forgetting her spoils. She did not sleep, and Mr Sekforde did not wake till the pale winter dawn showed between the curtains.

The Countess looked round on a chamber in disorder, but for Beau Sekforde everything was arranged, shaving water ready, his breakfast hot and tempting on a tray, his clothes laid out.

When he had dressed and come downstairs he found his wife yawning over a copy of the *Gazette*.

She remembered last night quite clearly, and considerably regretted what she had left behind in Beau Sekforde's room in her confusion. She gave him a glance, vicious with the sense of an opportunity lost.

He flung at her the question he had asked last night.

'Who is in this house?'

'Some woman has stayed,' she answered. 'I think it was Joanna, the housekeeper, but I did not see very clearly. She must be out now, as I have rung the bell and there has been no answer.'

'My breakfast was brought up to me,' said Mr Sekforde. 'So it is Joanna Mills, is it?'

The Countess was angry; she had had to go to the kitchen and pick among yesterday's scraps for her own food.

'And who is she?'

'You said, madam, the housekeeper.'

'She must be very fond of you,' sneered the lady.

He stared at that and turned on her a ghastly look.

'Oh, don't think I am jealous!' she grinned cynically.

'It was the word you used,' he muttered. 'I do not think anyone has been *fond* of me save one – '

He paused and passed his hand over his weary, heavy eyes. 'I dreamt of her last night.'

'Who?'

'Jane, my wife.'

The Countess remembered the ugly echo of her words last night.

'Your wife – do you forget that I and no other am your wife?'

'I do,' he replied sullenly; 'to me Jane is always my wife.'

'A pity,' said my lady sarcastically, 'that she did not live longer.'

He gave her a queer look.

'And now we have got to think of ourselves,' he said abruptly. 'I cannot keep these things much longer – you had better go.'

'Where?'

'What do I care!' he answered cruelly.

'I stay here,' she replied. 'Is the rent paid?'

'No.'

'Well, they will not disturb us till quarter-day,' said my lady calmly. 'You do not want to be parted from your loving wife, do you, dear?'

He stared at her as if her words had a double meaning.

'Cannot you be quiet about my wife?' he exclaimed.

'La! The man is off his head!' shrilled my lady. 'Jane Sekforde is dead.'

'That is why I think about her,' he retorted grimly.

'A model husband,' jeered the Countess, eyeing him viciously. 'I am sorry I never knew the sweet creature you regret so keenly and so touchingly.'

He raged at her like a man whose nerves are overwrought. 'Will you not let the matter be? Think of yourself, you monstrous horror! You will soon be in the Fleet!'

This picture was sufficiently realistic to make the Countess shiver. 'What are you going to do?' she asked with sudden feebleness.

He did not know; brooding and black-browed, he withdrew to the window-place and stared out at the leaden November sky that hung so heavily over the London streets.

'I suppose if you were free of me you would take your handsome face to market again?' added my lady, with a sudden flash of new fury.

He gave her a red look, at which she shrank away. 'Well, still we do not decide on anything,' she quavered.

He would not answer her, but flung out of the house. His unsteady steps were directed to St. Andrew's Church. It was a long time since Beau Sekforde had been near a church. Even when his wife had been buried here, he had not attended the service.

He stood now in the porch, biting his thumb; then presently he entered. Hesitating and furtive, he went round the walls until he came to the new, cheap tablet with the badly cut draped urn and the florid Latin setting forth the virtues of Jane Sekforde.

'They don't say anything about her being a good housekeeper,' he found himself saying aloud. 'Why, she told me once she would come back from the grave to set her house in order.'

He looked round as if to seek the answer of some companion, then laughed sullenly, drew his hat over his eyes, and left the church.

Towards dusk he wandered home.

The dining-room was neat and clean, the fire attended to, the dinner on the table. He managed to eat some of the food, but without appetite. The Countess was out; there was no trace any-where of her slovenly splendour.

The whole house was as clean and precise as it had been when that neglected drudge Jane Sekforde had ruled over it.

When the Countess returned he was almost glad to see her – he had been thinking so much, too much, of Jane. He had thought of her as he had seen her last, cold in her bed, clothed in her best grey gown, and how he had stared at her and hung over her and drawn suddenly away, so sharply that the button of cut steel on his cuff had left a scratch on her dead cheek.

'Where is Joanna Mills?' he abruptly asked his wife.

She stared at him. In such a moment as this could he think of nothing but the housekeeper? Was he losing his wits?

But she did not now much care; she had found a crony willing to shelter her and exploit her ancient glories.

'I am going away,' she said. 'I do not know who is in the house – I have seen no-one.'

He seemed to pay no attention at all to her first remark.

'What was that woman you saw last night like?'

'A very plain, shrewish-looking creature,' replied my lady, with some bitterness, as she recalled how she had been startled into dropping the filched money.

'Are you sure it was a woman?' asked Beau Sekforde with a ghastly grin.

'Why, what else could it have been?' she replied curiously.

'I do not think it has been a woman for – some months,' he said.

'Why, do you imagine there is a spectre in the place?'

He would not, could not answer; he left her, and went from room to room throwing everything into disorder, taking a horrid pleasure in making a confusion in the neatness of the house. And then he flung himself away from the dreary mansion, leaving the Countess, like an old, weary bird of prey, wandering among the untidy rooms to see if there were anything worth taking away.

When he returned in the dark hours before the dawn he found the candle on the hall table.

'Curse you!' he screamed. 'Cannot you let me alone?'

He hastened upstairs; everything was neat, his bed, his fire, his posset ready, his shoes warming, his candles lit. His terrified eyes cast a horrid glance round the room.

'The medicine cupboard – has she tidied that?' he muttered.

He crossed to where it hung in one corner, opened the door, and looked at the rows of pots and bottles. One he knew well had been stained – had been left with a broken stopper . . . a bottle of a peculiar, ugly look, holding a yellow liquid that stained linen purple.

Such a stain, very tiny, had been on Jane Sekforde's pillow.

As he stared into the cupboard he saw that the bottle had been cleaned and set in its place, while a new, neat label had been pasted on the front.

The writing was the writing of Jane Sekforde – it said in clear letters, '*Poison*.'

Beau Sekforde dropped the candle and ran into the Countess's room.

'Wake up!' he shouted. 'Wake up and hear me! She has come back.

I want to confess. I murdered her! Let them take me away . . . somewhere where – where she cannot tidy for me.'

The room was empty of the Countess, who had fled; an unnatural light came from the unshuttered windows and showed a woman sitting up in the great bed.

She had a pale, shrewish face, a grey garment on, and a scratch across her cheek.

As the shrieks of Beau Sekforde's confession echoed into the night and drew the watch to thunder on the door, the woman smiled.

Florence Flannery

An Ornament in Regency Paste

She who had been Florence Flannery noted with a careless eye
the stains of wet on the dusty stairs, and with a glance ill used
to observance of domesticities looked up for damp or dripping
ceilings. The dim-walled staircase revealed nothing but more
dust, yet this would serve as a peg for ill humour to hang on, so
Florence pouted.

'An ill, mouldy place,' said she, who loved gilding and gimcracks
and mirrors reflecting velvet chairs, and flounced away to the upper
chamber, lifting frilled skirts contemptuously high.

Her husband followed; they had been married a week and there
had never been any happiness in their wilful passion. Daniel Shute
did not now look for any; in the disgust of this draggled homecoming
he wondered what had induced him to marry the woman and how
soon he would come to hate her.

As she stood in the bedroom he watched her with dislike. Her
tawdry charms of vulgar prettiness had once been delightful to his
dazed senses and muddled wits; but here, in his old home, washed by
the fine Devon air, his sight was clearer and she appeared coarse as a
poppy at the far end of August.

'Of course you hate it,' he said cynically, lounging with his big
shoulders against one of the bedposts, his big hands in the pockets of
his tight nankeen trousers and his fair hair, tousled from the journey,
hanging over his mottled face.

'It is not the place you boasted to have,' replied Florence, but idly,
for she stood by the window and looked at the tiny leaded panes; the
autumn sun, gleaming sideways on this glass, picked out a name
scratched there:

Florence Flannery   Borne 1500

'Look here,' cried the woman, excited, 'this should be my an-
cestress!'

She slipped off a huge diamond ring she wore and scratched underneath the writing the present year, '1800'.

Daniel Shute came and looked over her shoulder.

'That reads strange – "Born 1500" – as if you would say died 1800,' he remarked. 'Well, I don't suppose she had anything to do with you, my charmer, yet she brought you luck, for it was remembering this name here made me notice you when I heard what you were called.'

He spoke uncivilly, and she responded in the same tone.

'Undervalue what is your own, Mr Shute. There was enough for me to choose from, I can swear.'

'Enough likely gallants,' he grinned, 'not so many likely husbands, eh?'

He slouched away, for, fallen as he was, it stung him that he had married a corybant of the opera, an unplaced, homeless, nameless creature for all he knew, for he could never quite believe that 'Florence Flannery' was her real name.

Yet that name had always attracted him; it was so queer that he should meet a real woman called Florence Flannery when one of the earliest of his recollections was tracing that name over with a curious finger in the old diamond pane.

'You have never told me who she was,' said Mrs Shute.

'Who knows? Three hundred years ago, m'dear. There are some old wives' tales, of course.'

He left the great bedroom and she followed him doggedly downstairs.

'Is this your fine manor, Mr Shute? And these your big rooms and noble grounds? And how am I to live here, Mr Shute, who left the gaieties of London for you?'

Her voice, shrill and edged, followed him down the stairs and into the vast, dismantled drawing-room, where they paused, facing each other like things caught in a trap, which is what they were.

For he had married her because he was a ruined man, driven from London by duns, and a drunken man who dreaded lonely hours and needed a boon companion to pledge him glass by glass, and a man of coarse desires who had bought with marriage what he was not rich enough to buy with money, and she had married him because she was past her meridian and saw no more conquests ahead and also was in love with the idea of being a gentlewoman and ruling in the great grand house by the sea – which was how she had thought of Shute Manor.

And a great grand house it had been, but for twenty years it had been abandoned by Daniel Shute, and stripped and mortgaged to pay for his vices, so that now it stood barren and desolate, empty and tarnished; and only a woman with love in her heart could have made a home of it. Never had there been love in Florence Flannery's heart, only greed and meanness.

Thus these two faced each other in the gaunt room with the monstrous chandelier hanging over them wrapped in a dusty brown holland bag, the walls festooned with cobwebs, the pale wintry sunshine showing the thick dust on the unpolished boards.

'I never can live here!' cried Mrs Shute. There was a touch of panic in her voice and she lifted her hands to her heart with a womanly gesture of grief.

The man was touched by a throb of pity; he did not himself expect the place to be so dilapidated. Some kind of a rascally agent had been looking after it for him, and he supposed some effort would have been made for his reception.

Florence saw his look of half-sullen shame and urged her point.

'We can go back, cannot we?' she said, with the rich drop in her voice so useful for coaxing. 'Back to London and the house in Baker Street? All the old friends and the old pleasures, Mr Shute, and a dashing little cabriolet to go round the park?'

'Curse it!' he answered, chagrined. 'I haven't the money, Flo; I haven't the damned money!' She heard the ring of sheer bitter truth in his voice, and the atrocious nature of the deception he had practised on her overwhelmed her shallow understanding.'You mean you've got no money, Mr Shute?' she screamed.

'Not enough for London, m'dear.'

'And I've to live in this filthy barn?'

'It has been good enough for my people, Mrs Shute,' he answered grimly. 'For all the women of my family, gentlewomen all of 'em, with quarterings, and it will be good enough for you, m'dear, so none of your Bartholomew Fair airs and graces.'

She was cornered and a little afraid of him; he had been drinking at the last place where they stopped to water the horses and she knew how he could be when he was drunk; she remembered that she was alone with him and what a huge man he was.

So she crept away and went down into the vast kitchens, where an old woman and a girl were preparing a meal.

The sight of this a little heartened Mrs Shute; in her frilled taffetas and long ringlets she sat down by the great open hearth, moving her hands to show the firelight flashing in her rings and shifting her petticoats so that the girl might admire her kid shoes.

'I'll take a cordial to stay my strength,' she said, 'for I've come a long way and find a sour welcome at the end of it, and that'll turn any woman's blood.'

The old dame smiled, knowing her type well enough; for even in a village you may find women like this.

So she brought Mrs Shute some damson wine and a plate of biscuits, and the two women became friendly enough and gossiped in the dim candlelit kitchen while Daniel Shute wandered about his old home, even his corrupt heart feeling many a pang to see the places of his childhood desolate, the walks overgrown, the trees felled, the arbours closed, the fountains dried, and all the spreading fields about fenced by strangers.

The November moon was high in a misted space of open heaven by the time he reached the old carp pond. Dead weeds tangled over the crumbling, moss-grown stone, trumpery and slime coated the dark waters.

'I suppose the carp are all dead?' said Mr Shute.

He had not been aware that he spoke aloud, and was surprised to hear himself answered.

'I believe there are some left, esquire.'

Mr Shute turned sharply and could faintly discern the figure of a man sitting on the edge of the pond so that it seemed as if his legs half dangled in the black water.

'Who are you?' asked Daniel Shute quickly.

'I'm Paley, sir, who looks after the grounds.'

'You do your work damned badly,' replied the other, irritated.

'It's a big place, esquire, for one man to work.'

He seemed to stoop lower and lower, as if any moment he might slip into the pond; indeed, in the half dark it seemed to Mr Shute that he was already half in the water. Yet, on this speech, he moved and showed that he was but bending over the sombre depths of the carp pond.

The moonlight displayed him as a drab man of middling proportions, with slow movements and a large languid eye which glittered feebly in the pale light; Mr Shute had an impression that this eye looked at him sideways as if it was set at the side of the man's head, but soon saw that this was an illusion.

'Who engaged you?' he asked acidly, hating the creature.

'Mr Tregaskis, the agent,' replied the man in what appeared to be a thick foreign accent or with some defect of speech, and walked away into the wintry undergrowth.

Mr Shute returned home grumbling; in the grim parlour Mr Tregaskis was waiting for him – a red Cornishman, who grinned at his employer's railings. He knew the vices of Mr Shute and the difficulties of Mr Shute, and he had seen Mrs Shute in the kitchen deep in maudlin gossip with old Dame Chase and the idiot-faced girl, drinking the alcoholic country wine till it spilled from her shaking fingers on to her taffeta skirt.

So he assumed a tone of noisy familiarity that Mr Shute was too sunken to resent; the last of the old squire's Oporto was sent for and the men drank themselves on to terms of easy goodfellowship.

At the last, when the candles were guttering, the bottles empty, and the last log's ashes on the hearth, Mr Shute asked who was the creature Paley he had found hanging over the carp pond.

Mr Tregaskis told him, but the next morning Mr Shute could not recollect what he had said – the whole evening had, in the recollection, an atmosphere of phantasmagoria – but he thought that the agent had said Paley was a deserted sailor who had wandered up from Plymouth and taken the work without pay, a peculiar individual who lived in a wattled hut that he had made himself and on food he caught with his own hands.

His sole explanation of himself was that he had waited for something a long time and was still waiting for it; useful he was, Mr Tregaskis had said, and it was better to leave him alone.

All this Mr Shute remembered vaguely, lying in the great bed staring at the pale sun glittering on the name 'Florence Flannery' scratched on the window with the two dates.

It was late in the autumnal morning, but his wife still lay beside him, heavily asleep, with her thick, heavy chestnut hair tossed over the pillow and her full bosom panting, the carnation of her rounded face flushed and stained, the coarse diamonds glowing on her plump hands, the false pearls slipping round her curved throat.

Daniel Shute sat up in bed and looked down at her prone sleep.

'Who is she? And where does she come from?' he wondered. He had never cared to find out, but now his ignorance of all appertaining to his wife annoyed him.

He shook her bare shoulder until she yawned out of her heavy sleep.

'Who are you, Flo?' he asked. 'You must know something about yourself.'

The woman blinked up at him, drawing her satin bed-gown round her breast.

'I was in the opera, wasn't I?' she answered lazily. 'I never knew my people.'

'Came out of an orphanage or the gutter, I suppose?' he returned bitterly.

'Maybe.'

'But your name?' he insisted. 'That is never your name – "Florence Flannery"?'

'I've never known another,' she responded indifferently.

'You're not Irish.'

'I don't know, Mr Shute. I've been in many countries and seen many strange things.'

He laughed; he had heard some of her experiences.

'You've seen so much and been in so many places, I don't know how you've ever got it all into one life.'

'I don't know myself. It's all rather like a dream and the most dreamlike of all is to be lying here looking at my own name written three hundred years ago.'

She moved restlessly and slipped from the bed, a handsome woman with troubled eyes.

' 'Tis the drink brings the dreams, m'dear,' said Mr Shute. 'I had some dreams last night of a fellow named Paley I met by the carp pond.'

'You were drinking in the parlour,' she retorted scornfully.

'And you in the kitchen, m'dear.'

Mrs Shute flung a fringed silk shawl, the gift of an Indian nabob, round her warm body and dropped, shivering and yawning, into one of the worn tapestry chairs.

'Who was this Florence Flannery?' she asked idly.

'I told you no-one knows. An Irish girl born in Florence, they said, when I was a child and listened to beldame's gossip. Her mother a Medici, m'dear, and he a groom! And she came here, the trollop, with some young Shute who had been travelling in Italy – picked her up and brought her home, like I've brought you.'

'He didn't marry her?' asked Mrs Shute indifferently.

'More sense,' said her husband coarsely. 'I'm the first fool of me family. She was a proper vixen. John Shute took her on his voyages; he'd a ship and went discovering. They talk yet at Plymouth of how she would sit among the parrots and the spices and the silks when the ship came into Plymouth Hoe.'

'Ah, the good times,' sighed Mrs Shute, 'when men were men and paid a good price for their pleasures!'

'You've fetched your full market value, Mrs Shute,' he answered, yawning in the big bed.

'I'd rather be John Shute's woman than your wife,' she returned.

'What do you know of him?'

'I saw his portrait on the back stairs last night. Goody Chase showed me. A noble man with a clear eye and great arms to fight and love with.'

'He used 'em to push Florence Flannery out with,' grinned Mr Shute, 'if half the tales are true. On one of their voyages they picked up a young Portuguese who took the lady's fancy, and she brought him back to Shute Court.'

'And what was the end of it?'

'I know no more, save that she was flung out – as I'd like to fling you out, my beauty!' foamed Mr Shute with gusty violence.

His wife laughed loud and discordantly.

'I'll tell the rest of the tale. She got tired of her new love, and he wasn't a Portuguese but an Indian, or partly, and his name was D'Ailey – Daly the people called it here. On one voyage she told John Shute about him, and he was marooned on a lonely island in the South Seas – tied up to a great stone image of a god, burning hot in the tropic sun. He must have been a god of fishes, for there was nothing else near that island but a monstrous fish.'

'Who told you this?' demanded Mr Shute. 'Old Dame Chase with her lies? I never heard of this before.'

' 'Tis the story,' resumed his wife. 'The last she saw of him was his bound figure tied tight, tight, to the gaping, grinning idol while she sat on the poop as the ship, *The Phoenix*, sailed away. He cursed her and called on the idol to let her live till he was avenged on her – he was of the breed, or partly of the breed, that these gods love, and Florence Flannery was afraid, afraid, as she sailed away . . . '

'Goody Chase in her cups!' sneered Mr Shute. 'And what's the end of your story?'

'There's no end,' said the woman sullenly. 'John Shute cast her off, for the bad luck that dogged him; and what became of her I don't know.'

'It's an ugly tale and a stupid tale,' grumbled Daniel Shute with a groan as he surveyed the bleak chill weather beyond the lattice panes. 'Get down and see what's to eat in the house and what's to drink in the cellar; and if that rogue Tregaskis is there, send him up to me.'

Mrs Shute rose and pulled fiercely at the long, wool-embroidered bell-rope so that the rusty bell jangled violently.

'What'll you do when the wine is all drunk and the boon companions have cleared out your pockets?' she asked wildly. 'Do your own errands, Mr Shute.'

He flung out of bed with a pretty London oath, and she remained huddled in the chair while he dressed and after he had left her, wringing her hands now and then and wailing under her breath, till Dame Chase came up with a posset and helped her to dress. The sight of her dishevelled trunks restored some of Mrs Shute's spirits; she pulled out with relish her furbelows and flounces, displaying to Goody Chase's amazed admiration the last fashions of Paris and London, mingling her display with fond reminiscences of gilded triumphs.

'Maybe you'd be surprised to learn that Mr Shute isn't my first husband,' she said, tossing her head.

The fat old woman winked.

'I'd be more surprised, m'lady, to learn he was your last.'

Mrs Shute laughed grossly, but her spirits soon fell; kneeling on the floor with her tumbled finery in her lap, she stared out through the window on which her name was written at the tossing bare boughs, the chill sky, the dry flutter of the last leaves.

'I'll never get away,' she said mournfully; 'the place bodes me no good. I've had the malaria in me time, Mrs Chase – in one of those cursed Italian swamps – and it affected me memory; there's much I can't place together and much I recall brokenly – dreams and fevers, Mrs Chase.'

'The drink, m'lady.'

'No,' returned the kneeling woman fiercely. 'Wasn't the drink taken to drown those dreams and fevers? I wish I could tell you half I know – there's many a fine tale in me head. When I begin to speak, it goes!'

She began to rock to and fro, lamenting.

'To think of the fine times I've had with likely young men drinking me health in me slipper, and the little cabriolet in Paris, and the walks in the Prater outside Vienna. So pleasant you would hardly believe!'

'You'll settle down, m'lady, like women do.'

Indeed, Mrs Shute seemed to make some attempt at 'settling

down'; there was something piteous in the despairing energy with which she set to work to make her life tolerable; there was a suite of rooms lined with faded watered green silk that she took for her own and had cleaned and furnished with what she could gather from the rest of the house – old gilt commodes and rococo chairs and threadbare panels of tapestries and chipped vases of Saxe Leunville, one or two pastel portraits that the damp had stained, together with some tawdry trifles she had brought in her own baggage.

She employed Mr Tregaskis to sell her big diamond in Plymouth and bought pale blue satin hangings for her bedroom and spotted muslin for her bed, a carpet wreathed with roses, a gaudy dressing-table and phials of perfume – opoponax, frangipane, musk – potent, searing, to dissipate, she said, the odours of must and mildew.

Arranging these crude splendours was her sole occupation. There were no neighbours in the lonely valley and Mr Shute fell into melancholy and solitary drinking; he hung on to this existence as just more tolerable than a debtor's prison, but the fury with which he met his fate expressed itself in curses awful to hear. Such part of the estate as still belonged to him he treated with complete contempt; Mr Tregaskis continued to supervise some rough farming and the man Paley worked in the garden; taciturn, solitary, and sullen, he made an ill impression on Mr Shute, yet he cost nothing and did some labour, as carrying up the firewood to the house and clearing away some of the thickets and dying weeds and vast clumps of nettles and docks.

Mrs Shute met him for the first time by the carp pond; she was tricked out in a white satin pelisse edged with fur and a big bonnet, and wandered forlornly in the neglected paths. Paley was sitting on the edge of the carp pond, looking intently into the murky depths.

'I'm the new mistress,' said Mrs Shute, 'and I'll thank you to keep better order in the place.'

Paley looked up at her with his pale eyes. 'Shute Court isn't what it was,' he said; 'there is a lot of work to do.'

'You seem to spend a power of time by the pond,' she replied. 'What are you here for?'

'I'm waiting for something,' he said. 'I'm putting in time, Mrs Shute.'

'A sailor, I hear?' she said curiously, for the draggled, nondescript man in his greenish-black clothes was difficult to place; he had a peculiar look of being boneless, without shoulders or hips, one slope slipping into another as if there were no framework under his flabby flesh.

'I've been at sea,' he answered, 'like yourself, Mrs Shute.'

She laughed coarsely. 'I would I were at sea again,' she replied; 'this is horror to me.'

'Why do you stay?'

'I'm wondering. It seems that I can't get away, the same as I couldn't help coming.' A wail came into her voice. 'Must I wait till Mr Shute has drunk himself to death?'

The wind blew sharp across the pond, cutting little waves in the placid surface, and she who had been Florence Flannery shuddered in the bite of it and turned away and went muttering up the path to the desolate house.

Her husband was in the dirty parlour playing at bezique with Mr Tregaskis, and she flared in upon them.

'Why don't you get rid of that man Paley? I hate him. He does no work – Mrs Chase told me that he always sits by the carp pond, and today I saw him – ugh!'

'Paley's all right, Mrs Shute,' replied Tregaskis; 'he does more work than you think.'

'Why does he stay?'

'He's waiting for a ship that's soon due in Plymouth.'

'Send him off,' insisted Mrs Shute. 'Isn't the place melancholic enough without you having that sitting about?'

Her disgust and distaste of the man seemed to amount to a panic, and her husband, whose courage was sapped by the drink, was infected by her fear.

'When did this fellow come?' he demanded.

'About a week before you did. He'd tramped up from Plymouth.'

'We've only his word for that,' replied Mr Shute with drunken cunning; 'maybe he's a Bow Street runner sent by one of those damned creditors! You're right, Flo, I don't like the wretch – he's watching me, split him! I'll send him off.'

Mr Tregaskis shrugged as Daniel staggered from his chair.

'The man's harmless, sir; halfwitted if you like, but useful.'

Still Mr Shute dragged on his greatcoat with the many capes and followed his wife out into the grey garden.

The carp pond was not near the house, and by the time that they had reached it a dull twilight had fallen in the cold and heavy air.

The great trees were quite bare now and flung a black tracing of forlorn branches against the bleak evening sky; patches and clumps of dead weeds obstructed every path and alley; by the carp pond showed the faint outline of a blind statue crumbling beneath the weight of dead mosses.

Paley was not there.

'He'll be in his hut,' said Mr Shute, 'sleeping or spying – the ugly old devil. I'll send him off.'

The dead oyster-white of Mrs Shute's pelisse gleamed oddly as she followed her husband through the crackling undergrowth.

There, in the thickening twilight, they found the hut, a queer arrangement of wattles cunningly interwoven in which there was no furniture whatever, nothing but a bare protection from the wind and weather.

Paley was not there.

'I'll find him,' muttered Mr Shute, 'if I have to stay out all night.'

For his half-intoxicated mind had fixed on this stranger as the symbol of all his misfortunes and perhaps the avenger of all his vices.

His wife turned back, for her pelisse was being caught on the undergrowth; she went moodily towards the carp pond.

A moment later a sharp shriek from her brought Mr Shute plunging back to her side. She was standing in a queer bent attitude, pointing with a shaking, plump hand to the murky depths of the pond.

'The wretch! He's drowned himself!' she screamed.

Mr Shute's worn-out nerves reacted to her ignoble panic; he clutched her arm as he gazed in the direction of her finger; there was something dark in the shallower side of the pond, something large and dark, with pale flat eyes that glittered malevolently.

'Paley!' gasped Mr Shute.

He bent closer in amazed horror, then broke into tremulous laughter. ' 'Tis a fish,' he declared, 'one of the old carp.'

Mrs Shute indeed now perceived that the monstrous creature in the water was a fish; she could make out the wide, gaping jaw, tall spines shadowing in the murk, and a mottled skin of deadly yellow and dingy white.

'It's looking at me,' she gasped. 'Kill it, kill it, the loathsome wretch!'

'It's – it's too big,' stammered Mr Shute, but he picked up a stone to hurl; the big fish, as if aware of his intentions, slipped away into the murky depths of the pond, leaving a sluggish ripple on the surface.

Daniel Shute now found his courage.

'Nothing but an old carp,' he repeated. 'I'll have the thing caught.'

Mrs Shute began to weep and wring her hands. Her husband

dragged her roughly towards the house, left her there, took a lantern, and accompanied now by Mr Tregaskis returned in search of Paley.

This time they found him sitting in his usual place by the side of the pond. Mr Shute had now changed his mind about sending him away; he had a muddled idea that he would like the pond watched, and who was to do this if not Paley?

'Look here, my man,' he said, 'there's a great carp in this pond – a very big, black old carp.'

'They live for hundreds of years,' said Paley. 'But this isn't a carp.'

'You know about it, then?' demanded Mr Shute.

'I know about it.'

'Well, I want you to catch it – kill it. Watch till you do. I loathe it – ugh!'

'Watch the pond?' protested Mr Tregaskis, who held the lantern and was chilled and irritable. 'Damme, esquire, what can the thing do? It can't leave the water.'

'I wouldn't promise you that,' muttered Mr Shute.

'You're drunk,' said the other coarsely.

But Mr Shute insisted on his point. 'Watch the pond, Paley, watch it day and night till you get that fish.'

'I'll watch,' answered Paley, never moving from his huddled position. The two men went back to the desolate house. When Mr Shute at last staggered upstairs he found his wife, with half a dozen candles lit, crouching under the tawdry muslin curtains with which she had disfigured the big bed.

She clutched a rosary that she was constantly raising to her lips as she muttered ejaculations.

Mr Shute lurched to the bedside. 'I didn't know that you were a Papist, Flo,' he sneered.

She looked up at him.

'That story's got me,' she whispered, 'the man tied up to the fish god – the curse – and he following her, tracking her down *for three hundred years*, till she was hounded back to the old place where they'd loved.'

Daniel Shute perceived that she had been drinking, and sank into a chair.

'Goody Chase's gossip,' he answered, yawning, 'and that damned ugly fish. I've set Paley to catch him – to watch the pond till he does.'

She looked at him sharply, and appeared relieved.

'Anyhow, what's it to do with you?' he continued. 'You ain't the jade who left the man on the island!' He laughed crudely.

Mrs Shute sank down on her pillows.

'As long as the pond is watched,' she murmured, 'I don't mind.'

But during the night she tossed and panted in a delirium, talking of great ships with strange merchandise, of lonely islands amid blazing seas, of mighty stone gods rearing up to the heavens, of a man in torture and a curse following a woman who sailed away, till her husband shook her and left her alone, sleeping on a couch in the dreary parlour.

The next day he spoke to Mrs Chase.

'Between your news and your ideas you've turned your mistress's head. Good God! She is like a maniac with your parcel of follies.'

But Goody Chase protested that she had told her nothing.

'*She* told *me* that story, esquire, and said she had found it in an old book. What did I know of Florence Flannery? Many a time you've asked me about her when you were a child and I've had no answer to give you – what did I know save she was a hussy who disgraced Shute Court?'

At this Daniel Shute vehemently demanded of his wife where she got the tales which she babbled about, but the woman was sullen and heavy and would tell him nothing; all the day she remained thus, but when the few hours of wintry light were over she fell again into unbridled terror, gibbering like a creature deprived of reason, beating her breast, kissing the rosary, and muttering, '*Mea culpa. Mea culpa. Mea maxima culpa*!'

Mr Shute was not himself in any state to endure this; he left his wife to herself and made Tregaskis sleep with him for company in another room.

Winter froze the bleak countryside; Paley kept guard by the pond and the Shutes somehow dragged on an intolerable existence in the deserted house.

In the daytime Mrs Shute revived a little and would even prink herself out in her finery and gossip with Mrs Chase over the vast log fire; but the nights always found her smitten with terror, shivering with cowardly apprehension; and the object of all her nightmare dread was the fish she had seen in the pond.

'It can't leave the water,' they told her, and she always answered: 'The first night I was here I saw wet on the stairs.'

'My God, my God!' Daniel Shute would say. 'This is like living with someone sentenced to death.'

'Get a doctor over from Plymouth,' suggested Mr Tregaskis.

But Mr Shute would not for fear of being betrayed to his creditors.

'Better rot here than in the Fleet,' he swore.

'Then take her away – and keep her from the bottle.'

The wretched husband could do neither of these things; he had no money, and no influence over Mrs Shute. He was indeed indifferent to her sufferings save in so far as they reacted on him and ever accustomed him to the spectacle of her breakdown; he knew that it was not really strange that a woman such as she was should collapse under conditions such as these, and his life was already so wretched that he cared little for added horrors.

He began to find a strange comfort in the man Paley, who, taciturn, slow, and queer, yet did his work and watched the pond with an admirable diligence.

One night in the blackest time of the year, the bitter dark nights before Christmas, the shrieks of Mrs Shute brought her husband cursing up the stairs.

Her door was unbolted and she sat up in bed, displaying, in the light of his snatched-up taper, some red marks on her arm.

'Let him kill me and done with it,' she jabbered.

Mr Tregaskis came pushing in and caught rudely hold of her arm.

'She's done it herself,' he cried, 'those are the marks of her own teeth!'

But Mrs Shute cried piteously: 'He came flopping up the stairs, he broke the bolts; he jumped on the bed! Oh! oh! oh! Isn't this the bed, the *very* bed I slept in then – and didn't he used to creep into this room when John Shute was away?'

'Still thinking of that damned fish,' said Mr Tregaskis; 'and it's my belief you neither of you saw it at all, esquire – that man Paley has been watching, and he's seen nothing.'

Mr Shute bit his fingernails, looking down on the writhing figure of his wife.

'Light all the candles, can't you?' he said. 'I'll stay with the poor fool tonight.'

While Mr Tregaskis obeyed he went to the door and looked out, holding his taper high.

There were pools of wet and a long trail of slime down the dusty, neglected stairs.

He called Mr Tregaskis.

'Ugh!' cried the Cornishman; then, 'It's from Goody Chase's water crock.'

On the following windy morning Mr Shute went out, shivering in the nipping air, to the carp pond.

'I don't want another night like last,' he said 'You'll sleep across my wife's door – she thinks that cursed carp is after her – '

Then, at the gross absurdity of what he said, he laughed miserably. 'This is a pretty pantomime I'm playing,' he muttered.

A horrid curiosity drove him up to look at his wife.

She sat between the draggled muslin curtains hugging her knees in the tumbled bed; a wretched fire flickered wanly in the chill depths of the vast room; a wind blew swift and remote round the window on which was scratched the name of Florence Flannery.

Mr Shute shivered.

'I must get you away,' he said, stirred above his fears for himself; 'this is a damned place – the Fleet would be better, after all.'

She turned lustreless eyes upon him.

'I can't *get* away,' she said dully. 'I've come here to die. Don't you see it on the window – "Died 1800"?'

He crossed the floor and peered at the scratching on the glass. Someone had indeed added the word 'Died' before the last date.

'These are the tricks of a Bedlamite,' he said nervously. 'Do you think there was only *one* Florence Flannery?'

'And do you think,' she returned harshly, 'that there were two?'

She looked so awful crouched up in bed with her hanging hair, her once plump face fallen in the cheeks, her soiled satin gown open over her labouring breast, her whole air and expression so agonised, so malevolent, so dreadful, that Daniel Shute passed his hand over his eyes as if to brush away a vision of unsubstantial horror.

He was shaken by an hallucination, by lightheadedness; he appeared to enter another world, in which many queer things were possible.

'What are you?' he asked uneasily. 'He's been after you for nearly three hundred years? Aren't you punished enough?'

'Oh! oh!' moaned the woman. 'Keep him out! Keep him out!'

'I'll put Paley at the door tonight,' muttered Mr Shute.

He crept out of the horrible chamber; he now detested his wife beyond all reason, yet somehow he felt impelled to save her from the invisible furies who were pursuing her in so gruesome a fashion.

'She's a lunatic,' said Mr Tregaskis brusquely. 'You'll have to keep her shut up in that room – it's not difficult to account for, with the life she's led and this place and the coincidence of the names.'

The first snow of the year began to fall that night, sullen flakes struggling in the coils of the leaping wind that circled round and round Shute Court.

In the last glimmer of daylight Paley came to take up his post.

Drab, silent, with his sloping shoulders and nondescript clothes, he went slowly upstairs and sat down outside Mrs Shute's door.

'He seems to know the way,' remarked Daniel Shute.

'Don't you know he works in the house?' retorted Mr Tregaskis.

The two men slept, as usual, in the parlour, on stiff horsehair couches bundled up with pillows and blankets; the litter of their supper was left on the table and they piled the fire up with logs before going to sleep. Mr Shute's nerves were in no state to permit him to risk waking up in the dark.

The wind dropped and the steady downdrift of the soft snow filled the blackness of the bitter night.

As the grandfather clock struck three Daniel Shute sat up and called to his companion.

'I've been thinking in my dreams,' he said, with chattering teeth. 'Is it Paley or Daley? You know the name was D'Ailey.'

'Shut up, you fool,' returned the agent fiercely; but he then raised himself on his elbow, for a hoarse, bitter scream, followed by some yelled words in a foreign language, tore through the stillness.

'The mad woman,' said Mr Tregaskis; but Daniel Shute dragged the clothes up to his chattering teeth. 'I'm not going up,' he muttered. 'I'm not going up!'

Mr Tregaskis dragged on his trousers and flung a blanket over his shoulders and so, lighting a taper at the big fire, went up the gaunt stairs to Mrs Shute's room. The glimmering beams of the rushlight showed him tracks of wet again on the dirty boards.

'Goody Chase with her crocks and possets,' he murmured; then, louder, 'Paley! Paley!'

There was no-one outside Mrs Shute's door, which hung open. Mr Tregaskis entered.

She who had been Florence Flannery lay prone on her tawdry couch; the deep wounds that had slain her appeared to have been torn by savage teeth; she looked infinitely old, shrivelled, and detestable.

Mr Tregaskis backed on to the stairs, the light lurching round him from the shaking of his taper, when Mr Shute came bustling up out of the darkness.

'Paley's gone,' whispered Mr Tregaskis dully.

'I saw him go,' gibbered Mr Shute 'as I ventured to the door, by the firelight – a great fish slithering away with blood on his jaws.'

Elsie's Lonely Afternoon

Elsie was always lonely, but her desolation seemed more poignant when the day was sunny.

Elsie lived with her grandmother in a large house at Hampstead. She thought that there could not be, anywhere, a house with more rooms, more stairs, more quiet and empty.

There were three servants. They lived in the day downstairs in a large basement, and nightly slept in attics at the top of the house. Both basement and attics were out of Elsie's reach; she was not allowed to speak to the servants. There was not, to Elsie's mind, a single thing in this great house that was cheerful or pleasant. A great many people must have lived there once, there were so many empty rooms. There was an empty schoolroom, the inky, tattered lesson-books still on the shelves round the walls, a globe in one corner, and a tattered map hanging between the windows, and worn cut desks and benches as if quite a number of children had once learnt their lessons there.

There was also an empty study, with a huge bookcase with a glass front, that was always locked; and there was a drawing-room in which no-one ever sat. The shutters were always closed in this room into which Elsie had only, just by chance, once peeped. It was full of mirrors with glass frames and little cabinets lined with quilted silk in which stood china figures.

Then there was the dining-room, so much too large for Elsie, who had her dinner and tea there alone on a little cloth laid at one end of the long, shining mahogany table.

But Grandmamma always had her meals in bed. She suffered from what Elsie had been told was a 'stroke'. When Elsie asked what that was, her grandmother replied, 'The hand of God'.

So Elsie thought of God's hand reaching out of heaven into Grandmamma's large bedroom and stroking her down one side and leaving that dead.

Elsie did not find Grandmamma's bedroom a pleasant place,

either. It was very large and had two windows which looked on to the garden at the back. Between the two windows was a dressing-table, covered in white spotted muslin over stiff pink stuff.

There were a great many engravings on the walls. They seemed to be all very much alike, with a smooth baby face, like a china doll, and each of these pictures had a little story.

One was of a young prince: the Prince Imperial, Grandmamma said, who had recently been killed by blackamoors. Another was of a girl, crying over a dead bird which she held in her hand, and there was a little hole at her feet where the bird was presently to be buried. And another was of a woman tying a scarf on to a man's arm, and Grandmamma explained that if he went out without the scarf he would be murdered.

Grandmamma's bed was very large. Grandpapa used to sleep there, too, before he had died. It had curtains at the back which looped on to the wall. Beside the curtain was Grandmamma's slipper-case and watch-case, made of stiff, white, perforated cardboard, tied up with dark ribbon. There were a great many objects in the room, but Elsie was forbidden to touch any of them. Grandmamma sat up in bed in a little wool jacket and knitted and crocheted all day long. She had on a lace cap with thick, pale mauve, velvet ribbons on it. Sometimes she would be helped to a chair and drawn to the window. The doctor used to come to see her every day; sometimes another man, whom Elsie heard referred to as a lawyer; and whenever these people were there, Elsie was sent out of the way.

Her grandmother used to tell her to 'efface herself', and Elsie soon became aware that this word meant that she was to act as if she didn't exist. She soon began to understand that she ought never to have existed. Her father, Grandpapa's son, was dead and her mother was poor, therefore neither of them were of any use to Elsie.

She was six years old and could neither read nor write, but she soon understood quite plainly that she ought never to have been born. Indeed, Mrs Parfitt, the cook, had once said as much in her hearing: 'Poor little thing, it was a pity she was ever born.'

Elsie thought so too. She had never enjoyed a moment of her short life, Father being dead and Mother being poor, and Elsie having to suffer for something very wrong which they had evidently both done.

Everything that Elsie did was wrong too. She knew that, and was resigned to the fact. Whenever her grandmother spoke to her it was nearly always to say something beginning with 'don't'.

The few people who ever came to the house and who ever took any notice of her nearly always also said something beginning with 'don't', or else 'run away'.

Elsie liked the servants, Grace and Sarah and Mrs Parfitt. Sometimes she opened the swing door at the top of the basement stairs and sat there listening to their talk and laughter; not that she could hear what they said, but the sound of voices was comforting in the large, empty house, with Grandmamma sleeping or dozing and no other company at all.

When Mrs Parfitt found Elsie one day at the top of the stairs, she too began to talk of 'don't' and 'mustn't'. She said that Elsie was a 'telltale' and a 'spy' and a 'nuisance' and would lose them all their places. Though Elsie did not understand what any of this meant, she realised that she had again done something wrong.

But sometimes, even after that, the servants were kind. Mrs Parfitt once brought her up an apple after her lunch, and on another occasion, in the middle of a long afternoon, some sandwiches. Once, when there was a thunderstorm and Grandmamma had had her sent to bed, the servants allowed Elsie to come down and sit by the kitchen fire. There was a cat on the hearth and a kettle, and rows of shining pots and plates on the walls and red curtains at the windows, and for a little while Elsie felt almost happy, though she shuddered whenever the door was opened to think of the stone passage without, and all the vaults and cellars and closets and presses, which, like the rest of the house, were disused.

But the moment came when Elsie had to go upstairs to her little bed in the dressing-room which opened out of Grandmamma's great room. Cook said it 'was a shame', but Elsie had to go just the same, and lie awake all night in the dark room, listening to the thunder and watching the lightning, her teeth chattering with terror, biting the pillow for fear she cried out.

She lay awake the most part of every night. She had only cried out once. That time she had disturbed Grandmamma and been punished, beaten very hard on the backs of her hands with a hairbrush, by Mary, who looked after Grandmamma, and made to stay in bed all the next day with nothing but bread and water to eat and drink. This diet was no such very great change for the little girl, for her fare was of the plainest and often such as she could not stomach. She was fastidious and preferred to go hungry rather than eat fat cold mutton, coarse boiled potatoes, stiff rice-puddings, and Normandy pippins boiled into a pulp. She did not know why she was living with

Grandmamma, but she understood it was very kind of Grandmamma to have her there. Indeed, it was very kind of anybody to endure her at all; nobody wanted her, and of course she must be, she was sure, quite useless and a nuisance.

Once she had contrived to creep into the wide hall when Sarah, who was good-humoured, was washing the black and red tiles, and Sarah began to talk to her. She was evidently smarting under some reprimand from Grandmamma, and Elsie understood from what Sarah said in a low, careful voice, that all Grandmamma's children had been useless and nuisances.

It seemed hard to believe that once that great house had been full of people. Grandmamma had had quite a lot of children, boys and girls. They were all dead or had gone away. None of them, so Elsie understood, was any good. Only Grandmamma remained, powerful and, of course, virtuous, always there and always right.

'Your poor papa was the favourite,' said Sarah. 'I shouldn't be surprised if you was to get the money after all.'

'But Grandmamma hasn't got any money,' said Elsie. 'When she talks to me she always says: "Mind, I haven't got a farthing!" '

At that Sarah laughed and pushed back a lock of hair from her forehead with her wet hand that still held the scrubbing brush. She said that Grandmamma was very rich, but a miser; that no doubt there was gold hidden all over the house if one only knew where to look for it.

Elsie asked what was the good of it? Sarah said that it was all the good in the world. If you had gold you could do anything. She said that that was what Master Tom used to come about. That's why the old lady had a stroke, quarrelling with him.

Elsie asked who was Master Tom? Sarah said: 'Why, your uncle of course, silly.' And then Mrs Parfitt called out to Sarah and Elsie had to go away.

After that, she used to look for gold for something to do in the long afternoons – she even ventured into those empty rooms which she held most in horror. One had a large hole in the floor. She used to lean down and bring her little face close to the hole and peer into the darkness and think that she might see gold lying there among the dust. She knew what gold was like – there was a gold clock in the drawing-room and her grandmamma had a gold watch, and her wedding ring, which moved round on her thin, knobby finger, was gold too. And on Grandmamma's kidney-shaped dressing-table were boxes that Grandmamma kept locked. Once, on a wet day, she had let Elsie bring them to the bed, and opened them, and there was this gold too, brooches and chains and earrings, and Elsie had played with them on the down coverlet.

Elsie never found any gold – gold which would do anything, even procure an escape from this house. She frightened herself very much wandering in and out of those empty rooms, some furnished, some unfurnished, but all silent, dusty, and desolate. The whole street, which was full of large houses with pillared porticoes like Grand-mamma's, seemed to Elsie to be always silent, desolate. Occasionally a carriage and pair passed, and sometimes, peering from the window in the midst of an afternoon that seemed endless, she would see some woman and child go by and her little heart would be pinched with an odd nostalgia for a happiness she had never known – no, not even the name of, and then for hours and hours the wide street would seem as silent, as empty as the house. Even the sunshine – and that summer there was a great deal of sunshine – could not lighten the tedium of that street and house to Elsie.

Even the flowering trees, lilac, laburnum, and may (for every house had before the basement a little square in which grew such trees and shrubs), could not give an air of cheerfulness and joy to those dreary sunny afternoons.

Every house had striped sunblinds out over the windows and striped curtains hanging in front of the door. The very sight of these awnings, mostly red and white, filled Elsie with an unutterable woe, born of complete loneliness. She had nothing to do, neither work nor play. Mrs Parfitt had said that she was getting a big girl and would soon be sent to school, and Elsie had hoped that as she was such a nuisance and ought to efface herself, she might indeed be sent away somewhere. She did not know what 'school' was; it could not be worse than the great house in Hampstead.

Once Mary turned her into the back garden, shut the door of the schoolroom that gave on to it, and told her to stay there all the afternoon. Elsie hated the garden almost as much as she hated the house. It had a dirty, high brick wall all round it and at the bottom a sloping bank on which were four tall poplar trees. The heart-shaped leaves fluttered continually to the ground; they were dirty and had a disagreeable smell and a harsh texture. The stems of the lilac bushes were thick with soot and the flowers were tarnished and brown almost as soon as they came out.

There were no other flowers in the garden. The square of grass in the middle was rusty and dirty. Everything in the garden was dirty;

Elsie never played in it, but she often got a scolding when she came in for having spoiled her pinafore. And this afternoon she began to amuse herself by trying to make a mud pie. The first digging with her fingers brought up some worms, and she left off, sick with disgust, that attempt at diversion.

When at last she was allowed into the house Mary scolded her, as she had expected to be scolded, as a naughty, naughty girl for getting herself into a mess. The servants all seemed rather excited. She was given her tea in the schoolroom, bread-and-butter and milk and a piece of seed cake, and scolded again because she did not like the seeds and tried to pull them out with her unskilful fingers.

When she had finished she tried to creep into the kitchen, with a hope of a sight of the cat or the kettle. She heard the servants talking about Master Tom and how he had been there that afternoon. There had been 'a scene', and Elsie wondered what 'a scene' was. It all seemed even more wrong and unhappy than before. It seemed to Elsie not only a pity that she had ever been born, but that anyone else had.

'He's a regular scapegrace, and will come to a bad end, you mark my words,' said Cook; and Elsie longed to ask what a bad end was, but she did not dare to be seen. She was discovered just the same, and smacked and turned out of the kitchen up into the lonely, empty passage, study, and dining-room, where she roamed at will all day, when she was not sitting by Grandmamma's bed or in her own room, which was quite bare, save for a bed and a tin wash-hand stand. Everything had been taken out of it when Elsie came to live there for fear she should touch something. She quite accepted the justice of this, because everything she touched was either spoilt or broken or soiled, for her hands were never clean and she seemed incredibly clumsy.

Except on those rare trembling expeditions when she had been looking for secret gold in a desperate hope that it might some-how procure her release from her present predicament, Elsie had never ventured up above her grandmother's bedroom, though there were three stories above that floor. The servants slept up there, but that did not seem to give an air of human habitation to those dreadful upper floors. One of them contained a large black oil painting the sight of which had made Elsie sick with terror. Some children, long ago, perhaps her own uncles and aunts, had used the picture for a target, and filled it full of small holes from toy arrows or darts.

It was the portrait of a dark man, and Elsie thought that he scowled in agony from his many wounds and that he would leap from the canvas to pursue her if she stared at him a second longer. Elsie had never looked into that room again, and besides that there were ghosts upstairs. Mrs Parfitt and Mary and Sarah had all said so.

Once, when she had lain awake listening to Grandmamma's snoring in the other room, she had certainly heard footsteps overhead, and unable at length to bear her torture any longer she had run downstairs in her nightgown and screamed out at the top of the basement stairs that she had heard steps overhead.

Mrs Parfitt had said good-humouredly: 'Nonsense! There's nobody up there.' Words which had filled Elsie with complete terror.

Sarah had laughed and said: 'The ghosts, I dare say.'

Mary had added: 'Of course – the ghosts!'

Mrs Parfitt, meaning to console, had assured Elsie that if she was a good girl and behaved herself and kept out of the way and didn't annoy Grandmamma ghosts would leave her alone.

Elsie had not returned to her own bed that night. She had not enough courage to do so. She had crept, instead, into her grandmother's room, and lain awake, curled, cold and sweating, on the outside of the coverlet, taking what comfort she could from the old lady's heavy snoring. And in the morning, just before Mary came in to bring Grandmamma her tea and wash her and comb her hair and put on her thick lace cap with the heavy, pale-violet, velvet ribbons, Elsie had crept away into her own bed and pretended to sleep.

All the next day she tried to make herself very agreeable to Grandmamma because she wanted to ask her about the ghosts upstairs. She held her wool for her and fetched her scissors and tried to remember to close the door quietly and not to raise her voice nor to talk too loud nor too fast.

Presently, in the afternoon, holding on her tiny hands the skein of orange wool, she asked: 'Have you ever seen the ghost upstairs, Grandmamma?'

Grandmamma was in a good humour that day. You would hardly have thought she was ill at all. She had been a very handsome woman and she still had an air of energy and vigour.

Propped up against her big pillows she laughed and said: 'I should think there are a good many ghosts in this house, my dear. Think of all the people who have been born and died here, even in my time, and only you and I left, eh, little Elsie!'

'How many people were there, Grandmamma?'

'Eh, I couldn't remember now. You see, this was your grandfather's father's house. He had it when it was first built and there
were a lot of children then. They died or scattered. Mostly died, I
think. I remember four of them went off in a week with typhus.
Then there were my own. Plenty of them, little Elsie. You wouldn't
think now, would you, there used to be such a noise here that I
often didn't know what to do. Children all over the place, boys and
girls – in the schoolroom, running up and down the stairs, playing
in the garden – '

She stopped and dropped her knitting needles on to the sheets.

'Plenty of noise then, little Elsie; quiet enough now, isn't it?'

'Are they all ghosts now?' asked Elsie, and she dropped the skein of
wool on to her lap.

'Ghosts – or worse,' said Grandmamma, with a sigh; 'most of them
seemed to go wrong somehow.'

'Were they nuisances, like I am?'

Grandmamma looked at her sharply, as if she suspected her of an
impertinence.

'Never mind what's become of them, Elsie, or whether they're
ghosts or not. Pick up that wool – it'll get tangled; and put the pillow
straight under my left arm. Mary knows I can't knit like this.'

Though Grandmamma was partially paralysed down one side, she
could, by a deft arrangement of pillows propping up one of her
elbows, still knit and crochet, which she did for hours every day with
a certain ferocity, making thick grey garments for the poor and the
heathen and squares and squares of crochet in bright colours, which
were going to be sewn together one day into a great quilt.

Elsie thought of the poor and the heathen with horror; she saw
armies and armies of them in grey woollen petticoats advancing on
her with hostile looks and menacing cries when she woke in the
middle of the night.

Cunningly she tried to get more information about the ghosts.

'Are there ghosts in the schoolroom, Grandmamma?'

'Aye, indeed, I should think there are ghosts in there. That's where
they learnt their lessons, all of them. Learnt no good, no, not one of
them. That's a strange thought, Elsie – all of them down there,
learning lessons year after year and not one of them learning anything good.'

'And the ghosts upstairs in the bedroom?' persisted Elsie.

'There'd be ghosts there. That's where a lot of them died. Your
grandfather died in this room, but I don't suppose you'll see his

ghost. Why are you so interested, little Elsie? It's a funny thing for a child to talk about, isn't it? Have you been gossiping with the servants?'

Elsie shook her head. She was accustomed to the quick lying of utter fear.

'I thought I heard one last night, Grandmamma. Walking about.' Her child's vivid imagination forced her to add: 'When I got out of bed and opened the door I thought I saw a ghost coming down the stairs and I wondered who it was.'

'Who would you like it to be?' grinned the old lady. 'Who would you like it to be out of all your uncles and aunts and great-uncles and aunts? Well, they weren't any of them any good, as I told you. Except your father, perhaps. Yes, that now, your father.'

'I'd like to see him,' said Elsie. 'Is he a ghost, too?'

Grandmamma was silent for a while. She seemed to be dozing, and Elsie felt even more afraid than she usually did when the old lady went off into one of her half-trances, half-sleeps, sitting propped up against the pillows, with her sharp chin on the little jacket of white Iceland wool she wore across her shoulder and breast.

Elsie began to whimper through fear of the ghosts and of Grandmamma and of loneliness of the great empty house. But Grandmamma was not asleep nor ill. She had only been thinking of the past.

'Your father would be a very pleasant sort of ghost. He was my youngest – the flower of the flock. Yes, if you saw him, Elsie, you would see a very handsome young man. Well, he wouldn't be so young now, I suppose. He died soon after you were born. How old are you, Elsie?'

'Nearly seven years old, Grandmamma.'

'Yes, he wouldn't be such a very young man, but he was handsome. Oh yes, my James was handsome. He had a mole on his left cheekbone.'

'I hope I won't see him,' said Elsie, shuddering, as she sat rigid on her little stool. 'I hope he'll stay upstairs. I wonder where he lived. I expect in that room with the big black picture all full of holes.'

'He used to amuse himself with that old canvas,' said Grandmamma, smiling, as if at a pleasant recollection. 'He used to have his games and sport there. He always was bold and spirited, and very loving to me, whatever they say about him.'

'And Uncle Tom?' asked Elsie. 'Was he loving too?'

At that name a convulsive spasm passed over Grandmamma's face.

She struck out angrily with her strongest hand, missing Elsie, who shrank back from the bedside.

'You have been gossiping with the servants! You haven't got an Uncle Tom! There's no such person! He doesn't exist! Who told you there was an Uncle Tom.?

'Nobody,' said Elsie, 'only you yourself, Grandmamma, the other day when you seemed half asleep you said something about Uncle Tom coming.'

The old woman looked at her dubiously, but was not able to contradict this, for she knew that she had not always full control over her senses.

'Well, perhaps I did, perhaps I did,' she grumbled. 'You shouldn't have taken any notice. I didn't know what I was saying. I dare say I've been dreaming about the ghosts upstairs, Elsie, just like you have – a lot of nonsense! There's no Uncle Tom. If you ever meet one who says he's your Uncle Tom or says he's any son of mine, you tell him that he's a scoundrel and a liar, Elsie. I've no son, do you hear? Do you hear? All my sons are dead – dead.'

Elsie said 'Yes' obediently and readily. Uncle Tom did not, after all, matter much to her. It was the ghost upstairs who concerned her and about whom she wanted to hear.

One afternoon in that odious June was more dreadful than any other afternoon to Elsie, for she was left quite alone in the house with her Grandmamma. Of course, this should never have happened and was not meant to happen. It occurred like this.

Mary and Sarah were, it seemed, both nieces of Mrs Parfitt, and when an uncle of theirs died all three wanted to go to the funeral. Grandmamma, of course, could not be left alone. Mrs Parfitt said she could easily arrange to send in a friend – a Mrs Skerrell – who would sit with Grandmamma and give Elsie her tea and do anything that was wanted until she, Mrs Parfitt, and the two girls came back about six o'clock, as they easily could, for the funeral was at Highgate.

So Mrs Parfitt told Elsie to be a good girl and Mary said, 'Don't get into mischief'; Sarah said, 'Don't you go telling no tales to your grandmother about what you haven't seen or heard'; and Elsie was left alone with Grandmamma and Mrs Skerrell, who was a dreary widow woman in a long black garment and a bonnet with jet flowers.

Elsie had taken advantage of this unusual confusion to get down into the kitchen. She was staring at Mrs Skerrell just untying the strings of the black bonnet when there was a sharp ring at the bell. Both the woman and the child started. Nothing was, as Mrs Parfitt had put it to Mrs Skerrell, 'expected'. All the tradespeople had called and visitors were rare.

Mrs Skerrell said 'Drat it', retied the strings of her bonnet, and ran up the stairs from the basement into the hall. Elsie remained alone in the kitchen. She wished she had the strength to get down one of the jars full of sultanas or sugar or motley biscuits and spice and eat large handfuls. She was always hungry. She had neither the strength nor the courage, so she remained standing beside the large, scrubbed, white-deal table, and looking up through the kitchen window into the area, she could just see a foot or so of the railings which divided the stone area, with its doors into coal cellars, from the square of garden where grew the ragged laburnum tree and the sooty lilac bushes.

Mrs Skerrell seemed to have been gone a very long time and loneliness increased and crystallised on the small figure of Elsie. She was shut into the desolation like a fly into a lump of amber, not daring to move for fear of finding worse things than loneliness in the other parts of the house. She peered up at the railings. Presently she saw the bottom of Mrs Skerrell's beaded mantle and black skirt going past. Then Elsie ran to the window and, pressing her face to the panes, looked up. Mrs Skerrell was certainly leaving the house. Elsie listened and heard the gate go 'click', the iron tongue of the lock into the iron socket. She knew that sound so well; indeed, she knew every sound in the large empty house in which she had spent her entire life.

She was, then, in the house alone with Grandmamma, who, about this time in the early afternoon, was always asleep. Elsie's first sensation was not one of added fear, but rather of deliverance. She now, given so much time, might be able to climb up on to the dresser and get down some of those canisters of things good to eat. She might be able to make a slow and careful hunt right through the kitchen and find out where the biscuits and the candied peel were kept; she might be able to tiptoe to the pantry, discover if there was a slice of pie or a portion of cake or a dish of fruit there. All things which she was not allowed and that were not good for Grandmamma, and off which the servants freely feasted.

Then she thought of an even fiercer temptation – an even more resplendent opportunity – the long, darkly gleaming sideboard in the dining-room. There was no speculation about that – there would not need to be any search. Elsie knew exactly where, on the top shelf when the large folding doors underneath the drawers were open, was kept jam, marmalade, and sugar. She was never allowed any of these delicacies. The marmalade used to go on her Grandmamma's breakfast tray, the jam on her afternoon tea tray. There were preserves, too, and cherry and quince, that were brought out for the rare visitors.

It was true that this cupboard, which was large enough to have contained a dozen Elsies, was usually locked, and Grandmamma had the keys. Elsie had seen her take them out of a little box on the table by her bedside and give them to Mary, and seen Mary give them back to her. And once Elsie had found the cupboard open. It was true she had been discovered before she had time to take anything, but perhaps, just perhaps, Mrs Parfitt, in the excitement of her day's outing, had left it open again, then Elsie would be able to help herself.

She would be discovered without doubt. She had little hope of being able to conceal the crime, there would be horrid stickiness on her fingers. When her fingers were sticky, she could, somehow, never get it off, even though she held them under the tap or wiped them on the towels.

But to satisfy her hungry craving for something sweet and delicious and delicate it would be worth enduring the punishment of being smacked on the backs of both her hands with a hard hairbrush, sent to bed in the daylight, or something worse if Grandmamma and Mrs Parfitt could think of a more severe punishment.

So she crept quietly up the stairs into the large, empty house. It was the very worst part of the afternoon, sunny, silent, with a feeling that it would be hours and hours and hours before the dark fell, as if the world had stopped and all life was in suspension and only she, Elsie, was alive and miserable.

As cautious as if she were certain that she would be overheard, Elsie went down the wide, black and red tiled corridor and into the dining-room, which was shuttered against the sun and full of dusty shadows, which lay in little straight lines of gold from the slats of the Venetian blinds.

Elsie had no luck. She found the sideboard locked. She had become by now reckless and daring; she would go upstairs, she decided, and take the key from the little box beside Grandmamma's bed. Grandmamma would be asleep, and she had heard Mrs Parfitt tell Mrs Skerrell the old lady 'had had her medicine and wouldn't give any trouble'.

The sunny, silent afternoon hung like a halter round Elsie's soul. She thought that if she could get the keys and open the cupboard, a pot of jam, yes, a whole pot of jam, eaten slowly and with relish, would do something to mitigate the horrible loneliness of her imprisonment.

Grandmamma was, as she had thought she would be, asleep. The clothes were drawn up over her face as usual, and only the top of her cap with violet ribbons could be seen against the pillow. There were the slippers in the slipper-case, the watch neatly in the watchcase, there was the box standing beside the bottle of medicine with the glasses, the spectacles in their case, the Bible with the bronze clasp, and the different balls of wool, the various pieces of knitting.

The sunblinds were drawn over Grandmamma's window; the poplars in the garden made a fluttering shadow on them. The little breeze lifted them now and then so that a spurt of golden sunlight would fall into the shadowed room. All the smooth-faced pictures on the wall seemed to be watching Elsie – the girl with the dead bird, the girl tying the bandage on the man's arm, the baby-faced boy who was called the 'Prince Imperial'; all these, in their pale, smooth, shining frames, seemed to turn and stare at Elsie, but she did not falter.

She lifted the lid of the key-box and was putting in her hand to take out the key when she heard, overhead, footsteps.

The ghost of course, undoubtedly the ghost, and she alone in the house and at its mercy. On a frantic impulse of terror she turned and tried to rouse her grandmother, even venturing, seldom as she dared to touch the invalid, to shake the gaunt shoulder that heaved up the clothes. Grandmamma was very soundly asleep and did not rouse. The steps came nearer, unmistakably descending the stairs from the upper room. Elsie thought only of hiding, of creeping under the bed or into the huge cupboard where Grandmamma kept hanks and hanks of brightly-coloured wool and skeins and skeins of grey wool. But before she had time to run farther than the length of the bed, the door, which she had left ajar, was pushed open and the ghost walked in.

It was a handsome man with red hair and a mole on the left cheekbone. Elsie remembered what Grandmamma had said about her father and stood still at the end of the bed, staring. The apparition gave her no special feeling of terror; it was, indeed, far less terrible than she had supposed it would be. She even thought that in the warm glint of the eyes, the half curl of the lips, she detected promise of an ally. He was, at least, younger and more attractive than any creature she had seen for a long time, nay, than she had ever seen before.

'Hullo, little nipper,' said the ghost. 'What are you doing here?' And as Elsie did not answer he advanced into the room and said in a low, steady voice, 'Oh, you're Elsie, I suppose, James's child.'

'And you're James,' said Elsie. 'Grandmother told me about you.'

'James,' said the ghost, 'your father do you mean? He's dead.'

'Yes, I meant that. I meant that you are my father and dead and a ghost. Isn't that right, please?'

The apparition seemed to reflect and gave a frown that made Elsie feel as if she were dwindling away with terror, then he said shortly, in the same low, cautious tone: 'Well, if you like. Come here and let me have a look at you.'

Elsie stood mute, shaking her head in terror. The ghost became at once angry.

'Don't be a little fool. I'm here for your good as well as my own. You don't have much of a life, do you? They've always packed you out of the way when I've been before.'

'Oh, you've been before?' whispered Elsie in a thin tone of curiosity.

'Yes, I don't suppose you heard anything about that. Well, I shan't come again. Come outside, anyway, I might help you. How old are you?'

'Seven,' replied Elsie, who felt that the extra six months gave her added importance. Not for anything would she have admitted to six and a half.

'I see. Well, you're old enough to have some sense. I've come here looking for something. Perhaps you could help me find it.'

'Grandmamma would know where it is,' said Elsie, pointing to the bed.

'I don't want to wake her,' said the man, with a queer look. 'She's asleep. I think she's going to sleep for a long time.'

'Mrs Skerrell ought to be looking after her,' whispered Elsie. 'What happened to Mrs Skerrell?'

'I sent her away with a cock-and-bull story. Never you mind that. I want a little time in this house to myself. I've been looking out for an opportunity for a long while. I had it today when the women went out. Now look here, if you'll help me, I'll do something for you. Is there anything you want?'

Elsie understood nothing of this except the last question. She did not know to what sort of creature she spoke; she was quite bewildered. She felt more confident than she had ever felt before, more happy than she had been since she had been brought, so long ago that she could not remember it, to this house.

'I came up for Grandmamma's keys.'

'Her keys?' asked the other sharply. 'Where are they?'

'In the little box by the bed.'

'What did you want with her keys?'

'I was going to take something out of the sideboard – jam.'

'I see.'

The man looked at her very shrewdly out of narrow eyes.

'I suppose the old miser – God forgive me – keeps you half-starved. Well, you shall have some jam, Elsie, and something else too. What else would you like?'

'Sixpence,' said Elsie, in wild bravado.

The stranger smiled sourly.

'I'll give you a gold sovereign. You could do a lot with that, couldn't you, a child of your age?'

Elsie's senses reeled. On rare occasions Mary or Sarah had taken her for short walks, but she had seen, oh, a long way off, shops in which, the servants had told her, almost anything could be purchased for money. There would not be any limit to what one could get with a golden sovereign.

'What do you want me to do?' she asked. Then her small shrewd face clouded. 'Have you come here looking for gold?'

He seemed startled.

'Gold! What made you think of that? I promised you a sovereign. I didn't say I'd come here looking for gold.'

'I thought perhaps you had, because there isn't any. Grand-mamma's only got farthings, she told me so herself. Mrs Parfitt said something about gold hidden in the house, but I looked, and there wasn't any. Grandmamma,' she repeated, 'has only farthings. I think they're hidden under her pillow.'

'No, I haven't come looking for gold. I want to know where your grandmother keeps her writing-desk, her papers. Has she got them here? Or does Furnival, that's the lawyer, have them all?'

Elsie shook her head, not understanding.

'Don't be a stupid,' said the man keenly, and with a certain desperation she had thought was impatience. 'How can I put it so that you'll understand? I'm looking for a piece of paper, do you see? And it's very important. It may not be here; but she used to, when I lived here, keep all her papers under her own eye and look at them secretly. Now, have you ever seen her sit up in bed and call for a little desk or a box and turn it over and look at the papers?'

Elsie nodded.

'Yes, she does that sometimes. And I have to fetch them.'

'Good girl.' The man seemed with difficulty to control an intense eagerness. 'Now, if you can find those papers and let me see them, I suppose the key's on the same bunch where the key for your jam cupboard is?'

Elsie nodded again. She began to feel herself important.

At least here was action, a chance to express oneself, to show one's quickness and courage. She opened the box, put her hand in, and took out the bunch of keys. She knew them all, through quick observation and a keen memory.

'This opens the cupboard downstairs, the jam and sugar cupboard. This is the key of the little box that Grandmamma keeps in her wool cupboard underneath her grey wool, and I bring it to her sometimes, and there are papers in it.'

'Give it to me.'

He held the keys in his hand, while Elsie went to the cupboard and quickly found this box of inlaid wood.

'Aren't you afraid she'll wake?' she said, as she came back and laid this on the quilted coverlet.

'No,' he said, tucking up his lips in a peculiar smile. 'I'm not afraid she'll wake. I'm not afraid of her at all.'

He quickly found the right key. His deft, swift fingers turned over the papers in the small box. The child stared at him, her peaked face taut with interest.

'I don't believe you're a ghost,' she said at length. 'I think you're Uncle Tom.'

At that he turned on her with a low snarl. 'Who told you there was an Uncle Tom?'

'Mrs Parfitt talked about him.'

'And she . . . ' The man pointed to the huddled outline of the sleeping woman in the bed. 'Did she say anything about me?'

'No,' said Elsie; 'she said there was no such person as Uncle Tom.'

'Well, isn't that right? Wouldn't she know? There is no such person. I am James, the ghost of James, your father, as you said just now when you saw me. That's right, isn't it?'

'I suppose so,' said Elsie, 'but I don't seem to be afraid like I should have been if you were a ghost.'

'You've forgotten your pot of jam, my dear,' he said, taking envelope after envelope out of the box and scanning them keenly. 'Yes, and the golden sovereign I promised you. Ah, here we are. I knew she'd keep it. She was always in two minds about everything.'

He had taken two documents that looked very dull to Elsie and laid them on the bed.

'You can't read, I suppose, my little dear, can you?'

The child shook her head.

'Will you give me the other key and I'll run downstairs and get the jam,' she said. 'If they punish me afterwards you might come back and say you let me take it.'

'They won't punish you. They'll have something else to think about.' He tossed her the keys. 'Bring them back here. You seem sharp and spry. You ought to know your way about.'

'What are those two pieces of paper?'

'Never you mind. I've found what I want. I'll give you two sovereigns, but you're not to tell anybody you saw me. You understand?'

'Oh, why mayn't I say I've seen a ghost? I said the other night I'd seen one and I hadn't really and nobody minded.'

He laughed and the tension of his dark face relaxed.

'Oh, well, you can say you've seen a ghost if you like. That will do very well. Why not?'

'Didn't Mrs Skerrell see you?' asked the child cunningly.

'No she didn't. What's that to you, anyway? Yet I ought to be grateful to you for reminding me. I suppose the hag'll be back soon.'

He stood staring at the two papers in his hand, then put one paper carefully back into the box, locked it, and watched Elsie while she cunningly returned it underneath the piles of grey wool in the cupboard. Then he tore the second piece of paper into small pieces and put them carefully in the inner breast pocket of his coat and followed Elsie downstairs and stood over her in a listening attitude while she unlocked the cupboard and took out a pot of apricot jam.

Her eyes glistened and her mouth watered so at the sight of the jam that she almost forgot about the two sovereigns and her bewilderment as to whether or not the man was an apparition or flesh and blood. Whoever he was, he took two sovereigns out of his pocket and placed them on the end of the shining mahogany table.

'There you are, my dear; you can't say I haven't kept my bargain. Now mind, I am a ghost. If you say anything about me I don't like, I shall come in the middle of the night and give you a fright. Perhaps carry you away to where it's all bogies and blue flames.'

'Oh, please,' said Elsie, nearly dropping the pot of jam in her terror, 'I'll do anything you like. What do you want me to say?'

'Nothing at all. Only that you've just seen a ghost. Better not mention the jam or the keys or those papers I took. See – not a word.'

He frowned and thrust his head forward and made himself look so menacing and hideous that Elsie began to weep.

'There, I know you're a good girl and won't say anything. Now take the jam somewhere you're not likely to be found and remember you've simply seen a ghost this afternoon – the ghost of your father, James.'

'Are you going away now? Where do you go? Through that step-ladder up on to the roof? I think that's the way the ghosts come.'

'No, I shall go out the back. Do you know who lives next door? Anybody likely to be about just now?'

'One house is empty,' said Elsie, 'there's only a caretaker there, and they don't come until the evening. The other side the people are away. There's never anyone there at all.'

'Good! My lucky day. Now remember what I told you about the ghost.'

Then he was gone.

When Elsie had finished her pot of jam she looked round for the sovereigns, but they had gone too. This caused her to weep bitterly, for it was the vanishing of the brightest dream of her life. Yet in her soul she felt that it was logical. What could a ghost leave but fairy gold? But she cried all the same in pure disappointment at the loss of the golden visions that the two golden coins had conjured up.

Mrs Skerrell, coming back hurried and panting, and out of temper, found her crying in the dining-room.

'Why aren't you up with your grandmother, you naughty girl? You're old enough – you might have been watching of her. What'll happen to me if the old lady's come to some harm while I was away?'

Mrs Skerrell, untying her bonnet and unfastening her cloak, began to mutter about a queer business – a boy had come with a message to say she was wanted at home, a matter of illness, serious and immediate. When she'd rushed back there had been nothing at all. The boy had said that it was a stranger whom he had never seen before had told him to give the message. He thought the gentleman was a doctor, he was very civil and had given him half a crown.

'All a lot of rubbish,' said Mrs Skerrell, going upstairs, considerably ruffled and discomposed, with Elsie behind her for the sake of company.

'Grandmamma's asleep,' said Elsie, 'Better leave her alone.' Then, because she could not keep her great secret any longer to herself: 'I've seen a ghost. He gave me two sovereigns, and as soon as he went the money went too.'

'Don't be a naughty wicked girl and tell a pack of lies,' scolded Mrs Skerrell. 'The old lady seems asleep,' she added with a sigh of relief. 'Better leave her, she won't want her tea before five, and by that time Mrs Parfitt will be home.'

Mrs Parfitt was punctual. At the usual appointed hour when she brought up Grandmamma's tea Elsie was sitting on her little stool sobbing to herself at the loss of the fairy gold, trying to wind the yellow wool. When Mrs Parfitt and Mrs Skerrell endeavoured to rouse Grandmamma they found they could not do so.

The old lady was dead.

When the doctor came he said she had been dead for some hours. Of course, it was quite likely that she might have had a sudden stroke. 'She passed away,' as the phrase went on, in her sleep. It was really not worth while making any question or raising any fuss. What else could have happened?

Mrs Skerrell did not admit that she had been decoyed away from the house and Elsie did not even mention the ghost. The doctor had thought that there were queer marks round the old woman's throat, as if her frail life had been impetuously shaken out of her, but of course, he assured himself, this must have been a delusion.

The lawyer said that Grandmamma had left a recent will leaving everything to Elsie, but as this could not be found he was quite prepared to believe that the old lady, in a capricious mood, had destroyed it. The earlier will, then, which was found quite readily in a box where the old lady kept her important papers hidden under the pile of grey wool which she knitted into petticoats for the poor, was proved.

Grandmamma's only surviving son, Mr Thomas, came into all her money and into the big lonely house at Hampstead. Grandmamma was a much wealthier woman than anyone had thought she was, and Mr Thomas behaved generously towards Elsie.

He paid for her to go into an orphanage for the daughters of decayed gentlefolk.

He did not come near the house at Hampstead himself, so Elsie never saw him.

She left the house with a great feeling of relief. She did not, of course, expect to be happy in the orphanage nor anywhere. She knew that she was a nuisance and not wanted and must always efface herself, but she was glad to get away from the house which was haunted by the ghost of her father, James. Though she had loyally kept her word to him, and never said a word about what he had done when he visited her the day Grandmamma died, she was filled with fear that his angry apparition might return one night under some hideous form.

And another reason for her relief at leaving the great house in Hampstead was the fact that now there was hardly any possibility that anyone would discover that she had stolen the pot of apricot jam.

The Bishop of Hell

'The Prince of Darkness is a Gentleman' – *King Lear*

England, 1790

This is the most awful story that I know; I feel constrained to write down the facts as they ever abide with me, praying, as I do so, a merciful God to pardon my small share therein.

God have mercy on us all!

In the hope, vain though I feel it to be, that when I have written down this tale it may cease to haunt me, I here begin.

It was twenty years ago, and never since, day nor night, have I had any respite from the thought of this story, through which you can hear the drums of Hell beat loudly and yet which has an awful beauty.

God have mercy on us all!

Hector Greatrix was my friend, yet to say friend is to profane a noble word; rather was he my counsellor, companion, and prop in all things evil.

His reputation was hideous even among the rakehelly crowd who flattered and followed him; he went lengths from which others shrank, and his excesses, his impiety, his boldness terrified even those hardened in wicked ways.

And what added a deeper edge of horror to his conduct was that he had been an ordained clergyman.

Younger son of a younger son, his father had placed him in the Church in the hope of rapid preferment, for the Greatrix were a highly placed family and the great Earl of Culvers was the head of it; but the scandal of young Hector's life was such that even in those days he was unfrocked. His intimates, in the clubs and gambling dens, called him, in bitter derision, *Bishop of Hell*.

I write of the year 1770, when this tale begins.

Hector Greatrix was then in the height of his fame and fashion. No-one could deny him certain splendour; he was literally in physical height head and shoulders above his companions, and mentally also;

his wit, his invention, his daring knew no bounds, but all these qualities were turned to evil. He was at this time about thirty years of age, of a magnificent figure, so graceful that his strength was hardly noticeable, tawny haired and tawny eyed, with features as yet unblemished from his debaucheries, the most elegant of hands and feet, the most exquisite taste in dress, and the most engaging of manners. There was not one honourable man nor respected woman among his acquaintances and all his intimates were villains; I do not except myself.

There was, however, one exception. Colonel Bulkeley, his cousin on the female side, had helped him by his countenance and by money. Why, I never understood, because William Bulkeley was the most austere, upright, and punctilious of men, of great wealth, of exceptional position, and of the most distinguished career.

I think now, as I thought then, that it was quite impossible for Colonel Bulkeley to realise what Hector Greatrix really was, or the set to which he belonged. The villain could be most plausible, and his cousin must have believed him to be wild, unfortunate, and blameable, but in no way vile or dishonoured.

In sum, Colonel Bulkeley effectually played the mediator between Greatrix and the chief of the family, Lord Culvers, who, no anchorite himself, was not ill-disposed towards his handsome and seductive nephew; but then his lordship, who was much disabled by gout, seldom left Greatrix Park and knew little of London society, so that he was by no means aware of his nephew's reputation.

I, as one of the most reputable of his disreputable friends, being, as I can truly say, more wild and young than vicious, was chosen to go with Hector to Greatrix Park when the old earl asked his company, and so I was able to see at close quarters how this charming knave pulled the wool over the eyes of his two kinsmen.

The end of the comedy was an allowance for Greatrix, a handsome subsidy from the earl most generously supplemented by a few hundreds more from the wealth of Colonel Bulkeley.

Greatrix was to study the law and live in chambers – suitable to his rank; he had no chance of accession to the family honours of the earl, whose heir, a dull, sickly youth enough, had lately married a blooming young woman of robust constitution, who had provided him with a couple of boys. So, Greatrix, thanks to Colonel Bulkeley, had done better than the most sanguine might have hoped. And he seemed more moved thereby than I had thought possible.

'Bulkeley has done me a good turn,' he swore, 'and damme if I'll ever do him a bad one.'

As for his allowance and the study of the law, he laughed at these things; what he really valued was the countenance of these two great, wealthy gentlemen.

'This visit will help my credit in London,' he declared. 'It is good for a couple of years' debt.'

'And what when two years are up and your credit and the patience of your relatives are alike exhausted?'

'Who am I,' smiled Greatrix, 'to think two years ahead?'

I think it was impossible for him to conceive of disaster or even common misfortune. His object gained, he was impatient to return to town; a woman with red hair was waiting for him. He had a curious and persistent passion for women with that bright shade of auburn, like burnt gold.

Colonel Bulkeley pressed us to stay a night with him on our way to town, and Greatrix, with an inner curse, for he wanted to be free of this formal, austere man, consented with a winning courtesy.

Moil Place was in Kent, quite near London, a commodious and elegant residence presided over by Mrs Bulkeley, who was some several years younger than her husband.

This type of woman was unknown to either Greatrix or myself. I have had no sisters and could not recall the character or the linea-ments of my mother; Greatrix had two sisters, but they were town ladies of smirched reputation, and his mother had been a passionate, reckless, uncommon woman.

To both of us Mrs Bulkeley appeared flat, childish, almost imbecile, almost incredible. She had been married direct from a Clapham boarding school and had there received several tokens (as the doting husband let slip) for deportment and good conduct.

It was June, and she wore a muslin gown with a wide blue silk sash and a wide straw hat tied under the chin with another ribbon of the same hue. She lisped a little and her small face was clearly and definitely coloured like a china ornament; she was, in fact, like the puppets children dress up and play with; then, when she had gone into the house and was pouring tea behind the Bulkeley silver – pieces that looked larger than herself – she suddenly took off her hat and showed a head overflowing with auburn curls, long, glossy, almost vermilion, yet soft and like burnt gold, all knotted up on the crown of her head.

With this revelation of her hair you saw her beauty – the golden eyes with blonde lashes, the features of such an exquisite delicacy, the pearly shades on throat and neck, the delicious carmine of faint carnation.

I did not care to look at Greatrix, and yet I felt that I need not have suffered this embarrassment.

Colonel Bulkeley was the one man in the world for whom Greatrix had expressed any respect or consideration and the lady obviously adored her husband. I was both amused and surprised to observe the manifestations of sentimental affection between them. There was one child too, a little doll in white lace just out of the cradle; what fondness Colonel Bulkeley could spare from his wife was devoted to the infant.

I was cloyed and thankful when we had taken our seats for town.

Greatrix, after the effort of the last few days, was in a surly mood. 'I have never passed a couple of days so tiresome,' he said.

And I, always minded to jeer at him when I could, replied: 'You have never seen a woman so beyond your reach, Hector. She never looked at you, I do believe.'

He laughed indifferently. 'Alicia Bulkeley is ready to the hand of any man who likes to reach out for her.'

What was yet good in me was shocked by this insult to our hostess, a woman who, commonplace and childish perhaps, had yet seemed to me to convey a sweet purity, a gentle fidelity, and an adoring affection beyond all reproach.

'She is in love with her husband,' I declared.

'The more reason she can be in love with another – 'tis your passionately attached wives who fall the easiest victims; that little creature is amorous as a lovebird. Take Bulkeley away for a month or so and she'd flutter into any arms held out –'

'By God, Hector,' I swore, 'if you can't believe in any nobility or decency, don't defame those qualities. Your words stick in my throat. These people have exerted themselves in kindness towards you. Mrs Bulkeley is silly, maybe, but a gentlewoman deserving of respect.'

'Since when have you turned Puritan?' he asked coldly.

I was not affected by his sneers; I felt a certain definite repulsion against him, and from that day I saw less of him and applied myself with some diligence to my studies.

We each of us had rooms in Paper Buildings, and the more I heard of Hector Greatrix the more I withdrew myself from his companionship. Two of his boon fellows shot themselves; the daughter of his laundress was found hanged; a married woman of his acquaintance was taken out of a Hampstead pond one winter morning. His name was associated, secretly and sombrely, with all these tragedies.

Some rumours of these matters must have reached the earl in his lofty retirement, for I heard from the associates of Greatrix who still continued to be mine that there had been a summons to Greatrix Park, quarrels, and the employment once more of Colonel Bulkeley as mediator.

I had seen little of the Bulkeleys; their severe and yet sentimental life, the chaste simplicity of their connubial bliss did not greatly attract me. I had been asked again to Moil Place and had needed all my fortitude to control my yawns. Mrs Bulkeley had now another infant at her breast and was more than ever infatuated with her husband.

Another six months and this idyllic family was rudely disturbed: Colonel Bulkeley's regiment was ordered to India for three years and he was forced to leave abruptly his wife and children he so tenderly loved.

That winter, to my surprise, I met Mrs Bulkeley in a London ballroom; it was only a few months since her husband had sailed and I imagined her consoling herself with her babies at Moil Place. When I spoke to her she seemed shy and confused; I learned that she had 'moped' in the country, that the doctor had ordered a change, and that these insufferable years of waiting would seem shorter amid the distractions of society. She was staying with a married brother at St. James's, and I could not doubt that she was well protected both by her own heart, her position, her relatives, her children; yet when I saw her dancing with Hector Greatrix I did not care to watch.

Needless to follow the course of an experienced and heartless seducer; suffice it to say that Greatrix was soon talked of in connection with Mrs Bulkeley, and, unattainable as I believed her to be, I could not forbear an appeal to her pursuer.

I found him, by rare luck, in his chambers.

'For God's sake, Hector,' I conjured him, 'stop your attentions to Mrs Bulkeley; even though it is impossible for you to destroy her peace of mind, you may blight her reputation.'

'What is this to me?' he asked coldly. 'Did I not tell you she would come at my whistle?'

I urged him to forbear. 'Never before have you compromised a woman of her position. Consider what it will mean to you – the fury of your uncle and of her husband, the scandal that will put you out of society – out of England.'

'And there,' he interrupted, 'I am likely to go in any case. I can keep the duns quiet no longer and my lord will be bled no more.'

I told him I hoped he would go before Mrs Bulkeley's good name was smirched by his detestable attentions and I reminded him solemnly of his obligations towards Colonel Bulkeley. He had no answer for me, and soon after I observed with relief that Mr Lambert, Alicia Bulkeley's brother, had taken alarm and that she was being kept from any opportunity of meeting Greatrix.

Yet what availed this?

Hector Greatrix, having spun his credit to the utmost and within a few hours of the Fleet Prison for debt, fled to the Continent and Alicia Bulkeley went with him.

Though I was never squeamish in these affairs, I will confess that this completely sickened me – the man was so vile, the woman so infantile, so pure, so attached to her husband.

The scandal was hideous. The earl cut Hector off with a curse; the Lamberts adopted the abandoned children; and as soon as they had news of Alicia, sent her a small allowance that was probably the main support of the wretched couple. This money was sent care of a bank in Genoa, but no-one knew where Mrs Bulkeley and her lover really were living.

Through the compassion of His Royal Highness, who had the chief command in India, Colonel Bulkeley was allowed to return to England on the receipt of the awful news and arrived in London something less than two years since he had sailed.

He immediately resigned his commission and returned with his children to Moil Place.

Declaring that he had no intention of following the fugitives, he said simply that if Greatrix ever returned to England one of the two would, in a few days, be dead; and Mr Lambert, with his next remittance, reported this message, advising his unfortunate sister and her paramour to keep clear of their native country for fear of further scandal and horror.

I avoided the possible chance of meeting Colonel Bulkeley. I had no desire to see this broken and outraged man, whose career, that had promised so splendidly, was broken in the middle and for whom life seemed to hold nothing but bitterness and humiliation. This, it might seem, should be the end of the story; it indeed appeared that nothing further could happen, either to the outcasts in their exile or to the betrayed husband, to alter the position of either or in any way bring them together again.

But who would have guessed at the turn Fate had in store?

Colonel Bulkeley had not been home much more than another two years when a severe epidemic of smallpox broke out in England; among the first victims were the wife and children of Lord Culvers; the son by his first marriage, always delicate, had lately died of a decline; and the old earl, then over seventy years of age, did not long endure the shock, but sank under the weight of his bereavement a few days after the funeral of his youngest child.

The estates and the money were both entailed, every portion of property having been strictly tied up by a preceding earl, and Hector Greatrix was now Earl of Culvers and one of the wealthiest noblemen in England.

Lord Culvers was summoned to London by his lawyers, and on the same day Colonel Bulkeley came up from Moil Place and took a house in Dover Street, Mayfair, not far from his lordship's town mansion, Culver House.

Hector came as far as Paris and there stopped. He still had Mrs Bulkeley with him; not, as I supposed, from any remnants of affection, but because of her allowance, which was till now his sole means of support. I winced to think what Alicia Bulkeley must be like now.

There had never been any talk of a divorce, but now people began to ask why Colonel Bulkeley did not permit his wife to marry her lover; they were people who did not know Hector.

I received, unexpectedly, a summons from my lord to attend him in Paris; he had not too many reputable acquaintances then, and I had become a respectable enough citizen while he was sliding down to pandemonium. Therefore, I supposed, this dubious honour.

I went, as one will, partly out of curiosity, partly out of complacence, and partly out of a faint pity for Alicia Bulkeley.

He had, of course, handled plenty of money already, and upset as the city still was, I found them elegantly installed in a *hôtel meublé* that had only lately become national property.

Hector was sumptuous to behold and cordial enough in his wild way; he had changed for the worse – the first bloom of his beauty had gone, the first fineness of his manners; but he was handsome enough, God help him.

She was with him.

I learnt afterwards that she had had and lost in the feverish heat of Italy three children, and never had she been without another woman sharing her lover's favours; often these lived under the same roof with her. She had known, I think, most of the humiliations possible to a refined woman who lives with a vile, brutal man; there could have been little of horror and squalor that she had not seen, nay, been in the midst of . . .

I could hardly keep curiosity from my eyes – this was the doll of Moil Place, with her lisp, her muslin, her babies.

She was, and this is perhaps the most horrible thing, much more beautiful, rich, opulent in line now, with a full bosom and flowing curves of thighs and shoulders, taller (she had been but eighteen), clever at dressing, clever of speech; gay, abandoned, and intolerably wretched. Her tone was one of bravado, but the look in her eyes was that of a whipped dog who creeps away from the lash.

As soon as we were alone she was down on her knees to me with a movement so passionately sudden that I could in no way prevent it – on her knees, Mrs Bulkeley of Moil Place!

'Tell me,' she implored, 'will not William divorce me? Surely you have some message from him?'

I told her, none.

She began to weep. 'If I were free Hector might marry me before he returned to England – that is my only hope.'

'Surely, madam,' said I in pity, 'a vain one?'

But she was not yet free of the illusion women are so slow to lose – that they have always some power over a man who has once loved them or been their lover, and she cherished the desperate hope that her husband might set her free and she regain something of all she had lost under the name of Lady Culvers.

Never was there a more futile and piteous hope even in the brain of a foolish woman. I could not forbear saying to her, when I had induced her to rise from her knees: 'Madam, has not your association with my lord shown you the manner of man he is?

'Indeed it has,' she answered bitterly, 'yet surely he could not, in these changed circumstances, abandon me – '

So she clung to the protection of that honour she had herself discarded, and a panic terror showed in her eyes as she added that she had now nothing with which to keep him – it had always been the money that had held him; the money the Lamberts sent, and, Heaven avert its face, other money, presents from Italian lovers of hers whom he had forced on her; she told me, with a wildness that made me fear for her reason, that she had paid for her last child's funeral by such means.

'And yet, madam,' I shuddered, 'you wish to continue your assoc-iation with such a monster? Indeed, I wonder that you have not already left him, if only for the protection of another man.'

As she was silent, I added: 'Is it possible that you love him?'

She replied: 'No, I have never loved any but William and my dear, dear children.'

But I doubt if she knew what love was, and I think that for months she had known no emotion save fear.

Seeking to abate her misery I asked her what she could dread worse than had yet befallen her.

'There's Hell,' she said.

'I should think,' I replied, 'that Hell is where my lord is.'

But no; to her, still at heart a religious, respectable English gentle-woman, anything was preferable to the life of open shame before her if my lord forsook her; she thought, in her narrow, ignorant mind, that if she could marry her lover her fault would be condoned; and I knew that in the eyes of many it would be.

I advised her that she could go into retreat somewhere with the money that the Lamberts allowed her, but she shook her head with a feeble laugh; she knew, she said with a dreadful accent, her own weakness, and she saw herself, once cast off by my lord, sinking to the lowest depths of degradation, till she reached Bridewell or a foreign lazar house.

And I could see this too. I promised to speak to my lord, but naturally with little hope; but the next day when I saw him, sitting over his breakfast playing with his dogs, he gave me no opening, for he plunged into his own affairs.

'Look 'ee here, Jack,' he said, 'I was too drunk yesterday to talk business and when I came back from the opera you'd gone. But this is the matter I've sent for you for – has Bulkeley seen reason? As I've no news, I take it he has gone to his prayers and his pumpkins at Moil Place and will give no trouble.'

'No,' I said, 'Colonel Bulkeley came up to London as soon as he heard of your fortune, and has taken lodgings in Dover Street – 'tis said that he keeps a watch posted by Culver House for your return.'

My lord's face turned ashy.

'What for?' he cried.

'That he may challenge you the moment that you set foot in England.'

My lord sprang up then; his rage was diabolic, there is no other word for this fury of a fiend outwitted at last; his oaths and blasphemies were detestable, atrocious, as he strode up and down with his dressing-gown flowing open and his locks, damp from last night's debauch, seeming to rise on his head.

'I never heard,' I said, wincing, 'that you were a coward, Hector, but it seems you are.'

'Coward!' he yelled. 'When I eloped with Bulkeley's wife I was a ruined man without a prospect in the world – did I think I'd ever want to return to England with the title and the money?'

He had been, in fact, exquisitely caught, but I could feel no spark of compassion for him.

'You'll have to meet the man,' I told him, not looking at his distorted face.

'I'll not. Bulkeley is a damned good shot. Do you think I want to go out when I've suddenly got everything to my hand?'

I could guess that he did not; to him the position, the money, meant the opening of Paradise. He would, no doubt, have a good life – fine flatterers, fine women, all that wealth could buy in London would be his; nay, there would be plenty who would receive him in the finest society of the town and not scruple to offer him their daughters in honourable matrimony; the hounded exile would be the great lord and at last able to get full value for his rank, his beauty, his audacity, his fascination.

'I stay in Paris,' he cried. 'People will come over to me here. I'll cheat the man that way. Paris is as well as London if you have money.'

'It were wiser, perhaps,' I said with disgust. 'But no-one will endure a man who is an avowed coward, my lord; you'll have to keep the company you've been used to lately if you stay out of England. People will know why – they're beginning to say already that you linger. I for one,' and I rose, 'would turn my back on you.'

'Blast your impudence, Jack,' he whispered. 'What is this tone to me?'

'You're a peer of England. Culvers is a great name; it'll cover much, but not cowardice.'

'Damn that word. I don't want to die – that's reasonable.'

'Yes; if I were you, my lord, I should not want to die.'

'Bah, you're thinking of my bishopric. Hell! As if I believed in Hell. There's nothing, not even Hell, Jack – one goes out like a snuffed candle – just blackness, blackness, nothingness, nothingness.'

The look on his face as he said this was one of such awful despair that I thought this was a moment when he might be softened by his own terrors.

'I can see one possible way out. Hector, if you were to let Colonel Bulkeley know that if he divorced his wife you would marry her – perhaps for her sake, he would forgo his revenge.'

He laughed in my face.

'The woman's been the harlot of half the rogues in Italy.'

I stopped him. 'Don't talk of that – even your corroded heart might blench there. Marry her, if you can, for your soul's sake and hers.'

His hideous pride was greater than his fear.

'A kept woman,' he mocked. 'My God, I'm Culvers now.'

'Remember it,' I recommended him. 'What do you mean to do with this poor creature?'

Then, as if he remembered that she was the original cause of his present predicament, he began to curse her, using those abominable names he so freely applied to women, and as for what he meant to do with her, his project was what the miserable wretch had herself guessed – complete abandonment; and his view of her future was her view – the streets and the *maison de Dieu*.

I reminded him of her birth and upbringing, of her relatives, but he only redoubled his blasphemies.

'Am I answerable if these Puritans breed women who run into the gutter?'

I left him; useless to contemplate a spectacle so frightful.

And I avoided any further interview with Alicia Bulkeley.

When I returned to London I observed the watcher set by Colonel Bulkeley near the shuttered gloom of Culver House.

In three months' time my lord returned to London; whether urged thereto by the jeers of his enemies, the flatteries of his friends, or his own pride, or whether unable to endure his tantalus position, or whether his nerve broke at the suspense and the waiting, I know not, but he came to London. I had heard that he had hopes of approaching Bulkeley with offers of apology or even money; of seeking in some way an accommodation. This sounded ridiculous, but from his nature it was possible to conclude that he cherished some such plan. He arrived in London secretly, with a horrid stealth, and slipped into Culver House under cover of a November evening.

Yet the next morning Lord Mildmay called on him with a challenge from Colonel Bulkeley.

That same evening I was summoned to Culver House.

My lord sat with some of his old boon companions in one of the dismantled rooms (for his coming had been sudden and unexpected);

the holland covers were yet over the great velvet and gilt chairs, muslin bags enveloped the candelabra, and where the bottles and glasses stood on the ornate table were rings in the dust; candles had been hastily stuck into tarnished sticks, and the only servants were the French rascals my lord had brought with him.

Rosy *amorini* and florid wreaths peeped from the shadows of the imposing walls, and the lordly pomp of this chill magnificence was a strange background for the men drinking by the huge fire on the marble hearth. Everyone was drunk but my lord, but he, this night, could find no oblivion in the wine cup; panic kept his head clear, and I could see by the ferocious anguish of his face that his thoughts were by no means dimmed.

He met me with bravado.

'If I go to Hell tomorrow, I'll pay you a visit to let you know what 'tis like.'

'Is Bulkeley so infallible?' asked one of his followers, and another, with tipsy malice: 'He's a damn good shot.'

'He has on his side justice at least,' I said coldly, for I had now come to detest my lord.

He looked at me in agony. 'Say I've a chance,' he muttered, and I smiled, always having believed him to be of an invincible courage.

For all that I thought his chance good enough; if Bulkeley was a fine marksman, so was my lord.

'Why don't you get to bed? What time is the meeting?' I looked with contempt at his hideous company; not one of them had set foot in Culver House, or any mansion like it, before.

'Seven o'clock tomorrow morning,' said one Hilton, the soberest of the wretched band and my lord's second.

It was now past midnight.

'Why have you sent for me?' I asked again.

He was pacing up and down the room in a very climax of terror and rage, while the drunken crew round the table condoled with and mocked him in a breath. He wore an almond-green velvet coat, overlaced, I recall, with silver – for that year the men's clothes began to be very plain – and his hair was long and powdered in the old-fashioned style still favoured in Italy. I think that the beauty of his lineaments rendered his expression the more awful – the despair, the dread, the fury expressed in that pale visage were awful indeed to contemplate.

'I will not go!' he cried. 'I'll not stand up to be killed!'

He then asked me to make his will (I was by then a lawyer of some modest standing), for the Culver property was his to dispose of since he was the last male of his family. Yet when it came to asking his wishes he would not reply, and finally refused to consider the matter; and so I left him staring into the huge mirror with a glass of brandy in his hand and cursing the clock for marking the passing of the time.

I had not dared to ask him anything of Alicia Bulkeley, but as I was leaving I did demand particulars of the lady from one of the servants, a man I had seen in Paris.

She had been left in Paris, quieted, I gathered, by some lie as to my lord's return. This affair and mainly the memory of my lord's face so wrought on my mind that I could not sleep that night and went out early for news of the duel.

I got this from the creature Hilton, the second.

The meeting had taken place in Hyde Park; at the first shot my lord had fallen. 'Killed?' asked Colonel Bulkeley.

'Sir,' said the surgeon, bending over the writhing man, 'death would have been more merciful – he is shot through the jaw.'

'He is marked where I aimed to mark him,' replied the implacable soldier coldly. 'He will never kiss another man's wife again; nor his own; nor even any drab from Whitefriars.'

With that remark he left the Park; his austere figure and his sombre countenance had never changed during the course of the encounter.

My lord was carried home in his carriage; he soon became unconscious, for the lower part of his face was shattered, half blown away, and, though he might well live, he would never be anything but a mask of terror.

Alicia Bulkeley, quieted for the moment by my lord's lies, no sooner lost sight of him than she fell into a fierce panic and resolved to follow him by the next packet. With little more than the price of her journey in her pocket and accompanied by a huge negress, who was her last attendant, she landed at Dover twenty-four hours after my lord, and took the night coach to London.

Arriving there, the demented creature could think of no asylum but Culver House; and, as she could hardly believe that the man for whom she had sacrificed everything and with whom she had lived for years would refuse her shelter, she directed her steps to the stately mansion of my lord.

The valet who opened to her knew her and was for refusing admission, but the negress said cunningly (Mrs Bulkeley being past coherent speech) that my lord had sent for them; and the servant, not knowing if this might be so, reluctantly admitted them. The two shuddering and draggled women had just reached the great doors on the first landing when my lord came home.

He had regained consciousness, and though his pain was fearful he had no tongue to make lament with; he walked between Hilton and the surgeon, who were indeed not well able to carry so large a man, and so slowly came up the wide treads of the stairs to where Mrs Bulkeley, who had heard the steps, cowered against the door, her silk shawl, her fallen hair, her bonnet disarranged, her face like milk, her lips ashy.

As my lord came into view, with his jaw swathed in bloody bandages and his terrible eyes above them, she broke into shriek after shriek; my lord sprang forward with a strength that made nothing of those who held him, took the frail wretch in his quivering hands and hurled her down the stairs. The surgeon tried to catch her, but she was weak and her high heel caught in her dress; she fell to the bottom of the flight and lay in the hall.

Whimpering, the negress scuttled after her; Hilton, to please his patron, from whom he still hoped favours, said: 'It's Alicia Bulkeley, the cause of the whole damn business – turn her out,' he added to the gibbering valet.

The surgeon, who was a fashionable man and fee'd by my lord, made no protest, and as the earl was led to his chamber, the servant and the negress picked up Mrs Bulkeley and carried her into the street. She stirred as they touched her and the black woman clamoured for pity, so that the valet consented to carry her to a pot-house nearby, where the landlady, after marking her rings and watch, took her in and let her lie in a back room, where the customers came and stared at her and the air was thick with the smell of smoke and beer.

She asked for her husband and a clergyman, but the negress was too ignorant to know what she meant; and so, about noon, she died, aged not quite twenty-three years.

It was a clear case of murder, but the landlady and her gossip, the slippered doctor, hushed the thing up, robbed her of her rings, watch, silk, and linen garments – and even the burnt gold hair that had first attracted my lord – and buried her in a pauper's grave. The negress they turned into the street; and she, distracted with terror, crept back to Culver House and begged for scraps at the kitchen door. There, out of compassion, they gave her my name and where I was to be found, and I discovered her on my stairs when I came home that night and so learnt from her the manner of Alicia Bulke-ley's death. I sent the poor wretch to a friend who had a house of servants, and debated whether or not I should write these matters to Colonel Bulkeley.

I was not encouraged to do so by the remembrance of his face on the morning of the duel, and while I hesitated I had news of the death of my lord. This was practically suicide, because his life had never been in danger, but he tore off the bandages with a ruthless hand, turned his mutilated face to the wall and furiously died – the day of the burial of Alicia Bulkeley.

Would that this were the end and that I, who believed in neither Heaven nor Hell, could have here finished with Hector Greatrix, seventh Earl of Culvers. I went out that day to a gathering of people who knew nothing of my lord, and stayed late, endeavouring to forget. I drank and danced and gambled, and fled the gossips who must mouth over the Culvers' scandal.

When I returned I found that the light on the stairs, commonly left there by my laundress, had gone out, so must fumble my way up in the dark and silence of the quiet building. When I reached my room I must fumble again in the dark for flint and tinder, feeling from one piece of furniture to another; it was cold, and through the tall window I could see the moon like an icicle in the dark sky. At last, when I had begun to be considerably oppressed by the dark, I found the tinderbox and struck a light.

As I set the flaming tinder to the candle I perceived that I was not alone in the room; someone was seated in the hooded chair that had its back towards me; a man. I could see the white hand hanging down, the skirt of a coat on which some bullion trimming gleamed. I concluded that a friend, minded to pay me a visit, had gone to sleep awaiting my return.

I approached, holding my light, and with I know not what feeling of unfathomable dread.

The figure turned as I neared.

It was my lord.

He wore the almond-green suit with the silver braiding in which I had seen him hold his ghastly vigil of terror and fury. God have mercy on us all!

His face was alight; where the visage should have been was a ripple of flames quivering upwards, and through this crimson veil of fire gleamed his infernal eyes with an expression of unutterable woe. The flames rose above his head, shaped into a peak; he wore a shining mitre glittering with lambent fires of green and blue like hellish jewels.

This fiend had been forced to keep his oath – to discover to another scoffer the truth of Hell.

My eyes could not long support this atrocious spectacle; as he raised his ashy hand in mock benediction, I fell senseless, seeing as I dropped the demoniacal mitre flare from his flaming brows to a man's height above his tortured eyes.

The Grey Chamber

ANONYMOUS

[*translated from the French by Marjorie Bowen*]

Young Blendau was travelling to Italy in the suite of a German princess to whom he acted as secretary. Arrived in the town in the north of Germany where the princess had decided to remain several days, he obtained permission to visit a certain M. Rebmann, who then held the office of chancellor to an adjacent royal estate. This gentleman lived several miles from the town where the princess and her train had halted.

Blendau had been educated with him and had not seen him since he was fourteen years old, that is to say, for about seven years. He thought, therefore, that he would make this visit a surprise to this friend and his family, and as he knew the country perfectly well he hired a horse and set out alone across the forests although it was the middle of winter.

The weather was very fine in the morning, but in the afternoon he perceived that the sky became covered over, and towards evening a heavy snow began to fall. This caused a considerable delay to Blendau: the path became heavy, large snowflakes blew into his eyes and blinded him so that he could not guide his horse properly; he mistook his way several times, and though he calculated on reaching M. Rebmann's early in the afternoon, it was not till nine o'clock at night that he at last arrived, cold and exhausted, at this friend's, having made a detour of twenty miles.

M. Rebmann hardly recognised him, so much had he changed since he had last seen him. When, however, he discovered who was this late guest he received him with great pleasure and only regretted that his wife and children had gone to the neighbouring town on the occasion of the marriage of a relative and would not return for several days.

He ordered a good meal for his friend and some of the best wine in his cellar, and after Blendau had drunk three bottles of Meersteiner and gossiped over all that had happened to him during the last seven years he felt the fatigue and vexation of his long cold ride pass. Nevertheless, an extreme lassitude overcame his spirits and he was forced at last to break off the hilarious conversation and demand permission to retire to bed.

M. Rebmann admitted with a laugh that this put him in a difficulty. His lady was away and all the chambers save those occupied by the family were dismantled, while the prudent housewife had taken with her the key to the coffers which held the sheets, the coverlets, and the mattresses. On calling the old servant, Bridget, and putting to her his difficulty, she replied: 'There is a bed already made in the Grey Chamber – you know, sir, the guest chamber. M. Blendau can sleep there if he pleases.'

'No,' replied Rebmann. 'My friend Blendau would not wish to pass the night in the Grey Chamber, of that I am sure.'

'And why not, sir?' asked the old woman.

'What, in the Grey Chamber! Have you already forgotten the Lady Gertrude?' Mr Rebmann turned slyly to his guest.

'Bah! That's such a long time ago that I thought no more of it,' cried Blendau. 'What, do you think I am still troubled by such childish follies? Go along with you! Let me pass the night in this famous chamber. I am no longer afraid of ghosts or evil spirits, and if the beautiful Gertrude should come to keep me company I am so tired that I don't think she'll prevent me from sleeping.'

M. Rebmann gave the young man a doubtful glance.

'Well, my friend, you've certainly singularly changed. Seven years ago nothing in the world would have made you consent to sleep in the Grey Chamber, even if you'd had two people to keep you company. Where did you find so much courage?'

'Seven years ago *is* seven years ago,' laughed Blendau. 'I have grown up since then. For five years I have lived in the capital, remember. Believe me, I now know too much to give any credit to old legends.'

'Very well, my friend, I've no more objection to make. May Heaven watch upon your rest. Bridget, take the light and conduct M. Blendau into the Grey Chamber.'

Blendau said good night to his old friend, then he followed Bridget to the famous Grey Chamber, situated at the second stage of the extremity of one of the wings of the castle.

Bridget put her two candles on a dressing-table on either side of a mirror of oval form surrounded by an interlaced antique border. The old woman seemed ill at ease in this vast chamber; she made a slight curtsey to Blendau and hurried away.

The young traveller stood for a moment considering the apartment which had once been familiar enough to him and had always, in the days of his youth, filled him with terror. It was still in the same state as it had been when he had seen it last. The enormous iron stove bore the date of 1616; a little beyond this, in the corner, was a narrow door the upper part of which was composed of squares of ancient glass, heavily leaded. This led to a long, sombre passage which wound round the tower to the subterranean dungeons.

The furniture consisted of six ormolu chairs, two tables in heavy brasswork supported by finely carved stag's feet, and a great bed with a baldaquin which was hung with curtains of heavy grey silk embroidered in tarnished gold. Nothing in the room had been changed for perhaps more than a hundred years, for the chancellorship of this royal domain had been confided from time immemorial to the family Rebmann.

The *châtelaine* Gertrude was of an even greater antiquity. How often had not Blendau heard her horrible story! According to this old legend, which he had heard whispered fearfully by his nurse in his boyhood, Gertrude had from an early age vowed to God her youth and beauty, and had been about to enclose herself for ever in a convent when the splendours of her youthful loveliness had aroused the base desires of a certain Graf Hugues, who one night broke into her room, this very Grey Chamber, and despoiled her by force of her honour.

Gertrude swore on the crucifix that she had called for help, but in this lonely part of the castle, so far from the other apartments, who could hear the cries of agony and innocence? The wickedness of Hugues did not entail any consequences that could reveal it, but the unhappy Gertrude avowed the crime to her confessor, who refused her permission to enter the convent and closed to her the door of the sanctuary of the virgins of the Lord. And as she had intended to tempt God by concealing her fault and taking the veil, he told her that in expiation she must suffer the torments of purgatory during three hundred years.

The wretched girl, a prey to despair, poisoned herself and expired in the Grey Chamber at the age of nineteen years. Her rigorous penitence was still lasting and would not be terminated for another forty years, that is to say in 1850, and until the expiration of the fatal term, Gertrude would continue to appear every night in the Grey Chamber.

Blendau had frequently heard this tale and he had even met several people who were ready to swear that they had seen Gertrude in the Grey Chamber. All these tales agreed that the phantom had a dagger in one hand, probably to pierce the heart of the perfidious lover, and a crucifix in the other, destined without doubt to reconcile the criminal with Heaven in offering him the image of the Saviour who died to expiate the sins of mankind.

The ghostly apparition only showed itself in the Grey Chamber, and for this reason this apartment had long remained uninhabited. But when M. Rebmann inherited the castle and the post of chancellor, he had turned the haunted room into a guest-chamber as a proof of his complete disbelief in phantom or legend.

Blendau looked steadily round the room. Although he had boasted of not believing any longer in ghosts, he was not too much at ease. He locked the door by which he had entered and the glass door which gave on to the long, obscure passage. He put out one of the candles, placed the other near the bed, undressed, and slipped beneath the sheets and under the warm coverlet, recommending his soul to God, then extinguished the other candle, sunk his head upon the pillow, and at once fell into a profound sleep.

But about two hours afterwards he woke and heard a clock in the neighbouring tower strike midnight. He opened his eyes and saw that there was a faint light in the chamber. He raised himself on his elbow – extreme terror caused him to become immediately wide awake. The curtains at the end of the bed were half-pulled and his glance fell on the mirror on the dressing-table directly in front of him. In this he could see the reflection of the spectre of Gertrude wrapped in a shroud, a crucifix in the left hand and a dagger in the right.

Blendau's blood froze in his veins: this that he saw before him was not a dream, a vision, but a frightful reality, it was not a skeleton or a shade, it was Gertrude herself, the face discoloured with the livid tint of death. A garland of ivy and rosemary was interlaced among her dry, colourless locks, and as she moved Blendau heard the rustle of the leaves of this dead chaplet and the sound of the hem of the shroud dragging on the floor. He saw in the mirror by the light of the two candles, both of which were now brightly burning, the fixed brilliancy of the eyes of Gertrude, the pallor of her lips.

He tried to leap from his bed and to run to the door by which he had entered, but the fright had paralysed him – he found that he could not move.

Gertrude kissed the crucifix. She seemed to be praying under her breath; Blendau distinguished the movement of her lips which still carried the marks of the burning poison. He saw the eyes of the unfortunate wretch turned towards heaven; she raised her dagger and advanced towards the bed with a terrible glance.

Blendau was about to lose consciousness as she opened the curtains of the bed. Horror was painted in her fixed and inanimate eyes as she perceived a man crouching on the pillows, and she pressed her little dagger on the bosom of him whom she took for her false lover. As she did so a cold drop of poison fell from her garland on to Blendau's pallid face. At this he gave a piercing cry, flung himself from the bed, and rushed to the window to cry for help.

But Gertrude prevented him. When he reached the window she was there with one hand on the catch so that he could not open it. With the other she caught him round the waist and he gave a piercing cry, for he felt through his nightshirt the glacial impression of the cold sweat of death coming from her clasp.

He observed that she had now neither crucifix nor dagger, and that she seemed no longer to wish for the life of the unhappy Blendau, but, what was more horrible, that she appeared to offer and to expect the embraces of love.

As the icy spectre folded him in her arms Blendau dragged himself away with long shudders of terror and hurled himself towards the little glass door.

As he opened this (it was not locked, though he had turned the key himself the night before) he found himself face to face with a skeleton that blocked the long passage – that of Graf Hugues, without doubt. His ghastly face, on which still clung a remnant of skin and muscle, was distorted in a frightful grimace. He entered the chamber, letting the door fall behind him with a sound that echoed like thunder throughout the tower.

Blendau, between the two phantoms, that of Gertrude and that of the skeleton, sank to the ground unconscious into darkness.

When he recovered, the cold wintry dawn was showing through the unshuttered windows. Blendau, stiff and chilled, his shirt still bathed with sweat, rose from the floor and with trembling hands searched for his clothes. Though unutterably weary and shaken by nausea, nothing would have persuaded him to endeavour to obtain any repose in that apartment.

At first he endeavoured to persuade himself he had been the victim of some frightful dream, but such an idea was no longer plausible when he perceived, on the dressing-table in front of the mirror, the second candle that he had placed near his bed and put out after he had got between the sheets. He remarked that these candles were half burnt down, although they had only just been lit for a second the night before. He also discovered that the two doors which he had locked the night before were again fastened as he had left them.

Blendau had not the courage to relate his adventure to anyone. He did not wish to be laughed at for a susceptible fool and made the subject of the pleasantries of the family of Rebmann. On the other hand, if he was able to persuade his host of the reality of his vision, who would dare to continue to inhabit the castle where Gertrude and the hideous skeleton of her lover had a rendezvous every evening?

Then, again, if he was silent, he would be asked to spend another night in the Grey Chamber and that he felt he had not the strength to do.

He therefore dressed himself in haste, crept through the castle while everyone was still asleep, went to the stable, mounted his horse, and without taking leave of anyone rode away through the snowy forest towards the city.

The Extraordinary Adventure of
Mr John Proudie

Mr John Proudie kept a chemist's shop in Soho Fields, Monmouth Square; it was a very famous shop, situated at the corner, so that there were two fine windows of leaded glass, one looking on Dean Street and one on the Square, and at the corner the door, with a wooden portico by which two steps descended into the shop.

A wooden counter, polished and old, ran round this shop, and was bare of everything save a pair of gleaming brass scales; behind, the walls were covered from floor to ceiling by shelves which held jars of Delft pottery, blue and white, and Italian majolica, red and yellow, on which were painted the names of the various drugs; in the centre the shelves were broken by a door that led into an inner room.

On a certain night in November when the shop was shut, the old housekeeper abed, and the fire burning brightly in the parlour, Mr John Proudie was busy in his little laboratory compounding some medicines, in particular a mixture of the milky juice of blue flag root and pepper which he had found very popular for indigestion.

He was beginning to feel cold, and, not being a young man (at this time, the year 1690, Mr Proudie was nearly sixty), a little tired, and to think with pleasure of his easy chair, his hot drink of mulled wine on the hearth, his *Gazette* with its exciting news of the war and the Commons and the plots, when a loud peal at the bell caused him to drop the strainer he was holding – not that it was so unusual for Mr Proudie's bell to ring after dark, but his thoughts had been full of these same troubles of plots and counter-plots of the late Revolution, and the house seemed very lonely and quiet.

'Fine times,' thought Mr Proudie indignantly, 'when an honest tradesman feels uneasy in his own home!'

The bell went again, impatiently, and the apothecary wiped his hands, took up a candle, and went through to the dark shop. As he passed through the parlour he glanced up at the clock and was surprised to see that it was nearly midnight. He set the candle in its great pewter stick on the counter, whence the light threw glistening reflections on the rows of jars and their riches, and opened the door. A gust of wind blew thin cold sleet across the polished floor, and the apothecary shivered as he cried out: 'Who is there?'

Without replying a tall gentleman stepped down into the shop, closing the door behind him.

'Well, sir?' asked Mr Proudie a little sharply.

'I want a doctor,' said the stranger, 'at once.'

He glanced round the shop impatiently, taking no more notice of Mr Proudie than if he had been a servant.

'And why did you come here for a doctor?' demanded the apothecary, not liking his manner and hurt at the insinuation that his own professional services were not good enough.

'I was told,' replied the stranger, speaking in tolerable English, but with a marked foreign accent, 'that a doctor lodged over your shop.'

'So he does,' admitted Mr Proudie grudgingly; 'but he is abed.'

The stranger approached the counter and leant against it in the attitude of a man exhausted; the candlelight was now full on him, but revealed nothing of his features, for he wore a black mask such as was used for travelling on doubtful rendezvous; a black lace fringe concealed the lower part of his face.

Mr Proudie did not like this; he scented mystery and underhand intrigue, and he stared at the stranger very doubtfully.

He was a tall, graceful man, certainly young, wrapped in a dark blue mantle lined with fur and wearing riding gloves and top boots; the skirts of a blue velvet coat showed where the mantle was drawn up by his sword, and there was a great deal of fine lace and a diamond brooch at his throat.

'Well,' he said impatiently, and his black eyes flashed through the mask holes, 'how long are you going to keep me waiting? I want Dr Valletort at once.'

'Oh, you know his name?'

'Yes, I was told his name. Now, for God's sake, sir, fetch him – tell him it is a woman who requires his services!'

Mr Proudie turned reluctantly away and picked up the candle, leaving the gentleman in the dark, mounted the stairs to the two rooms above the shop, and roused his lodger.

'You are wanted, Dr Valletort,' he said through the door; 'there is a man downstairs come to fetch you to a lady – a bitter night and he a foreign creature in a mask,' finished the old apothecary in a grumble.

Dr Francis Valletort at once opened the door; he was not in bed, but had been reading by the light of a small lamp. Tall and elegant, with the pallor of a scholar and the grace of a gentleman, the young doctor stood as if startled, holding his open book in his hand.

'Do not go,' said Mr Proudie on a sudden impulse; 'these are troubled times and it is a bitter night to be abroad.'

The doctor smiled.

'I cannot afford to decline patients, Mr Proudie – remember how much I am in your debt for food and lodging,' he added with some bitterness.

'Tut, tut!' replied Mr Proudie, who had a real affection for the young man. 'But no doubt I am an old fool – come down and see this fellow.'

The doctor took up his shabby hat and cloak and followed the apothecary down into the parlour and from there into the shop.

'I hope you are ready,' said the voice of the stranger from the dark; 'the patient may be dead through this delay.'

Mr Proudie again placed the candle on the counter; the red flame of it illuminated the tall, dark figure of the stranger and the shabby figure of the doctor against the background of the dark shop and the jars – labelled 'Gum Camphor', 'Mandrake Root', 'Dogwood Bark', 'Blue Vervain', 'Tansy', 'Hemlock', and many other drugs, written in blue and red lettering under the glazing.

'Where am I to go and what is the case?' asked Francis Valletort, eyeing the stranger intently.

'Sir, I will tell you all these questions on the way; the matter is urgent.'

'What must I take with me?'

The stranger hesitated.

'First, Dr Valletort,' he said, 'are you skilled in the Italian?'

The young doctor looked at the stranger very steadily. 'I studied medicine at the University of Padua,' he replied.

'Ah! Well, then, you will be able to talk to the patient, an Italian lady who speaks no English. Bring your instruments and some antidotes for poisoning, and make haste.'

The doctor caught the apothecary by the arm and drew him into the parlour. He appeared in considerable agitation.

'Get me my sword and pistols,' he said swiftly, 'while I prepare my case.'

He spoke in a whisper, for the door was open behind them into the shop, and the apothecary, alarmed by his pale look, answered in the same fashion: 'Why are you going? Do you know this man?'

'I cannot tell if I know him or not – what shall I do? God help me!'

He spoke in such a tone of despair and looked so white and ill that Mr Proudie pushed him into a chair by the fire and bade him drink some of the wine that was warming.

'You will not go out tonight,' he said firmly.

'No,' replied the doctor, wiping the damp from his brow, 'I cannot go.'

John Proudie returned to the shop to take this message to the stranger, who, on hearing it, broke into a passionate ejaculation in a foreign language, then thrust his hand into his coat pocket.

'Take this to Francis Valletort,' he answered, 'and then see if he will come.'

He flung on the counter, between the scales and candle, a ring of white enamel, curiously set with alternate pearls and diamonds very close together, and having suspended from it a fine chain from which hung a large and pure pearl.

Before the apothecary could reply Francis Valletort, who had heard the stranger's words, came from the parlour and snatched at the ring. While he was holding it under the candle flame and gazing at the whiteness of diamond, pearl, and enamel, the masked man repeated his words.

'Now will you come?'

The doctor straightened his thin shoulders, his hollow face was flushed into a strange beauty.

'I will come,' he said; he pushed back the brown locks that had slipped from the black ribbon on to his cheek and turned to pick up his hat and cloak, while he asked Mr Proudie to go up to his room and fetch his case of instruments.

The apothecary obeyed; there was something in the manner of Francis Valletort that told him that he was now as resolute in undertaking this errand as hitherto he had been anxious to avoid it; but he did not care for the adventure. When the stranger had thrust his hand into his pocket to find the ring that had produced such an effect on the doctor, Mr Proudie had noticed something that he considered very unpleasant. The soft doeskin glove had fallen back, caught in the folds of the heavy mantle as the hand was withdrawn, and Mr Proudie had observed a black wrist through the lace ruffles: the masked cavalier was a negro. Mr Proudie had seen few coloured men and regarded them with suspicion and aversion; and what seemed to him so strange was that what he styled a 'blackamoor' should be thus habited in fashionable vestures and speaking with an air of authority.

However, evidently Francis Valletort knew the man or at least his errand – doubtless from some days of student adventure in Italy; and the apothecary did not feel called upon to interfere. He returned with the case of instruments to find the stranger and the doctor both gone, the parlour and the shop both empty, and the candle on the counter guttering furiously in the fierce draught from the half-open door.

Mr Proudie was angry; there had been no need to slip away like that, sending him away by a trick, and still further no need to leave the door open at the mercy of any passing vagabond.

The apothecary went and peered up and down the street; all was wet darkness; a north wind flung the stinging rain in his face; a distant street lamp cast a fluttering flame but no light on the blackness.

Mr Proudie closed the door with a shudder and went back to his fire and his *Gazette*.

'Let him,' he said to himself, still vexed, 'go on his fool's errand.'

He knew very little of Francis Valletort, whose acquaintance he had made a year ago when the young doctor had come to him to buy drugs. The apothecary had found his customer earnest, intelligent, and learned, and a friendship had sprung up between the two men which had ended in the doctor renting the two rooms above the shop, and, under the wing of the apothecary, picking up what he could of the crumbs let fall by the fashionable physicians of this fashionable neighbourhood.

'I hope he will get his fee tonight,' thought Mr Proudie, as he stirred the fire into a blaze; then, to satisfy his curiosity as to whether this were really a medical case or only an excuse, he went to the dispensary to see if the doctor had taken any drugs. He soon discovered that two bottles, one containing an antidote against arsenic poisoning, composed of oxide of iron and flax seed, the other a mixture for use against lead poisoning, containing oak bark and green tea, were missing.

'So there *was* someone ill?' cried Mr Proudie aloud, and at that moment the door bell rang again.

'He is soon back,' thought the apothecary, and hastened to undo the door; 'perhaps he was really hurried away and forgot his case.'

He opened the door with some curiosity, being eager to question the doctor, but it was another stranger who stumbled down the two steps into the dark shop – a woman, whose head was wrapped in a cloudy black shawl.

The wind had blown out the candle on the counter and the shop was only lit by the illumination, faint and dull, from the parlour; therefore, Mr Proudie could not see his second visitor clearly, but only sufficiently to observe that she was richly dressed and young; the door blew open, and wind and rain were over both of them; Mr Proudie had to clap his hand to his wig to keep it on his head.

'Heaven help us!' he exclaimed querulously. 'What do you want, madam?'

For answer she clasped his free hand with fingers so chill that they struck a shudder to the apothecary's heart, and broke out into a torrent of words in what was to Mr Proudie an incomprehensible language; she was obviously in the wildest distress and grief, and perceiving that the apothecary did not understand her, she flung herself on her knees, wringing her hands and uttering exclamations of despair.

The disturbed Mr Proudie closed the door and drew the lady into the parlour; she continued to speak, rapidly and with many gestures, but all he could distinguish was the name of Francis Valletort.

She was a pretty creature, fair and slight, with braids of seed pearls in her blonde hair showing through the dark net of her lace shawl, an apple-green silk gown embroidered with multitudes of tiny roses, and over all a black Venetian velvet mantle; long corals were in her ears, and a chain of amber round her throat; her piteously gesticulating hands were weighted with large and strange rings.

'If you cannot speak English, madam,' said Mr Proudie, who was sorry for her distress, but disliked her for her outlandish appearance and because he associated her with the blackamoor, 'I am afraid I cannot help you.'

While he spoke she searched his face with eager haggard brown eyes, and when he finished she sadly shook her head to show that she did not understand. She glanced round the homely room impatiently, then, with a little cry of despair and almost stumbling in her long silken skirts, which she was too absorbed in her secret passion to gather up, she turned back into the shop, making a gesture that Mr Proudie took to mean she wished to leave. The apothecary was not ill-pleased at this; since they could not understand each other her presence was but an embarrassment. He would have liked to have asked her to wait the doctor's return, but saw that she understood no word of English; he thought it was Italian she spoke, but he could not be even sure of that.

As swiftly as she had come she had gone, unbolting the door herself and disappearing into the dark; as far as Mr Proudie could see, she had neither chair nor coach; in which case she must have come from nearby, for there was but little wet on her clothes.

Once more the apothecary returned to his fire, noticing the faint perfume of iris the lady had left on the air to mingle with the odours of Peruvian bark and camomile, rosemary and saffron, beeswax and turpentine, myrrh and cinnamon that rendered heavy the air of the chemist's shop.

'Well, she knows her own business, I have no doubt,' thought Mr Proudie, 'and as I cannot help her I had better stay quietly here till Francis Valletort returns and elucidates the mystery.'

But he found that he could not fix his thoughts on the *Gazette*, nor, indeed, on anything whatever but the mysterious events of the evening.

He took up an old book of medicine and passed over the pages, trying to interest himself in old prescriptions of blood root, mandrake and valerian, gentian, flax seed and hyssop, alum, poke root and black cherry, which he knew by heart, and which did not now distract him at all from the thought of the woman in her rich foreign finery, her distress and distraction, who had come so swiftly out of the night.

Now she had gone, uneasiness assailed him – where had she disappeared? Was she safe? Ought he not forcibly to have kept her till the return of Francis Valletort, who spoke both French and Italian? Certainly he had been the cause of the lady's visit; she had said, again and again, 'Valletort – Francis Valletort.' The apothecary drank his spiced wine, trimmed and snuffed his candles, warmed his feet on the hearth and his hands over the blaze, and listened for the bell that should tell of the doctor's return.

He began to get sleepy, almost dozed off in his chair, and was becoming angry with these adventures that kept him out of his bed when the bell rang a third time, and he sat up with that start that a bell rung suddenly in the silence of the night never fails to give.

'Of course it will be Francis Valletort back again,' he said, rising and taking up the candle that had now nearly burnt down to the socket; it was half an hour since the doctor had left the house.

Once again the apothecary opened the door on to the wet, windy night; the candle was blown out in his hand.

'You – must come,' said a woman's voice out of the darkness; he could just distinguish the figure of his former visitor, standing in the doorway and looking down on him; she spoke the three English words with care and difficulty, and with such a foreign accent that the apothecary stared stupidly, not understanding, at which she broke out into her foreign ejaculations, caught at his coat, and dragged at him passionately.

Mr Proudie, quite bewildered, stepped into the street, and stood there hatless and cloakless, the candlestick in his hand.

'If you could only explain yourself, madam!' he exclaimed in despair.

While he was protesting she drew the door to behind him and, seizing his arm, hurried along down Dean Street.

Mr Proudie did not wish to refuse to accompany her, but the adventure was not pleasing to him; he shivered in the night air and felt apprehensive of the darkness; he wished he had had time to bring his hat and cloak.

'Madam,' he said, as he hurried along, 'unless you have someone who can speak English, I fear I shall be no good at all, whatever your plight.'

She made no answer; he could hear her teeth chattering and feel her shivering; now and then she stumbled over the rough stones of the roadway. They had not gone far up the street when she stopped at the door of one of the mansions and pushed it gently open, guiding Mr Proudie into a hall in absolute silence and darkness. Mr Proudie thought that he knew all the houses in Dean Street, but he could not place this; the darkness had completely confused him.

The lady opened another door and pushed Mr Proudie into a chamber where a faint light burned.

The room was unfurnished, covered with dust and in disrepair; only in front of the shuttered windows hung long, dark blue silk curtains. Against the wall was hung a silver lamp of beautiful workmanship, which gave a gloomy glow over the desolate chamber.

The apothecary was about to speak when the lady, who had been standing in an attitude of listening, suddenly put her hand over his mouth and pushed him desperately behind the curtains. Mr Proudie would have protested, not liking this false position, but there was no mistaking the terrified entreaty in the foreign woman's blanched face, and the apothecary, altogether unnerved, suffered himself to be concealed behind the flowing folds of the voluminous curtains that showed so strangely in the unfurnished room.

A firm step sounded outside and Mr Proudie, venturing in the shadow to peer from behind the curtain, saw his first visitor of the evening enter the room. He was now without mask, hat, or wig, and his appearance caused Mr Proudie an inward shudder.

Tall and superb in carriage, graceful, and richly dressed, the face and head were those of a full-blooded negro; his rolling eyes, his twitching lips, and an extraordinary pallor that rendered greenish his dusky skin showed him to be in some fierce passion. His powerful black hands grasped a martingale of elegant leather, ornamented with silver studs.

With a fierce gesture he pointed to the lady's draggled skirts and wet shawl, and in the foreign language that she had used questioned her with a flood of invective – or such it seemed to the terrified ears of Mr Proudie.

She seemed to plead, weep, lament, and defy all at once, sweeping up and down the room and wringing her hands, and now and then, it seemed, calling on God and his saints to help her, for she cast up her eyes and pressed her palms together. To the amazed apothecary, to whom nothing exciting had ever happened before, this was like a scene in a stage play; the two brilliant, fantastic figures, the negro and the fair woman, going through this scene of incomprehensible passion in the empty room, lit only by the solitary lamp.

Mr Proudie hoped that there might be no violence in which he would be called upon to interfere on behalf of the lady: neither his age nor his strength would give him any chance with the terrible blackamoor – he was, moreover, totally unarmed.

His anxieties on this score were ended; the drama being enacted before his horrified yet fascinated gaze was suddenly cut short. The negro seized the lady by the wrist and dragged her from the room.

Complete silence fell; the shivering apothecary was straining his ears for some sound, perhaps some call for help, some shriek or cry.

But nothing broke the stillness of the mansion, and presently Mr Proudie ventured forth from his hiding-place.

He left the room and proceeded cautiously to the foot of the stairs. Such utter silence prevailed that he began to think he was alone in the house and that anyhow he might now return – the front door was ajar, as his conductress had left it; the way of escape was easy.

To the end of his days Mr Proudie regretted that he had not taken it; he never could tell what motives induced him to return to the room, take down the lamp, and begin exploring the house. He rather thought, he would say afterwards, that he wanted to find Francis

Valletort; he felt sure that he must be in the house somewhere and he had a horrid premonition of foul play; he was sure, in some way, that the house was empty and the lady and the blackamoor had fled, and an intense curiosity got the better of his fear, his bewilderment, and his fatigue.

He walked very softly, for he was startled by the creaking of the boards beneath his feet; the lamp shook in his hand so that the fitful light ran wavering over walls and ceiling; every moment he paused and listened, fearful to hear the voice or step of the blackamoor.

On the first floor all the doors were open, the rooms all empty, shuttered, desolate, covered with dust and damp.

'There is certainly no-one in the house,' thought Mr Proudie, with a certain measure of comfort. 'Perhaps Valletort has gone home while I have been here on this fool's errand.'

He remembered with satisfaction his fire and his bed, the safe, comfortable shop with the rows of jars, the shining counter, and the gleaming scales, and the snug little parlour beyond, with everything to his hand, just as he liked to find it. Yet he went on up the stairs, continuing to explore the desolate, empty house, the chill atmosphere of which caused him to shiver as if he was cold to the marrow.

On the next landing he was brought up short by a gleam of light from one of the back rooms. In a panic of terror he put out his own lamp and stood silent and motionless, staring at the long, faint ray of yellow that fell through the door that was ajar.

'There is someone in the house, then,' thought Mr Proudie. 'I wonder if it is the doctor.'

He crept close to the door, but dared not look in; yet could not go away. The silence was complete; he could only hear the thump of his own heart.

Curiosity, a horrible, fated curiosity, urged him nearer, drove him to put his eye to the crack. His gaze fell on a man leaning against the wall; he was dressed in a rich travelling dress and wore neither peruke nor hat; his superb head was bare to the throat, and he was so dark as to appear almost of African blood; his features, however, were handsome and regular, though pallid and distorted by an expression of despair and ferocity.

A candle stuck into the neck of an empty bottle stood on the bare floor beside him and illuminated his sombre and magnificent figure, casting a grotesque shadow on the dark, panelled wall.

At his feet lay a heap of white linen and saffron-coloured brocade, with here and there the gleam of a red jewel. Mr Proudie stared at this; as his sight became accustomed to the waving lights and shades, he saw that he was gazing at a woman.

A dead woman.

She lay all dishevelled, her clothes torn and her black hair fallen in a tangle – the man had his foot on the end of it; her head was twisted to one side and there were dreadful marks on her throat.

Mr John Proudie gave one sob and fled, with the swiftness and silence of utter terror, down the stairs, out into the street, and never ceased running until he reached home.

He had his key in his pocket, and let himself into his house, panting and sighing, utterly spent. He lit every light in the place and sat down over the dying fire, his teeth chattering and his knees knocking together. Like a man bewitched he sat staring into the fire, raking the embers together, rubbing his hands and shivering, with his mind a blank for everything but that picture he had seen through the crack of the door in the empty house in Dean Street.

When his lamp and candles burnt out he drew the curtains and let in the colourless light of the November dawn; he began to move about the shop in a dazed, aimless way, staring at his jars and scales and pestle and mortar as if they were strange things he had never seen before.

Now came a young apprentice with a muffler round his neck, whistling and red with the cold; and as he took down the shutters and opened the dispensary, as the housekeeper came down and bustled about the breakfast and there was a pleasant smell of coffee and bacon in the place, Mr Proudie began to feel that the happenings of last night were a nightmare indeed that had no place in reality; he felt a cowardly and strong desire to say nothing about any of it, but to try to forget the blackamoor, the foreign lady, and that horrible scene in the upper chamber as figments of his imagination.

It was, however, useless for him to take cover in the refuge of silence – old Emily's first remark went to the root of the matter. 'Why, where is the doctor? He has never been out so late before.'

Where, indeed, was Francis Valletort?

With a groan Mr Proudie dragged himself together; his body was stiff with fatigue, his mind amazed, and he wished that he could have got into bed and slept off all memories of the previous night.

Bur he knew the thing must be faced and, snatching up his hat and coat, staggered out into the air, looking by ten years an older man than the comfortable, quiet tradesman of last night.

He went to the nearest magistrate and told his story; he could see that he was scarcely believed, but a couple of watchmen were sent with him to investigate the scene of last night's adventure, which, remarked the magistrate, should be easily found, since there was, it seemed, but one empty house in Dean Street.

The house was reached, the lock forced, and the place searched, room by room.

To Mr Proudie's intense disappointment and amazement absolutely nothing was found: the blue silk curtains had gone, as had the silver lamp the apothecary had dropped on the stairs in his headlong flight; in the upper chamber where he had stared through the crack of the door nothing was to be found – not a stain on the boards, not a mark on the wall. Dusty, neglected, desolate, the place seemed as if it had not been entered for years.

Mr Proudie began to think that he had been the victim of a company of ghosts or truly bewitched. Then, inside the door, was found the pewter candlestick he had held mechanically in his hand when hurried from his shop and as mechanically let fall here as he had afterwards let fall the lamp.

This proved nothing beyond the fact that he had been in the house last night; but it a little reassured him that he was not altogether losing his wits.

The fullest inquiries were made in the neighbourhood, but without result. No-one had seen the foreigners, no-one had heard any noise in the house, and it would have been generally believed that Mr Proudie had really lost his senses but for one fact – *Francis Valletort never returned*!

There was, then, some mystery, but the solving of it seemed hopeless. No search or inquiries led to the discovery of the whereabouts of the young doctor, and as he was of very little importance and had no friends but the old apothecary, his disappearance was soon forgotten.

But Mr Proudie, who seemed very aged and, the neighbours said, strange since that November night, was not satisfied with any such reasoning. Day and night he brooded over the mystery, and hardly ever out of his mind was the figure of the young scholar in his shabby clothes, with the strange face of one doomed as he stood putting his heavy hair back from his face and staring at the little white ring on the old, polished counter.

As the years went by the rooms over the chemist's shop were occupied by another lodger and Mr Proudie took possession of the poor effects of Francis Valletort – a few shabby clothes, a few shabby books; nothing of value or even of interest. But to the apothecary these insignificant articles had an intense if horrid fascination.

He locked them away in his cabinet and when he was alone he would take them out and turn them over. In between the thick, yellow leaves of a Latin book on medicine he found the thin leaves of what seemed to be the remains of a diary – fragments torn violently from the cover – mostly half-effaced and one torn across and completely blotted with ink.

There was no name, but Mr Proudie recognised the handwriting of Francis Valletort. With pain and difficulty the dim old eyes of the apothecary made out the following entries:

July 15th, 1687 – I saw her in the church today – Santa Maria Maggiore. He is her husband, a Calabrere.' Several lines were blotted out, then came these words – 'a man of great power; some mystery – his half-brother is an African . . . children of a slave . . . that such a woman . . .

July 27th – I cannot see how this is going to end; her sister is married to the brother – Vittoria, the name – *hers* Elena della Cxxxxxx.

August 3rd – She showed me the ring today. I think she has worn it since she was a child; it only fits her little finger.'

Again the manuscript was indecipherable; then followed some words scratched out, but readable –

As if I would not come to her without this token! But she is afraid of a trick. *He* is capable of anything – they, I mean; the brother is as his shadow. I think she trusts her sister. My little love!

On another page were found further entries:

October 10th – She says that if he discovered us he would kill her – us together. He told her he would kill her if she angered him; showed her a martingale and said *they* would strangle her. My God, why do I not murder him? Carlo Fxxxxxx warned me today.

October 29th – I must leave Padua. For her sake – while she is safe – if she is in trouble she will send me the ring. I wonder why we go on living – it is over, the farewells.

Mr Proudie could make out nothing more; he put down the pages with a shudder. To what dark and secret tale of wrong and passion did they not refer? Did they not hold the key to the events of that awful night?

Mr Proudie believed that he had seen the husband and brother-in-law of some woman Francis Valletort had loved, who had followed him to England after the lapse of years; having wrung the secret and the meaning of the white ring from the wretched wife, the husband had used it to lure the lover to his fate; in his other visitor the apothecary believed he had seen the sister Vittoria, who, somehow, had escaped and endeavoured to gain help from the house where she knew Francis Valletort lived, only to be silenced again by her husband. And the other woman – and the martingale?

'I saw her, too,' muttered Mr Proudie to himself, shivering over the fire, *'but what did they do with Frank?'*

He never knew, and died a very old man with all the details of this mystery unrevealed; the fragments of diary were burnt by some careless hand for whom they had no interest; the adventure of Mr Proudie passed into the realms of forgotten mystery, and there was no-one to tell of them when, a century later, repairs to the foundations of an old house in Dean Street revealed two skeletons buried deep beneath the bricks. One was that of a man, the other that of a woman, round whose bones still hung a few shreds of saffron-coloured brocade; and between them was a little ring of white enamel and white stones.

The Scoured Silk

This is a tale that might be told in many ways and from various points of view; it has to be gathered from here and there – a letter, a report, a diary, a casual reference. In its day the thing was more than a passing wonder, and it left a mark of abiding horror on the neighbourhood.

The house in which Mr Orford lived has finally been destroyed; the mural tablet in St. Paul's, Covent Garden, may be sought for in vain by the curious; but little remains of the old Piazza where the quiet scholar passed on his daily walks. The very records of what was once so real have become blurred, almost incoherent in their dealings with things forgotten; but this thing happened to real people, in a real London, not so long ago that the last generation had not spoken with those who remembered some of the actors in this terrible drama.

It is round the person of Humphrey Orford that this tale turns, as, at the time, all the mystery and horror centred; yet until his personality was brought thus tragically into fame, he had not been an object of interest to many; he had, perhaps, a mild reputation for eccentricity, but this was founded merely on the fact that he refused to partake of the amusements of his neighbours and showed a dislike for much company.

But this was excused on the ground of his scholarly predilections; he was known to be translating, in a leisurely fashion, as became a gentleman, Ariosto's great romance into English couplets, and to be writing essays on recondite subjects connected with grammar and language, which were not the less esteemed because they had never been published.

His most authentic portrait, taken in 1733 and intended for a frontispiece for the Ariosto when this should come to print, shows a slender man with reddish hair, rather severely clubbed, a brown coat, and a muslin cravat; he looks straight out of the picture, and the face is long, finely shaped, and refined, with eyebrows rather heavier than one would expect from such delicacy of feature.

When this picture was painted Mr Orford was living near Covent Garden, close to the mansion once occupied by the famous Dr Radcliffe, a straight-fronted house, dark, of obvious gentility, with a little architrave portico over the door and a few steps leading up to it; a house with neat windows and a gloomy air, like every other residence in that street and most other streets of the same status in London.

And if there was nothing remarkable about Mr Orford's dwelling-place or person, there was nothing, as far as his neighbours knew, remarkable about his history.

He came from a good Suffolk family, in which county he was believed to have considerable estates (though it was a known fact that he never visited them), and he had no relations, being the only child of an only child and his parents dead; his father had purchased this town house in the reign of King William, when the neighbourhood was very fashionable; and up to it he had come twenty years ago – nor had he left it since.

He had brought with him an ailing wife, a housekeeper, and a manservant, and to the few families of his acquaintance near, who waited on him, he explained that he wished to give young Mrs Orford, who was of a mopish disposition, the diversions of a few months in town.

But soon there was no longer this motive for remaining in London, for the wife, hardly seen by anyone, fell into a short illness and died – just a few weeks after her husband had brought her up from Suffolk. She was buried very simply in St. Paul's, and the mural tablet, set up with a draped urn in marble and just her name and the date, ran thus:

FLORA, WIFE OF HUMPHREY ORFORD, Esq.
of this Parish
Died November, 1713, aged 27 years

Mr Orford made no effort to leave the house; he remained, people thought, rather stunned by his loss, kept himself close in the house, and for a considerable time wore deep mourning.

But this was twenty years ago, and all had forgotten the shadowy figure of the young wife, whom so few had seen and whom no-one had known anything about or been interested in; and all trace of her seemed to have passed out of the quiet, regular, and easy life of Mr Orford when an event that gave rise to some gossip caused the one-time existence of Flora Orford to be recalled and discussed among the curious. This event was none other than the sudden betrothal of Mr Orford and the announcement of his almost immediate marriage.

The bride was one who had been a prattling child when the groom had first come to London; one old lady, who was for ever at her window watching the little humours of the street, recollected and related how she had seen Flora Orford, alighting from the coach that had brought her from the country, turn to this child, who was gazing from the railing of the neighbouring house, and touch her bare curls lovingly and yet with a sad gesture. And that was about the only time anyone ever did see Flora Orford, she so soon became ailing; and the next the inquisitive old lady saw of her was the slender brown coffin being carried through the dusk towards St. Paul's Church.

But that was twenty years ago, and here was the baby grown up into Miss Elisa Minden, a very personable young woman, soon to be the second Mrs Humphrey Orford. Of course there was nothing very remarkable about the match; Elisa's father, Dr Minden, had been Mr Orford's best friend (as far as he could be said to have a best friend or indeed any friend at all) for many a long year, both belonged to the same quiet set, both knew all about each other. Mr Orford was not much above forty-five or so, an elegant, well-looking man, wealthy, with no vices and a calm, equable temper; while Miss Elisa, though pretty and well-mannered, had an insufficient dowry, no mother to fend for her, and the younger sisters to share her slender advantages. So what could anyone say save that the good doctor had done very well for his daughter and that Mr Orford had been fortunate enough to secure such a fresh, capable maiden for his wife. It was said that the scholar intended giving up his bookish ways – that he even spoke of going abroad a while, to Italy, for preference; he was, of course, anxious to see Italy, as all his life had been devoted to preparing the translation of an Italian classic.

The quiet betrothal was nearing its decorous conclusion when one day Mr Orford took Miss Minden for a walk and brought her home round the piazza of Covent Garden, then took her across the cobbled street, past the stalls banked up with the first spring flowers (it was the end of March), under the portico built by the great Inigo Jones, and so into the church.

'I want to show you where my wife Flora lies buried,' said Mr Orford.

And that is really the beginning of the story.

Now, Miss Minden had been in this church every Sunday of her life and many weekdays and had been used since a child to see that tablet to Flora Orford; but when she heard these words in the quiet voice of her lover and felt him draw her out of the sunlight into the darkness of the church, she experienced a great distaste that was almost fear. It seemed to her both a curious and a disagreeable thing for him to do, and she slipped her arm out of his as she replied: 'Oh, please let us go home!' she said. 'Father will be waiting for us and your good Mrs Boyd vexed if the tea is over-brewed.'

'But first I must show you this,' he insisted, and took her arm again and led her down the church, past his seat, until they stood between his pew end and the marble tablet in the wall which was just a hand's space above their heads.

'That is to her memory,' said Mr Orford. 'And you see, there is nothing said as to her virtues.'

Now, Elisa Minden knew absolutely nothing of her predecessor and could not tell if these words were spoken in reverence or irony, so she said nothing, but looked up rather timidly from under the shade of her Leghorn straw at the tall figure of her lover, who was staring sternly at the square of marble.

'And what have you to say to Flora Orford?' he asked sharply, looking down at her quickly.

'Why, sir, she was a stranger to me,' replied Miss Minden.

Mr Orford pressed her arm. 'But to me she was a wife,' he said. 'She is buried under your feet, quite close to where you are standing. Why, think of that, Lizzie, if she could stand up and put out her hand she could catch hold of your dress – she is as near as that.'

The words and his manner of saying them filled Miss Minden with shuddering terror, for she was a sensitive and fanciful girl, and it seemed to her a dreadful thing to be thus standing over the bones of the poor creature who had loved the man who was now to be her own husband, and horrible to think that the handful of decay so near them had once clung to this man and loved him.

'Do not tremble, my dear girl,' said Mr Orford. 'She is dead.'

Tears were in Elisa Minden's eyes, and she answered coldly: 'Sir, how can you speak so?'

'She was a wicked woman,' he replied, 'a very wicked woman.'

The girl could not reply as to that; this sudden disclosing of a painful secret abashed her simple mind.

'Need we talk of this?' she asked; then, under her breath – 'Need we be married in this church, sir?'

'Of course,' he answered shortly, 'everything is arranged. To-morrow week.'

Miss Minden did not respond; hitherto she had been fond of the church, now it seemed spoiled for her – tarnished by the thought of Flora Orford.

Her companion seemed to divine what reflection lay behind her silence. 'You need not be afraid,' he said rather harshly. 'She is dead. Dead.'

And he reached out the light cane he carried and tapped on the stone above his wife's grave, and slowly smiled as the sound rang hollow in the vaults beneath.

Then he allowed Elisa to draw him away, and they returned to Mr Orford's comfortable house, where in the upper parlour Dr Minden was awaiting them together with his sister and her son, a soldier cousin whom the quick perceptions of youthful friends had believed to be devoted to Elisa Minden. They made a pleasant little party, with the red curtains drawn and the fire burning up between the polished andirons, and all the service for tea laid out with scones and Naples cake, and Mrs Boyd coming to and fro with plates and dishes. And everyone was cheerful and friendly and glad to be indoors together, for it was a bleak afternoon, grey out of doors, with a snowstorm coming up and people hurrying home with heads bent before a cutting wind.

But to Elisa's mind had come an unbidden thought: 'I do not like this house – it is where Flora Orford died.'

And she wondered in which room and also why this had never occurred to her before, and glanced rather thoughtfully at the fresh young face of the soldier cousin as he stood by the fire in his scarlet and white, with his glance on the flames.

But it was a cheerful party, and Elisa smiled and jested with the rest as she served the dishes at tea.

There is a miniature of her painted about this time, and one may see how she looked, with her bright brown hair and bright brown eyes, rosy complexion, pretty nose and mouth, and her best gown of lavender blue tabinet with a lawn tucker, and a lawn cap fastened under the chin with frilled lappets showing now that the big Leghorn hat with the velvet strings was put aside.

Mr Orford also looked well tonight; he did not look his full age in the ruddy candle-glow, the grey did not show in his abundant hair nor the lines in his fine face, but the elegance of his figure, the grace of his bearing, the richness of his simple clothes were displayed to full advantage; Captain Hoare looked stiff and almost clumsy by contrast.

But now and then Elisa Minden's eyes would rest rather wistfully on the fresh face of this young man who had no dead wife in his life. And something was roused in her meek youth and passive innocence, and she wondered why she had so quietly accepted her father's arrangement of a marriage with this elderly scholar, and why Philip Hoare had let her do it. Her thoughts were quite vague and amounted to no more than a confused sense that something was wrong, but she lost her satisfaction in the tea-drinking and the pleasant company and the warm room with the drawn curtains and the bright fire, and rose up saying they must be returning, as there was a great store of mending she had promised to help her aunt with; but Mrs Hoare would not help her out, but protested, laughing, that there was time enough for that; and the good doctor, who was in a fine humour and in no mood to go out into the bleak streets even as far as his own door, declared that now was the time they must be shown over the house.

'Do you know, Humphrey,' he said, 'you have often promised us this, but never done it, and all the years that I have known you, I have never seen but this room and the dining-room below; and as to your own particular cabinet – '

'Well,' said Mr Orford, interrupting in a leisurely fashion, 'no-one has been in there save Mrs Boyd now and then, to announce a visitor.'

'Oh, you scholars!' smiled the doctor. 'A secretive tribe – and a fortunate one; why, in my poor room I have had to have three girls running to and fro!'

The soldier spoke, not so pleasantly as his uncle. 'What have you so mysterious, sir, in this same cabinet that it must be so jealously guarded?' he asked.

'Why, nothing mysterious,' smiled the scholar; 'only my books and papers and pictures.'

'You will show them to me?' asked Elisa Minden, and her lover gave graceful consent; there was further amiable talk, and then the whole party, guided by Mr Orford holding a candle, made a tour of the house and looked over the fine rooms.

Mrs Hoare took occasion to whisper to the bride-to-be that there were many alterations needed before the place was ready for a lady's use and it was time these were put in hand – why, the wedding was less than a fortnight off!

And Elisa Minden, who had not had a mother to advise her in these matters, suddenly felt that the house was dreary and old-fashioned and an impossible place to live in; the very rooms that had so pleased her good father – a set of apartments for a lady – were to her the most hateful in the house, for they, her lover told her, had been furnished and prepared for Flora Orford twenty years ago.

She was telling herself that when she was married she must at once go away and that the house must be altered before she returned to it, when the party came crowding to the threshold of the library, or private cabinet, and Mr Orford, holding the candle aloft, led them in. Then as this illumination was not sufficient, he went very quickly and lit the two candles on the mantelpiece.

It was a pleasant apartment, lined with books from floor to ceiling, old, valuable, and richly bound books, save only in the space above the chimney-piece, which was occupied by a portrait of a lady, and the panel behind the desk – this was situated in a strange position, in the farthest corner of the room fronting the wall, so that anyone seated there would be facing the door with the space of the room between; the desk was quite close to the wall, so that there was only just space for the chair at which the writer would sit, and to accommodate this there were no bookshelves behind it, but a smooth panel of wood on which hung a small picture; this was a rough, dark painting, and represented a man hanging on a gallows on a wild heath; it was a subject out of keeping with the luxurious room, with its air of ease and learning, and while Mr Orford was showing his first editions, his Elzevirs and Aldines, Elisa Minden was staring at this ugly little picture.

As she looked she was conscious of such a chill of horror and dismay as nearly caused her to shriek aloud. The room seemed to her to be full of an atmosphere of terror and evil beyond expression. Never had such a thing happened to her before; her distaste at her visit to the tomb in the afternoon had been nothing to this. She moved away, barely able to disguise an open panic. As she turned, she half-stumbled against a chair, caught at it, and noticed, hanging over the back, a skirt of peach-coloured silk. Elisa, not being mistress of herself, caught at this garment.

'Why, sir,' cried she hysterically, 'what is this?'

All turned to look at her; her tone, her obvious fright were out of proportion to her discovery.

'Why child,' said Mrs Hoare, 'it is a silk petticoat, as all can see.'

'A gift for you, my dear,' said the cheerful doctor.

'A gift for me?' cried Elisa. 'Why, this has been scoured, and turned, and mended, and patched a hundred times!'

And she held up the skirt, which had indeed become like tinder and seemed ready to drop to pieces.

The scholar now spoke. 'It belongs to Mrs Boyd,' he said quietly. 'I suppose she has been in here to clear up and has left some of her mending.'

Now, two things about this speech made a strange impression on everyone: first, it was manifestly impossible that the good house-keeper would ever have owned such a garment as this, that was a lady's dress and such as would be worn for a ball; and, secondly, Mr Orford had only a short while before declared that Mrs Boyd only entered his room when he was in it, and then of a necessity and for a few moments. All had the same impression, that this was some garment belonging to his dead wife and as such cherished by him; all, that is, but Elisa, who had heard him call Flora Orford a wicked woman.

She put the silk down quickly (there was a needle sticking into it and a spool of cotton lying on the chair beneath) and looked up at the portrait above the mantelpiece.

'Is that Mrs Orford?' she asked.

He gave her a queer look. 'Yes,' he said.

In a strange silence all glanced up at the picture.

It showed a young woman in a white gown, holding a crystal heart that hung round her neck; she had dark hair and a pretty face; as Elisa looked at the pointed fingers holding the pretty toy, she thought of the tablet in St. Paul's Church and Mr Orford's words – 'She is so near to you that if she could stretch out her hand she could touch you,' and without any remark about the portrait or the sitter, she advised her aunt that it was time to go home. So the four of them left, and Mr Orford saw them out, standing framed in the warm light of the corridor and watching them disappear into the grey darkness of the street.

It was little more than an hour afterwards when Elisa Minden came creeping down the stairway of her home and accosted her cousin, who was just leaving the house. 'Oh, Philip,' said she, clasp-ing her hands, 'if your errand be not a very important one, I beg you to give me an hour of your time. I have been watching for you to go out that I might follow and speak to you privately.'

The young soldier looked at her keenly as she stood in the light of the hall lamp, and he saw that she was very agitated.

'Of course, Lizzie,' he answered kindly, and led her into the little parlour off the hall, where there were neither candles nor fire, but leisure and quiet to talk.

Elisa, being a housekeeper, found a lamp and lit it and apologised for the cold, but she would not return upstairs, she said, for Mrs Hoare and the two girls and the doctor were all quiet in the great parlour, and she had no mind to disturb them.

'You are in trouble,' said Captain Hoare quietly.

'Yes,' replied she in a frightened way, 'I want you to come with me now to Mr Orford's house – I want to speak to his house-keeper.'

'Why, what is this, Lizzie?'

She had no very good explanation; there was only the visit to the church that afternoon, her impression of horror in the cabinet, the discovery of the scoured silk.

'But I must know something of his first wife, Philip,' she concluded. 'I could never go on with it if I did not . . . something has happened today – I hate that house, I almost hate . . . *him*.'

'Why did you do it, Lizzie?' demanded the young soldier sternly. 'This was a nice homecoming for me . . . a man who might be your father, a solitary, one who frightens you.'

Miss Minden stared at her cousin; she did not know why she had done it – the whole thing seemed suddenly impossible.

'Please, you must come with me now,' she said.

So overwrought was she that he had no heart to refuse her, and they took their warm cloaks from the hall and went out into the dark streets. It was snowing now and the ground slippery underfoot, and Elisa clung to her cousin's arm. She did not want to see Mr Orford or his house ever again, and by the time they reached the doorstep she was in a tremble; but she rang the bell boldly.

It was Mrs Boyd herself who came to the door; she began explaining that the master was shut up in his cabinet, but the soldier cut her short. 'Miss Minden wishes to see you,' he said, 'and I will wait in the hall till she is ready.'

So Elisa followed the housekeeper down to her basement sitting-room; the manservant was out and the two maids were quickly dismissed to the kitchen.

Mrs Boyd, a placid soul, near seventy years, waited for the young lady to explain herself, and Elisa Minden, flushing and paling by turns and feeling foolish and timid, put forth the object of her coming.

She wanted to hear the story of Flora Orford – there was no-one else whom she could ask – and she thought that she had a right to know.

'And I suppose you have, my dear,' said Mrs Boyd, gazing into the fire, 'though it is not a pretty story for you to hear – and I never thought I should be telling it to Mr Orford's second wife!'

'Not his wife yet,' said Miss Minden.

'There, there, you had better ask the master yourself,' replied Mrs Boyd placidly. 'Not but that he would be fierce at your speaking of it, for I do not think a mention of it has passed his lips, and it's twenty years ago and best forgotten, my dear.'

'Tell it me and then I will forget,' begged Miss Minden.

So then Mrs Boyd, who was a quiet, harmless soul, with no dislike to telling a tale (though no gossip, as events had proved, she having kept her tongue still on this matter for so long), told her the story of Humphrey Orford's wife; it was told in very few words.

'She was the daughter of his gamekeeper, my dear, and he married her out of hand, just for her pretty face. But they were not very happy together that I could ever see; she was afraid of him and that made her cringe, and he hated that; and she shamed him with her ignorant ways. And then one day he found her with a lover – saving your presence, mistress – one of her own people, just a common man. And he was just like a creature possessed; he shut up the house and sent away all the servants but me, and brought his lady up to town, to this house here. And what passed between her and him no-one will know, but she ever looked like one dying of terror. And then the doctor began to come – Dr Thursby, it was, that is dead now – and then she died. And no-one was able to see her even when she was in her coffin, nor to send a flower. 'Tis likely she died of grief, poor, fond wretch. But, of course, she was a wicked woman and there was nothing to do but pity the master.'

And this was the story of Flora Orford.

'And the man?' asked Miss Minden, after a while.

'The man she loved, my dear? Well, Mr Orford had him arrested as a thief for breaking into his house – he was wild, that fellow, with not the best of characters. Well, he would not say why he was in the house, and Mr Orford, being a Justice of the Peace, had some power, so he was just condemned as a common thief. And there are few to this day know the truth of the tale, for he kept his counsel to the last, and no-one knew from *him* why he had been found in the squire's house.'

'What was his end?' asked Miss Minden in a still voice.

'Well, he was hanged,' said Mrs Boyd. 'Being caught red-handed, what could he hope for?'

'Then that is a picture of him in the cabinet!' cried Elisa, shivering for all the great fire; then she added desperately, 'Tell me, did Flora Orford die in that cabinet?'

'Oh, no, my dear, but in a great room at the back of the house that has been shut up ever since.'

'But the cabinet is horrible,' said Elisa; 'perhaps it is her portrait and that picture.'

'I have hardly been in there,' admitted Mrs Boyd, 'but the master lives there – he always has his supper there, and he talks to that portrait, my dear: "Flora, Flora," he says, "how are you tonight?" and then he imitates her voice, answering.'

Elisa Minden clapped her hand to her heart. 'Do not tell me those things or I shall think that you are hateful too, to have stayed in this dreadful house and endured them!'

Mrs Boyd was surprised. 'Now, my dear, do not be put out,' she protested. 'They were wicked people, both of them, and got their deserts, and it is an old story best forgotten; and as for the master, he has been just a good creature ever since we have been here, and he will not go talking to any picture when he has a sweet young wife to keep him company.'

But Elisa Minden had risen and had her fingers on the handle of the door.

'One thing more,' said she breathlessly; 'that scoured silk, of a peach colour – '

'Why, has he got that still? Mrs Orford wore it the night he found her with her sweetheart. I mind I was with her when she bought it – fine silk at forty shillings the yard. If I were you, my dear, I should burn that when I was mistress here.'

But Miss Minden had run upstairs to the cold hall.

Her cousin was not there; she heard angry voices overhead and saw the two maidservants affrighted on the stairs – a disturbance was unknown in this household.

While Elisa stood bewildered, a door banged and Captain Hoare came down red in the face and fuming; he caught his cousin's arm and hurried her out of the house. In an angry voice he told her of the unwarrantable behaviour of Mr Orford, who had found him in the hall and called him 'intruder' and 'spy' without waiting for an explanation; the soldier had followed the scholar up to his cabinet and there had been an angry scene about nothing at all, as Captain Hoare said.

'Oh, Philip,' broke out poor Elisa as they hastened through the cold darkness, 'I can never, never marry him!'

And she told him the story of Flora Orford. The young man pressed her arm through the heavy cloak.

'And how came such a one to entangle thee?' he asked tenderly. 'Nay, thou shalt not marry him.'

They spoke no more, but Elisa, happy in the protecting and whole-some presence of her kinsman, sobbed with a sense of relief and gratitude. When they reached home they found they had been missed and there had to be explanations; Elisa said there was something that she wished to say to Mrs Boyd and Philip told of Mr Orford's rude-ness and the quarrel that had followed. The two elder people were disturbed and considered Elisa's behaviour strange, but her manifest agitation caused them to forbear pressing her for an explanation; nor was it any use addressing themselves to Philip, for he went out to his delayed meeting with companions at a coffee-house.

That night Elisa Minden went to bed feeling more emotion than she had ever done in her life: fear and disgust of the man whom hitherto she had placidly regarded as her future husband and a yearning for the kindly presence of her childhood's companion united in the resolute words she whispered into her pillow during that bitter night: 'I can never marry him now!'

The next day it snowed heavily, yet a strange elation was in Elisa's heart as she descended to the warm parlour, bright from the fire and light from the glow of the snow without.

She was going to tell her father that she could not carry out her engagement with Mr Orford and that she did not want ever to go into his house again.

They were all gathered round the breakfast-table when Captain Hoare came in late (he had been out to get a newsletter) and brought the news that was the most unlooked for they could conceive, and that was soon to startle all London.

Mr Orford had been found murdered in his cabinet.

These tidings, though broken as carefully as possible, threw the little household into the deepest consternation and agitation; there were shrieks and cryings and runnings to and fro. Only Miss Minden, though of a ghastly colour, made no especial display of grief; she was thinking of Flora Orford.

When the doctor could get away from his agitated womenkind, he went with his nephew to the house of Mr Orford.

The story of the murder was a mystery. The scholar had been found in his chair in front of his desk with one of his own bread-knives sticking through his shoulders; and there was nothing to throw any light as to how or through whom he had met his death. The story, sifted from the mazed incoherency of Mrs Boyd, the hysterics of the maids, the commentaries of the constables, and the chatter of the neighbours, ran thus.

At half-past nine the night before, Mrs Boyd had sent one of the maids up with the master's supper; it was his whim to have it always thus, served on a tray in the cabinet. There had been wine and meat, bread and cheese, fruit and cakes, the usual plates and silver – among these the knife that had killed Mr Orford. When the servant left, the scholar had followed her to the door and locked it after her; this was also a common practice of his, a precaution against any possible interruption; for, he said, he did the best part of his work in the evening.

It was found next morning that his bed had not been slept in and that the library door was still locked; as the alarmed Mrs Boyd could get no answer to her knocks, the manservant was sent for someone to force the lock, and Humphrey Orford had been found in his chair, leaning forward over his papers with the knife thrust up to the hilt between his shoulders. He must have died instantly for there was no sign of any struggle, nor any disarrangement of his person or his papers. The first doctor to see him, a passer-by, attracted by the commotion about the house, said he must have been dead some hours – probably since the night before; the candles had all burnt down to the socket, and there were spillings of grease on the desk; the supper tray stood at the other end of the room, most of the food had been eaten, most of the wine drunk, the articles were all there in order excepting only the knife sticking between Mr Orford's shoulder-blades.

When Captain Hoare had passed the house on his return from buying the newsletter, he had seen the crowd and gone in and been able to say that he had been the last person to see the murdered man alive, as he had had his sharp encounter with Mr Orford about ten o'clock, and he remembered seeing the supper things in the room. The scholar had heard him below, unlocked the door, and called out such impatient resentment of his presence that Philip had come angrily up the stairs and followed him into the cabinet; a few angry words had passed, when Mr Orford had practically pushed his visitor out, locking the door in his face and bidding him take Miss Minden home.

This threw no light at all on the murder; it only went to prove that at ten o'clock Mr Orford had been alive and locked in his cabinet.

Now here was the mystery: in the morning the door was still locked, *on the inside*; the window was, as it had been since early evening, shuttered and fastened across with an iron bar, on the inside, and the room being on an upper floor, access would have been in any case almost impossible by the window, which gave on to the smooth brickwork of the front of the house.

Neither was there any possible place in the room where anyone might have hidden – it was just the square lined with the shallow bookshelves, the two pictures (that sombre little one looking strange now above the bent back of the dead man), the desk, one or two chairs and side tables; there was not so much as a cupboard or bureau – not a hiding-place for a cat.

How, then, had the murderer entered and left the room?

Suicide, of course, was out of the question owing to the nature of the wound – but murder seemed equally out of the question; Mr Orford sat so close to the wall that the handle of the knife touched the panel behind him. For anyone to have stood between him and the wall would have been impossible; behind the back of his chair was not space enough to push a walking-stick.

How, then, had the blow been delivered with such deadly precision and force? Not by anyone standing in front of Mr Orford – first because he must have seen him and sprung up; and secondly because, even had he been asleep with his head down, no-one, not even a very tall man, could have leant over the top of the desk and driven in the knife, for experiment was made and it was found that no arm could possibly reach such a distance.

The only theory that remained was that Mr Orford had been murdered in some other part of the room and afterwards dragged to his present position. But this seemed more than unlikely, as it would have meant moving the desk, a heavy piece of furniture that did not look as if it had been touched, and also because there was a paper under the dead man's hand, a pen in his fingers, a splutter of ink where it had fallen, and a sentence unfinished. The thing remained a complete and horrid mystery, one that seized the imagination of men; the thing was the talk of all the coffee-houses and clubs.

The murder seemed absolutely motiveless; the dead man was not known to have an enemy in the world, yet robbery was out of the question, for nothing had been touched. The early tragedy was opened out. Mrs Boyd told all she knew, which was just what she had told Elisa Minden – the affair was twenty years ago and the gallows-bird had no kith or kin left.

Elisa Minden fell into a desperate state of agitation, a swift change from her first stricken calm. She wanted Mr Orford's house pulled down – the library and all its contents burnt. Her own wedding dress she did burn, in frenzied silence, and none dared stop her. She resisted her father's entreaties that she should go away directly after the inquest; she would stay on the spot, she said, until the mystery was solved.

Nothing would content her but a visit to Mr Orford's cabinet; she was resolved, she said wildly, to come to the bottom of this mystery and in that room, which she only had entered once and which had affected her so terribly. She believed she might find some clue.

The doctor thought it best to allow her to go; he and her cousin escorted her to the house that now no-one passed without a shudder and into the chamber that all dreaded to enter.

Good Mrs Boyd was sobbing behind them; the poor soul was quite mazed with this sudden and ghastly ending to her orderly life. She spoke incoherently, explaining, excusing, lamenting all in a breath; yet through all her trouble she showed plainly and artlessly that she had had no affection for her master, and that it was custom and habit that had been wounded, not love.

Indeed, it seemed that there was no-one who did love Humphrey Orford; the lawyers were already looking for a next-of-kin. It seemed likely that this property and the estates in Suffolk would go into Chancery.

'You should not go in, my dear, you should not go in,' sobbed the old woman, catching at Miss Minden's black gown (she was in mourning for the murdered man) and yet peering with a fearful curiosity into the cabinet.

Elisa looked ill and distraught, but also resolute. 'Tell me, Mrs Boyd,' said she, pausing on the threshold, 'what became of the scoured silk?'

The startled housekeeper protested that she had never seen it again; and here was another touch of mystery – the old peach-coloured silk skirt that four persons had observed in Mr Orford's cabinet the night of his murder had completely disappeared.

'He must have burnt it,' said Captain Hoare; and though it seemed unlikely that he could have consumed so many yards of stuff without leaving traces in the grate, still it was the only possible solution.

'I cannot think why he kept it so long,' murmured Mrs Boyd, 'for it could have been no other than Mrs Orford's best gown.'

'A ghastly relic,' remarked the young soldier grimly.

Elisa Minden went into the middle of the room and stared about her; nothing in the place was changed, nothing disordered; the desk had been moved round to allow of the scholar being carried away, his chair stood back, so that the long panel on which hung the picture of the gallows was fully exposed to view.

To Elisa's agitated imagination this portion of the wall, sunk in the surrounding bookshelves, long and narrow, looked like the lid of a coffin.

'It is time that picture came down,' she said; 'it cannot interest anyone any longer.'

'Lizzie, dear,' suggested her father gently, 'had you not better come away? This is a sad and awful place.'

'No,' replied she. 'I must find out about it – we must know.'

And she turned about and stared at the portrait of Flora Orford.

'He hated her, Mrs Boyd, did he not? And she must have died of fear – think of that! – died of fear, thinking all the while of that poor body on the gallows. He was a wicked man and whoever killed him must have done it to revenge Flora Orford.'

'My dear,' said the doctor hastily, 'all that was twenty years ago and the man was quite justified in what he did, though I cannot say I should have been so pleased with the match if I had known this story.'

'How did we ever like him?' muttered Elisa Minden. 'If I had entered this room before, I should never have been promised to him – there is something terrible in it.'

'And what else can you look for, my dear,' snivelled Mrs Boyd, 'in a room where a man has been murdered?'

'But it was like this before,' replied Miss Minden; 'it *frightened* me.'

She looked round at her father and cousin, and her face was quite distorted. 'There is something here now,' she said, 'something in this room.'

They hastened towards her, thinking that her overstrained nerves had given way; but she took a step forward.

Shriek after shriek left her lips.

With a quivering finger she pointed before her at the long panel behind the desk. At first they could not tell at what she pointed; then Captain Hoare saw the cause of her desperate terror.

It was a small portion of faded, peach-coloured silk showing above the ribbed line of the wainscot, protruding from the wall like a fragment of stuff shut in a door.

'She is in there!' cried Miss Minden. 'In there!'

A certain frenzy fell on all of them; they were in a confusion, hardly knowing what they said or did. Only Captain Hoare kept some presence of mind and, going up to the panel, discerned a fine crack all round.

'I believe it is a door,' he said, 'and that explains how the murderer must have struck – from the wall.'

He lifted up the picture of the hanged man and found a small knob or button, which, as he expected, sent the panel back into the wall, disclosing a secret chamber no larger than a cupboard.

And directly inside this hidden room, that was dark to the sight and noisome to the nostrils, was the body of a woman, leaning against the inner wall with a white kerchief knotted tightly round her throat, showing how she had died; she wore the scoured silk skirt, the end of which had been shut in the panel, and an old ragged bodice of linen that was like dirty parchment; her hair was grey and scanty, her face past any likeness to humanity, her body thin and dry.

The room, which was lit by a window only a few inches square looking on to the garden, was furnished with a filthy bed of rags and a stool, with a few tattered clothes; a basket of broken bits was on the floor.

Elisa Minden crept closer. 'It is Flora Orford,' she said, speaking like one in a dream.

They brought the poor body down into the room, and then it was clear that this faded and terrible creature had a likeness to the pictured girl who smiled from the canvas over the mantelpiece.

And another thing was clear, and for a moment they did not dare speak to each other.

For twenty years this woman had endured her punishment in the wall chamber in the library that no-one but her husband entered; for twenty years he had kept her there, behind the picture of her lover, feeding her on scraps, letting her out only when the household was abed, amusing himself with her torture – she mending the scoured silk she had worn for twenty years, sitting there, cramped in the almost complete darkness, a few feet from where he wrote his elegant poetry.

'Of course she was crazy,' said Captain Hoare at length, 'but why did she never cry out?'

'For a good reason,' whispered Dr Minden, when he had signed to Mrs Boyd to take his fainting daughter away. 'He saw to that – *she has got no tongue.*'

The coffin bearing the nameplate 'Flora Orford' was exhumed, and found to contain only lead; it was substituted by another containing the wasted body of the woman who died by her own hand twenty years after the date on the mural tablet to her memory. Why or how this creature, certainly become idiotic and dominated entirely by the man who kept her prisoner, had suddenly found the resolution and skill to slay her tyrant and afterwards take her own life (a thing she might have done any time before) was a question never solved.

It was supposed that he had formed the hideous scheme to complete his revenge by leaving her in the wall to die of starvation while he left with his new bride for abroad, and that she knew this and had forestalled him; or else that her poor lunatic brain had been roused by the sound of a woman's voice as she handled the scoured silk which the captive was allowed to creep out and mend when the library door was locked. But over these matters and the details of her twenty years' suffering, it is but decent to be silent.

Lizzie Minden married her cousin, but not at St. Paul's, Covent Garden. Nor did they ever return to the neighbourhood of Humphrey Orford's house.

The Avenging of Ann Leete

This is a queer story, the more queer for the interpretation of passions of the strong human heart that have been put upon it and for glimpses of other motives and doings not, it would seem, human at all.

The whole thing is seen vaguely, brokenly, a snatch here and there: one tells the tale, strangely another exclaims amazed, a third points out a scene, a fourth has a dim memory of a circumstance, a nine days' (or less) wonder, an old print helps, the name on a mural tablet in a deserted church pinches the heart with a sense of confirmation, and so you have your story; when all is said it remains a queer tale.

It is seventy years odd ago, so dating back from this present year of 1845, you come to nearly midway in the last century, when conditions were vastly different from what they are now.

The scene is in Glasgow and there are three points from which we start, all leading us to the heart of our tale.

The first is the portrait of a woman that hangs in the parlour of a respectable banker: he believes it to be the likeness of some connection of his wife's, dead this many a year, but he does not know much about it; some while ago it was discovered in a lumber room and he keeps it for the pallid beauty of the canvas, which is much faded and rubbed.

Since as a young man I had the privilege of my worthy friend's acquaintance, I have always felt a strange interest in this picture; and, in that peculiar way in which the imagination will seize on trifles, I was always fascinated by the dress of the lady. This is of dark-green very fine silk, an uncommon colour to use in a portrait and, perhaps, in a lady's dress; it is very plain, with a little scarf of a striped Roman pattern, and her hair is drawn up over a pillow in the antique mode; her face is expressionless yet strange, the upper lip very thin, the lower very full, the light-brown eyes set under brows that slant. I cannot tell why this picture to me was always full of such a great attraction; but I used to think of it a vast deal and often to note, secretly, that never had I chanced to meet, in real life or in any other painting, a lady in a dark-green silk dress.

In the corner of the canvas is a little device put in a diamond, as a gentlewoman might bear arms yet with no pretensions to heraldry, just three little birds, the topmost with a flower in its beak.

It was not so long ago that I came upon the second clue that leads into the story, and that was a mural tablet in an old church near the Rutherglen road, a church that had lately fallen into disrepute or neglect, for it was deserted and impoverished; but I was assured that a generation ago it had been a most famous place of worship, fashionable and well frequented by the better class.

This mural tablet was to one 'Ann Leete', and there was just the date (seventy odd years old) given with what seemed a sinister brevity. And underneath the lettering, lightly cut on the time-stained marble, was the same device as that on the portrait of the lady in the green silk dress.

I was curious enough to make enquiries, but no-one seemed to know anything of or wished to talk about Ann Leete.

It was all so long ago, I was told, and there was no-one now in the parish of the name of Leete. And all who had been acquainted with the family of Leete seemed to be dead or gone away; the parish register (my curiosity went so far as an inspection of this) yielded me no more information than the mural tablet.

I spoke to my friend the banker and he said he thought that his wife had had some cousins by the name of Leete, and that there was some tale of a scandal or great misfortune attached to them, which was the reason of a sort of ban on their name so that it had never been mentioned.

When I told him I thought the portrait of the lady in the dark-green silk might picture a certain Ann Leete he appeared uneasy and even desirous of having the likeness removed, which roused in me the suspicion that he knew something of the name and that not pleasant; but it seemed to me indelicate and perhaps useless to question him.

It was a year or so after this incident that my business, which was that of silversmith and jeweller, put into my hands a third clue. One of my apprentices came to me with a rare piece of work which had been left at the shop for repair.

It was a thin medal of the purest gold on which was set in fresh-water pearls, rubies, and cairngorms the device of the three birds, the plumage being most skilfully wrought in the bright jewels and the flower held by the topmost creature accurately designed in pearls. It was one of these pearls that was missing, and I had some difficulty in matching its soft lustre.

An elderly lady called for the ornament, the same person who had left it; I saw her in person and ventured to admire and praise the workmanship of the medal.

'Oh,' she said, 'it was worked by a very famous jeweller, my great-uncle, and he had a peculiar regard for it – indeed, I believe it has never before been out of his possession, but he was so greatly grieved by the loss of the pearl that he would not rest until I offered to take it to be repaired. He is, you will understand,' she added with a smile, 'a very old man. He must have made that jewellery – why, seventy-odd years ago.'

Seventy-odd years ago – that would bring one back to the date on the tablet to Ann Leete, to the period of the portrait.

'I have seen this device before,' I remarked. 'On the likeness of a lady – and on the mural inscription in memory of a certain Ann Leete.' Again this name appeared to make an unpleasant impression.

My customer took her packet hastily.

'It is associated with something dreadful,' she said quickly. 'We do not speak of it – a very old story, I did not know anyone had heard of it – '

'I certainly have not,' I assured her. 'I came to Glasgow not so long ago as apprentice to this business of my uncle's, which I now own.'

'But you have seen a portrait?' she asked.

'Yes, in the house of a friend of mine.'

'This is queer. We did not know that any existed. Yet my great-uncle does speak of one – in a green silk dress.'

'In a green silk dress,' I confirmed.

The lady appeared amazed.

'But it is better to let the matter rest,' she decided. 'My relative, you will realise, is very old – nearly, sir, a hundred years old, and his wits wander and he tells queer tales. It is all very strange and horrible – but one cannot tell how much my old uncle dreams.'

'I should not think to disturb him,' I replied.

But my customer hesitated. 'If you know of this portrait – perhaps he should be told – he laments after it so much, and we have always believed it an hallucination . . . '

She returned the packet containing the medal. 'Perhaps,' she added dubiously, 'you are interested enough to take this back to my relative yourself and judge that you shall or shall not tell him.'

I eagerly accepted the offer and the lady gave me the name and residence of the old man, who, although possessed of considerable means, had lived for the past fifty years in the greatest seclusion in that lonely part of the town beyond the Rutherglen Road and near to the Green, the once pretty and fashionable resort for youth and pleasure, but now a deserted and desolate region. Here, on the first opportunity, I took my way, and found myself well out into the country, nearly at the river, before I reached the lonely mansion of Eneas Bretton, as the ancient jeweller was called.

A ferocious dog troubled my entrance in the dark overgrown garden where the black glossy laurels and bays strangled the few flowers, and a grim woman in an old-fashioned fitch or cap at length answered my repeated peals at the rusty chain-bell.

It was not without considerable trouble that I was admitted into the presence of Mr Bretton, and only, I think, by the display of the jewel and the refusal to give it into any hands but those of its owner.

The ancient jeweller was seated on a southern terrace that received the faint and fitful rays of the September sun.

He was wrapped in shawls that disguised his natural form and a fur and leather cap was fastened under his chin. I had the impression that he had been a fine man, of a vigorous and handsome appearance; even now, in the extreme of decay, he showed a certain grandeur of line and carriage, a certain majestic power in his personality. Though extremely feeble, I did not take him to be imbecile nor greatly wanting in his faculties. He received me courteously, though obviously ill used to strangers.

I had, he said, a claim on him as a fellow craftsman and he was good enough to commend the fashion in which I had repaired his medal. This, as soon as he had unwrapped it, he fastened to a fine gold chain he drew from his breast and slipped inside his heavy clothing.

'A pretty trinket,' I said, 'and of an unusual design.'

'I fashioned it myself,' he answered, 'over seventy years ago – the year, sir, before she died.'

'Ann Leete?' I ventured.

The ancient man was not in the least surprised at the use of this name. 'It is a long time since I heard those words with any but my inner ear,' he murmured; 'to be sure, I grow very old. You'll not remember Ann Leete?' he added wistfully.

'I take it she died before I was born,' I answered.

He peered at me. 'Ah, yes, you are still a young man, though your hair is grey.'

I noticed now that he wore a small tartan scarf inside his coat and shawl; this fact gave me a peculiar, almost unpleasant shudder.

'I know this about Ann Leete – she had a dark-green silk dress – and a Roman or tartan scarf.'

He touched the wisp of bright coloured silk across his chest. 'This is it. She had her likeness taken so – but it is lost.'

'It is preserved,' I answered. 'And I know where it is – I might, if you desired, bring you to a sight of it.'

He turned his grand old face to me with a civil inclination of his massive head. 'That would be very courteous of you, sir, and a pleasure to me. You must not think,' he added with dignity, 'that the lady has forsaken me or that I do not often see her. Indeed, she comes to me more frequently than before. But it would delight me to have the painting of her to console the hours of her absence.'

I reflected what his relative had said about the weakness of his wits and recalled his great age, which one was apt to forget in face of his composure and reasonableness.

He appeared now to doze and to take no further notice of my presence, so I left him. He had a strange look of lifelessness as he slumbered there in the faintish rays of the cloudy autumn sun. I reflected how lightly the spirit must dwell in this ancient frame, how easily it must take flight into the past, how soon into eternity.

It did not cost me much persuasion to induce my friend the banker to lend me the portrait of Ann Leete, particularly as the canvas had been again sent up to the attics.

'Do *you* know the story?' I asked him.

He replied that he had heard something; that the case had made a great stir at the time; that it was all very confused and amazing, and that he did not desire to discuss the matter.

I hired a carriage and took the canvas to the house of Eneas Bretton.

He was again on the terrace, enjoying with a sort of calm eagerness the last warmth of the failing sun.

His two servants brought in the picture and placed it on a chair at his side.

He gazed at the painted face with the greatest serenity. 'That is she,' he said, 'but I am glad to think that she looks happier now, sir. She still wears that dark-green silk. I never see her in any other garment.'

'A beautiful woman,' I reflected quietly, not wishing to agitate or disturb his reflections, which were clearly detached from any considerations of time and space.

'I have always thought so,' he answered gently, 'but I, sir, have peculiar faculties. I saw her, and see her still, as a spirit. I loved her as a spirit. Yet our bodily union was necessary for our complete happiness. And in that my darling and I were baulked.'

'By death?' I suggested, for I knew that the word had no terrors for him.

'By death,' he agreed, 'who will soon be forced to unite us again.'

'But not in the body,' I said.

'How, sir, do you know that?' He smiled. 'We have but finite minds. I think we have but little conception of the marvellous future.'

'Tell me,' I urged, 'how you lost Ann Leete.'

His dim, heavy-lidded, many-wrinkled eyes flickered a glance over me. 'She was murdered,' he said.

I could not forbear a shudder. 'That fragile girl?' I exclaimed. My blood had always run cool and thin and I detested deeds of violence; my even mind could not grasp the idea of the murder of women save as a monstrous enormity.

I looked at the portrait and it seemed to me that I had always known that it was the likeness of a creature doomed.

'Seventy years ago and more,' continued Eneas Bretton, 'since when *she has wandered lonely betwixt time and eternity*, waiting for me. But very soon I shall join her, and then, sir, we shall go where there is no recollection of the evil things of this earth.'

By degrees he told me the story; not in any clear sequence nor at any one time, nor without intervals of sleep and pauses of dreaming, nor without assistance from his servants and his great niece and her husband, who were his frequent visitors.

Yet it was from his own lips and when we were alone together that I learned all that was really vital in the tale.

He required very frequent attendance; altogether, all human passion was at the utmost ebb with him; he had, he said, a kind of regard for me in that I had brought him his lady's portrait, and he told me things of which he had never spoken to any human being before – I say human on purpose because of his intense belief that he was, and always had been, in communication with powers not of this earth.

In these words I put together his tale.

As a young man, said Eneas Bretton, I was healthy, prosperous, and happy.

My family had been goldsmiths as long as there was any record of their existence and I was an enthusiast in this craft, grave withal and studious, over-fond of books and meditation. I do not know how or when I first met Ann Leete. To me, she was always there, like the sun; I think I have known her all my life, but perhaps my memory fails.

Her father was a lawyer and she an only child, and though her social station was considered superior to mine, I had far more in the way of worldly goods, so there was no earthly obstacle to our union.

The powers of evil, however, fought against us; I had feared this from the first, as our happiness was the complete circle ever hateful to friends and devils, who try to break the mystic symbol.

The mistress of my soul attracted the lustful attention of a young doctor, Rob Patterson, who had a certain false charm of person, not real comeliness, but a trick of colour, of carriage, and a fine taste in clothes. His admiration was whetted by her coldness and his intense dislike of me. We came to scenes in which he derided me as no gentleman, but a beggarly tradesman, and I scorned him as an idle voluptuary designing a woman's ruin for the crude pleasure of the gratification of fleeting passions.

For the fellow made not even any pretence of being able to support a wife and was of that rakehelly temperament that made an open mock of matrimony.

Although he was but a medical student he was of what they call noble birth, and his family, though decayed, possessed considerable social power, so that his bold pursuit of Ann Leete and his insolent flaunting of me had some licence, the more so that he did not lack tact and address in his manner and conduct.

Our marriage could have stopped this persecution or given the right to publicly resent it, but my darling would not leave her father, who was of a melancholy and querulous disposition.

It was shortly before her twenty-first birthday, for which I had made her the jewel I now wear (the device being the crest of her mother's family and one for which she had a great affection), that her father died suddenly. His last thoughts were of her, for he had this very picture painted for her birthday gift. Finding herself thus unprotected and her affairs in some confusion, she declared her intention of retiring to some distant relative in the Highlands until decorum permitted of our marriage.

And upon my opposing myself to this scheme of separation and delay she was pleased to fall out with me, declaring that I was as importunate as Dr Patterson and that I, as well as he, should be kept in ignorance of her retreat.

I had, however, great hopes of inducing her to change this resolution, and it being then fair spring weather, engaged her to walk with me on the Green, beyond the city, to discuss our future.

I was an orphan, like herself, and we had now no common meeting-place suitable to her reputation and my respect.

By reason of a pressure of work, to which by temperament and training I was ever attentive, I was a few moments late at the tryst on the Green, which I found as usual empty; but it was a lovely afternoon of May, very still and serene, like the smile of satisfied love.

I paced about, looking for my darling.

Although she was in mourning, she had promised me to wear the dark-green silk I so admired under her black cloak, and I looked for this colour among the brighter greens of the trees and bushes.

She did not appear, and my heart was chilled with the fear that she was offended with me and therefore would not meet, and an even deeper dread that she might, in vexation, have fled to her unknown retreat.

This thought was sending me, hotfoot, to seek her at her house when I saw Bob Patterson coming across the close-shaven grass of the Green.

I remember that the cheerful sun seemed to me to be at this moment darkened, not by any natural clouds or mists but as it is during an eclipse, and that the fresh trees and innocent flowers took on a ghastly and withered look.

It may appear a trivial detail, but I recall clearly his habit, which was of a luxury beyond his means – fine grey broadcloth with a deep edging of embroidery in gold thread, little suited to his profession.

As he saw me he cocked his hat over his eyes, but took no other notice of my appearance, and I turned away, not being wishful of any encounter with this gentleman while my spirit was in a tumult.

I went at once to my darling's house and learnt from her maid that she had left home two hours previously.

I do not wish to dwell on this part of my tale; indeed, I could not, it becomes very confused to me. The salient facts are these, that no-one saw Ann Leete in bodily form again.

And no-one could account for her disappearance; yet no great comment was aroused by this, because there was no-one to take much interest in her and it was commonly believed that she had disappeared from the importunity of her lovers, the more so as Rob Patterson swore that the day of her disappearance he had had an interview with her in which she had avowed her intention of going where no-one could discover her; this, in a fashion, was confirmed by what she had told me, and I was the more inclined to believe it, as my inner senses told me that she was not dead.

Six months of bitter search, of sad uneasiness, that remain in my memory blurred to one pain, and then, one autumn evening as I came home late and dispirited, I saw her before me in the gloaming, tripping up the street wearing her dark-green silk dress and tartan or Roman scarf.

I did not see her face, as she disappeared before I could gain on her, but she held to her side one hand and between the long fingers I saw the haft of a surgeon's knife.

I knew then that she was dead. And I knew that Rob Patterson had killed her.

Although it was well known that my family were all ghost-seers, to speak in this case was to be laughed at and reprimanded.

I had no single shred of evidence against Dr Patterson. But I resolved that I would use what powers I possessed to make him disclose his crime. And this is how it befell.

In those days in Glasgow it was compulsory to attend some place of worship on the Sabbath, the observation of the holy day being enforced with peculiar strictness and no-one being allowed to show themselves in any public place during the hours of the church services, and to this end inspectors and overseers were employed to patrol the streets on a Sabbath and take down the names of those who might be found loitering there.

But few were the defaulters, Glasgow on a Sunday being as bare as the Arabian desert.

Rob Patterson and I both attended the church in Rutherglen Road, towards the Green and the river.

And the Sunday after I had seen the phantom of Ann Leete, I changed my usual place and seated myself behind this young man.

My intention was to work on his spirit so as to cause him to make public confession of his crime. And I crouched there, behind him, with a concentration of hate and fury forcing my will on his during the whole of the long service. I noticed he was pale and that he glanced several times behind him, but he did not change his place or open his lips, but presently his head fell forward on his arms as if he was praying, and I took him to be in a kind of swoon brought on by the resistance of his spirit against mine. I did not for this cease to pursue him; I was, indeed, as if in an exaltation and I thought my soul had his soul by the throat, somewhere above our heads, and was shouting out: 'Confess! confess!'

One o'clock struck and he rose with the rest of the congregation, but in a dazed kind of fashion; it was almost side by side that we issued from the church door.

As the stream of people came into the street they were stopped by a little procession that came down the road.

All immediately recognised two of the inspectors employed to search the Sunday streets for defaulters from church attendance, followed by several citizens who appeared to have left their homes in haste and confusion.

These people carried between them a rude bundle which some compassionate hand had covered with a white linen cloth; below this fell a swathe of dark-green silk and the end of a Roman scarf.

I stepped up to the rough bier. 'You have found Ann Leete,' I said.

'It is a dead woman,' one answered me. 'We know not her name.'

I did not need to raise the cloth; the congregation was gathering round us, and amongst them was Rob Patterson.

'Tell me, who was her promised husband, how you found her,' I said.

And one of the inspectors answered: 'Near here, on the Green, where the wall bounds the grass, we saw, just now, the young surgeon Rob Patterson lying on the sward, and put his name in our books, besides approaching him to enquire the reason of his absence from church. But he, without excuse for his offence, rose from the ground, exclaiming, "I am a miserable man! Look in the water!"

'With that he crossed a stile that leads to the river and disappeared, and we, going down to the water, found the dead woman, deep tangled between the willows and the weeds – '

'And,' added the other inspector gravely, 'tangled in her clothes is a surgeon's knife.'

'Which,' said the former speaker, 'perhaps Dr Patterson can explain, since I perceive he is amongst this congregation – he must have found some quick way round to have got here before us.'

Upon this all eyes turned on the surgeon, but more with amaze than reproach.

And he, with a confident air, said: 'It is known to all these good people that I have been in the church the whole of the morning, especially to Eneas Bretton, who sat behind me and, I dare swear, never took his eyes from me during the whole of the service.'

'Aye, your *body* was there,' I said.

With that he laughed angrily and, mingling with the crowd, passed on his way.

You may believe there was a great stir. The theory put abroad was that Ann Leete had been kept a prisoner in a solitary ruined hut that was up the river, and then, through fury or fear, slain by her jailor and cast into the river.

To me all this is black; I only know that she was murdered by Rob Patterson.

He was arrested and tried on the circuit. He there proved beyond all cavil that he had been in the church from the beginning of the service to the end of it; his *alibi* was perfect. But the two inspectors never wavered in their tale of seeing him on the Green, of his self-accusation in his exclamation; he was very well known to them and they showed his name written in their books.

He was acquitted by the tribunal of man, but a higher power condemned him. Shortly after he died by his own hand, which God armed and directed.

This mystery, as it was called, was never solved to the public satisfaction, but I know that I sent Rob Patterson's soul out of his body, to betray his guilt and to procure my darling Christian burial.

This is the tale Eneas Bretton, that ancient man, told me on the old terrace as he sat opposite the picture of Ann Leete.

'You must think what you will,' he concluded; 'they will tell you that the shock unsettled my wits or even that I was always crazed. As they would tell you that I dream when I say that I see Ann Leete now and babble when I talk of my happiness with her for fifty years.'

He smiled faintly; a deeper glory than that of the autumn sunshine seemed to rest on him. 'Explain it yourself, sir. *What was it those inspectors saw on the Green?*'

He slightly raised himself in his chair and peered over my shoulder. '*And what is this,*' he asked triumphantly, in the voice of a young man, 'coming towards us now?'

I rose, I looked over my shoulder.

Through the gloom I saw a dark-green silk gown, a woman's form, a pale hand beckoning.

My impulse was to fly from the spot, but a happy sigh from my companion reproved my cowardice. I looked at the ancient man, whose whole figure appeared lapped in warm light, and as the apparition of the woman moved into this glow, which seemed too glorious for the fading sunshine, I heard his last breath flow from his body, with a glad cry. I had not answered his questions; I never can.

Kecksies

Two young esquires were riding from Canterbury; jolly and drunk, they shouted and trolled, and rolled in their saddles as they followed the winding road across the downs.

A dim sky was overhead and shut in the wide expanse of open country that one side stretched to the sea and the other to the Kentish Weald.

The primroses grew in thick posies in the ditches, the hedges were full of fresh hawthorn green, the new grey leaves of eglantine and honeysuckle, the long boughs of ash with the hard black buds, the wand-like shoots of sallow willow hung with catkins and the smaller red tassels of the nut and birch. Little the two young men heeded of any of these things, for they were in their own country that was thrice familiar; but Nick Bateup blinked across to the distant purple hills and cursed the gathering rain.

'Ten miles more of the open,' he muttered, 'and a great storm blackening upon us.'

Young Crediton, who was more full of wine, laughed drowsily. 'We'll lie at a cottage on the way, Nick – think you I've never a tenant who'll let me share board and bed?' He maundered into singing:

> There's a light in the old mill
> Where the witch weaves her charms,
> But dark is the chamber
> Where you sleep in my arms.
> Now come you by magic, by trick, or by spell
> I have you and hold you,
> And love you right well!

The clouds overtook them like an advancing army; the wayside green looked vivid under the purplish threat of the heavens and the birds were all still and silent.

'Split me if I'll be soaked,' muttered young Bateup. 'Knock up

one of these boors of thine, Ned – but damn me if I see as much
as hut or barn.'

'We come to Banells farm soon – or have we passed it?' answered
the other confusedly. 'What's the pother? A bold bird as thou art and
scared of a drop of rain?'

'My lungs are not as lusty as thine,' replied Bateup, who was
indeed of a delicate build and more carefully dressed in greatcoat
and muffler.

'But thy throat is as wide!' laughed Crediton. 'And God help you,
you are shawled like an old woman – and as drunk as a Spanish
parrot.

> Tra la la, my sweeting,
>   Tra la la, my May,
> If now I miss the meeting
>   I'll come some other day.

His companion took no notice of this nonsense, but with as
much keenness as his muddled faculties would allow, was looking
out for some shelter, for he retained sufficient perception to en-
able him to mark the violence of the approaching storm and the
loneliness of the vast stretch of country where the only human
habitations appeared to be some few poor cottages far distant in
the fields.

Ned lost his good humour and as the first drops of stinging cold
rain began to fall, he cursed freely, using the terms common to the
pot-houses where he had intoxicated himself on the way from
Canterbury.

Urging their tired horses, they came on to the top of the little
hill they ascended; immediately before them was the silver ashen
skeleton of a blasted oak, polished like worn bone, standing over a
small pool of stagnant water (for there had been little rain and much
east wind), where a few shivering ewes crouched together from the
oncoming storm.

Just beyond this, rising out of the bare field, was a humble cottage
of black timber and white plaster and a deep thatched roof. For the
rest the crest of the hill was covered by a hazel copse and then dipped
lonely again to the clouded lower levels that now began to slope into
the marsh.

'This will shelter us, Nick,' cried Crediton.

' 'Tis a foul place and the boors have a foul reputation,' objected
the lord of the manor. 'There are those who swear to seeing the

devil's own fizz leer from Goody Boyle's windows – but anything to please thee and thy weak chest.'

They staggered from their horses, knocked open the rotting gate, and leading the beasts across the hard dry grazing field, knocked with their whips at the tiny door of the cottage.

The grey sheep under the grey tree looked at them and bleated faintly; the rain began to fall like straight yet broken darts out of the sombre clouds.

The door was opened by a woman very neatly dressed, with large scrubbed hands, who looked at them with fear and displeasure; for if her reputation was bad, theirs was no better. The lord of the manor was a known roisterer and wild liver who spent his idleness in rakish expeditions with Sir Nicholas Bateup from Bodiam, who was easily squandering a fine property. Neither were believed to be free of bloodshed, and as for honour they were as stripped of that as the blasted tree by the lonely pool was stripped of leaves.

Besides they were both now, as usual, drunk.

'We want shelter, Goody Boyle,' cried Crediton, pushing his way in as he threw her his reins. 'Get the horses into the barn.'

The woman could not deny the man, who could make her homeless in a second; she shouted hoarsely an inarticulate name and a loutish boy came and took the horses, while the two young men stumbled into the cottage, which they filled and dwarfed with their splendour.

Edward Crediton had been a fine young man, and though he was marred with insolence and excess, he still made a magnificent appearance, with his full, blunt features, his warm colouring, the fair hair rolled and curled, and all his bravery of blue broadcloth, buckskin breeches, foreign lace, topboots, French sword, and gold rings and watch-chains.

Sir Nicholas Bateup was darker and more effeminate, having a cast of weakness in his constitution that betrayed itself in his face; but his dress was splendid to the point of foppishness and his manners even more arrogant and imposing.

Of the two he had the more evil repute; he was unwed and, therefore, there was no check upon his mischief; whereas Crediton had a young wife, whom he loved after his fashion and who checked some of his doings and softened others, and stayed very faithful to him and adored him still after five years of a wretched marriage, as is the manner of some women.

The rain came down with slashing severity; the little cottage panes were blotted with water.

Goody Boyle put logs on the fire and urged them with the bellows. It was a gaunt white room with nothing in it but a few wooden stools, a table, and an eel-catcher's prong.

On the table were two large, fair, wax candles.

'What are these for, Goody?' asked Crediton.

'For the dead, sir.'

'You've dead in the house?' cried Sir Nicholas, who was leaning by the fireplace and warming his hands. 'What do you want with dead men in the house, you trollop?'

'It is no dead of mine, my lord,' answered the woman with evil civility, 'but one who took shelter here and died.'

'A curse, witch!' roared Crediton. 'You hear that, Nick? Came here – died. And now you'll put spells on us, you ugly slut – '

'No spells of mine,' answered the woman quietly, rubbing her large clean hands together. 'He had been long ailing and died here of an ague.'

'And who sent the ague?' asked Crediton with drunken gravity. 'And who sent him here?'

'Perhaps the same hand that sent us,' laughed Sir Nicholas. 'Where is your corpse, Goody?'

'In the next room – I have but two.'

'And two too many – you need but a bundle of faggots and a tuft of tow to light it – an arrant witch, a confest witch,' muttered Crediton; he staggered up from the stool. 'Where is your corpse? I've a mind to see if he looks as if he died a natural death.'

'Will you not ask first who it is?' asked the woman, unlatching the inner door.

'Why should I care?'

'Who is it?' asked Sir Nicholas, who had the clearer wits, drunk or sober.

'Robert Horne,' said Goody Boyle.

Ned Crediton looked at her with the eyes of a sober man.

'Robert Horne,' said Sir Nicholas. 'So he is dead at last – your wife will be glad of that, Ned.'

Crediton gave a sullen laugh. 'I'd broken him – she wasn't afraid any longer of a lost wretch cast out to die of ague on the marsh.'

But Sir Nicholas had heard differently; he had been told, even by Ned himself, how Anne Crediton shivered before the terror of Robert Horne's pursuit, and would wake up in the dark crying out for fear of him like a lost child; for he had wooed her before her marriage and persisted in loving her afterwards with mad boldness and insolent confidence, so that justice had been set on him and he had been banished to the marsh, a ruined man.

'Well, sirs,' said Goody Boyle in her thin voice, that had the pinched accents of other parts, 'my lady can sleep of nights now – Robert Horne will never disturb her again.'

'Do you think he ever troubled us?' asked Crediton with a coarse oath. 'I flung him out like an adder that had writhed across the threshold – '

'A wonder he did not put a murrain on thee, Ned. He had fearful ways and a deep knowledge of unholy things.'

'A warlock – God help us!' added the woman.

'The devil's proved an ill master then,' laughed Crediton. 'He could not help Robert Horne into Anne's favour – nor prevent him lying in a cold bed in the flower of his age.'

'The devil,' smiled Sir Nicholas, 'was over-busy, Ned, helping *you* to the lady's favour and a warm bed. You were the dearer disciple.'

'Oh, good lords, will you talk less wildly with a lost man's corpse in the house and his soul riding the storm without?' begged Goody Boyle; and she latched again the inner door.

Murk filled the cottage now; waves of shadow flowed over the landscape; without the rain blotted the window and drowned the valley; in the bitter field the melancholy ewes huddled beneath the blasted oak beside the bare pool, the stagnant surface of which was now broken by the quick rain drops; a low thunder grumbled from the horizon and all the young greenery looked livid in the ghastly light of heaven.

'I'll see him,' said Ned Crediton swaggering. 'I'll look at this gay gallant in his last smock – so that I can swear to Anne he has taken his amorous smile to the earthworms – surely.'

'Look as you like,' answered Sir Nicholas, 'glut your eyes with looking – '

'But you'll remember, sirs, that he was a queer man and died queerly, and there was no parson or priest to take the edge off his going or challenge the fiends who stood at his head and feet.'

'Saw you the fiends?' asked Ned curiously.

'Question not what I saw,' muttered the woman. 'You'll have your own familiars, Esquire Crediton.'

She unlatched the inner door again and Ned passed in, bowing low on the threshold.

'Good day, Robert Horne,' he jeered.' We parted in anger; but my debts are paid now and I greet you well.'

The dead man lay on a pallet bed with a coarse white sheet over him that showed his shape but roughly; the window was by his head and looked blankly on to the rain-bitten fields and dismal sky; the light was cold and colourless on the white sheet and the miserable room.

Sir Nicholas lounged in the doorway; he feared no death but his own, and that he set so far away it was but a dim dread.

'Look and see if it is Robert Horne,' he urged, 'or if the beldame lies.'

And Crediton turned down the sheet. ' 'Tis Robert Horne,' he said.

The dead man had his chin uptilted, his features sharp and horrible in the setting of the spilled hair on the coarse pillow.

Ned Crediton triumphed over him, making lewd jests of love and death and sneering at this great gallant who had been crazed for love and driven by desire, and who now lay impotent.

And Sir Nicholas in the doorway listened and laughed and had his own wicked jeers to add; for both of them had hated Robert Horne as a man who had defied them.

But Goody Boyle stole away with her fingers in her ears.

When these two were weary of their insults they replaced the flap of the sheet over the dead face and returned to the outer room. And Ned asked for drink, declaring that Goody Boyle was a known smuggler and had cellars of rare stuff.

So the lout brought up glasses of cognac and a bottle of French wine, and these two drank grossly, sitting over the fire; and Goody Boyle made excuse for the drink by saying that Robert Horne had given her two gold pieces before he died (not thin pared coins, but thick and heavy) for his funeral and the entertainment of those who should come to his burying.

'What mourners could he hope for?' laughed Ned Crediton. 'The crow and the spider and the death-watch beetle?'

But Goody Boyle told him that Robert Horne had made friends while he had lived an outcast on the marshes; they were no doubt queer and even monstrous people, but they were coming tonight to sit with Robert Horne before he was put in the ground.

'And who, Goody, have warned this devil's congregation of the death of Robert Horne?' asked Sir Nicholas.

She answered him – that Robert Horne was not ill an hour or a day, but for a long space struggled with fits of marsh fever, and in between these bouts of the ague he went abroad like a well man and his friends would come up and see him, and the messenger who came up to enquire after him was Tora, the Egyptian girl who walked with her bosom full of violets.

The storm was in full fury now, muttering low and sullen round the cottage with great power of beating rain.

'Robert Horne was slow in dying,' said Sir Nicholas. 'Of what did he speak in those days?'

'Of a woman, good sir.'

'Of my wife!' cried Ned.

Goody Boyle shook her head with a look of stupidity. 'I know nothing of that. Though for certain he called her Anne, sweet Anne, and swore he would possess her yet – in so many words and very roundly.'

'But he died baulked,' said Ned, swaying on his stool, 'and he'll rot outside holy ground.'

'They'll lay him in Deadman's Field, which is full of old bones none can plough and no sheep will graze,' answered the woman; 'and I must set out to see lame Jonas, who promised to have the grave ready – but maybe the rain has hindered him.'

She looked at them shrewdly as she added: 'That is, gentles, if you care to remain alone with the body of Robert Horne.'

'I think of him as a dead dog,' replied Ned Crediton.

And when the woman had gone, he, being loosened with the French brandy, suggested a gross jest.

'Why should Robert Horne have all this honour, even from rogues and Egyptians? Let us fool them – throwing his corpse out into the byre, and I will lie under the sheet and presently sit up and fright them all with the thought it is the devil!'

Sir Nicholas warmly cheered this proposal and they lurched into the inner chamber, which was dark enough now by reason of a great northern cloud that blocked the light from the window.

They pulled the sheet off Robert Horne and found him wrapped in another that was furled up under his chin, and so they carried him to the back door and peered through the storm for some secret place where they might throw him.

And Ned Crediton saw a dark bed of rank hemlock and cried, 'Cast him into the kecksies!' that being the rustic name for the weed.

So they flung the dead man into the hemlocks, which were scarce high enough to cover him, and to hide the whiteness of the sheet, broke off boughs from the hazel copse and put them over him, and went back laughing to the cottage, and there kept a watch out from the front window, and when they saw Goody Boyle toiling along through the rain, Ned took off his hat and coat and sword and folded them away under the bed; then Sir Nicholas wrapped him in the under sheet, so that he was shrouded to the chin, and he lay on the pillow and drew the other sheet over him.

'If thou sleepst, do not snore,' said Nicholas, and went back to the fire and lit his long clay full of Virginian tobacco.

When Goody Boyle entered with her wet shawl over her head, she had two ragged creatures behind her who stared malevolently at the fine gentleman with his fine clothes and dark curls lolling by the fire and watching the smoke rings rise from his pipe.

'Esquire Crediton has ridden for home,' he said, 'but I am not minded to risk the ague.'

And he sipped more brandy and laughed at them, and they, muttering, for they knew his fame, went into the death chamber and crouched round the couch where Sir Nicholas had just laid Ned Crediton under the sheet.

And presently others came up, Egyptians, eel-catchers, and the like, outcasts and vagrants who crept in to watch by the corpse.

Sir Nicholas presently rolled after them to see the horror and shriekings for grace there would be when the dead man threw aside his shroud and sat up.

But the vigil went on till the night closed in and the two wax candles were lit, and still Ned Crediton gave no sign, nor did he snore or heave beneath the sheet; and Sir Nicholas became impatient, for the rain was over and he was weary of the foul air and the grotesque company.

'The fool,' he thought (for he kept his wits well even in his cups), 'has gone into a drunken sleep and forgot the joke.'

So he pushed his way to the bed and turned down the sheet, whispering, 'This jest will grow stale with keeping.'

But the words withered on his lips, for he looked into the face of a dead man. At the cry he gave they all came babbling about him and he told them of the trick that had been put upon them.

'But there's devil's work here,' he ended. 'For here is the body back again – or else Ned Crediton dead and frozen into a likeness of the other.' And he flung the sheet end quickly over the pinched face and fair hair.

'And what did ye do with Robert Horne, outrageous darefiend that ye be?' demanded an old vagrant.

And the young lord passed the ill words and answered with whitened lips: 'We cast him into yon bed of kecksies.'

And they all beat out into the night, the lout with a lantern.

And there was nothing at all in the bed of kecksies . . . and Ned Crediton's horse was gone from the stable.

'He was drunk,' said Sir Nicholas, 'and forgot the part – and fled that moment I was in the outer room.'

'And in that minute did he carry Robert Horne in alone and wrap him up so neatly?' queried Goody Boyle.

'We'll go in,' said another hag, 'and strip the body and see which man it be – '

But Sir Nicholas was in the saddle.

'Let be,' he cried wildly; 'there's been gruesome work enough for tonight – it's Robert Horne you have there – let be. I'll back to Crediton Manor – '

And he rode his horse out of the field, then more quickly down the darkling road, for the fumes of the brandy were out of his brain and he saw clearly and dreaded many things. At the crossroads when the ghastly moon had suddenly struck free of the retreating clouds he saw Ned Crediton ahead of him riding sharply, and he called out: 'Eh, Ned, what have you made of this jest? This way it is but a mangled folly.'

'What matter now for the jest or earnest?' answered the other. 'I ride home at last.'

Sir Nicholas kept pace with him; he was hatless and wore a shabby cloak that was twisted about him with the wind of his riding.

'Why did not you take your own garments?' asked Sir Nicholas. 'Belike that rag you've snatched up belonged to Robert Horne – '

'If Crediton could steal his shroud, he can steal his cloak,' replied Ned, and his companion said no more, thinking him wrought into a frenzy with the brandy and the evil nature of the joke.

The moon shone clear and cold with a faint stain like old blood in the halo, and the trees, bending in a seaward wind, cast the recent rain that loaded them heavily to the ground as the two rode into the gates of Crediton Manor.

The hour was later than even Sir Nicholas knew (time had been blurred for him since the coming of the storm) and there was no light save a dim lamp in an upper window.

Ned Crediton dropped out of the saddle, not waiting for the mounting-block, and rang the iron bell till it clattered through the house like a madman's fury.

'Why, Ned, why this panic homecoming?' asked Sir Nicholas; but the other answered him not, but rang again.

There were footsteps within and the rattle of chains, and a voice asked from the side window: 'Who goes there?'

And Ned Crediton dragged at the bell and screamed: 'I! The master !'

The door was opened and an old servant stood there, pale in his bed-gown.

Ned Crediton passed him and stood by the newel-post, like a man spent yet alert.

'Send someone for the horses,' said Nick Bateup, 'for your master is crazy drunk. I tell you Mathews, he has seen Robert Horne dead tonight – '

Crediton laughed: the long rays of the lamplight showed him pale, haggard, distorted, with tumbled fair hair and a torn shirt under the mantle, and at his wrist a ragged bunch of hemlock thrust into his sash.

'A posy of kecksies for Anne,' he said. The sleepy servants who were already up began to come into the hall, and looked at him with dismay.

'I'll lie here tonight,' said Sir Nicholas; 'bring me lights into the parlour. I've no mind to sleep.'

He took off his hat and fingered his sword and glanced uneasily at the figure by the newel-post with the posy of kecksies.

Another figure appeared at the head of the stairs. Anne Crediton holding her candle, wearing a grey lute-string robe and a lace cap with long ribbons that hung on to her bosom; she peered over the baluster and some of the hot wax from her taper fell on to the oak treads.

'I've a beau pot for you, Anne,' said Crediton, looking up and holding out the hemlocks. 'I've long been dispossessed, Anne, but I've come home at last.'

She drew back without a word and her light flickered away across the landing; Crediton went up after her and they heard a door shut.

In the parlour the embers had been blown to flames and fresh logs put on, and Sir Nicholas warmed his cold hands and told old Mathews, in a sober manner for him, the story of the jest they had striven to put on Goody Boyle and the queer monstrous people from the marsh and the monstrous ending of it, and the strangeness of Ned Crediton; it was not his usual humour to discourse with servants or to discuss his vagrant debaucheries with any, but tonight he seemed to need company and endeavoured to retain the old man, who was not reluctant to stay, though usually he hated to see the dark face and bright clothes of Nick Bateup before the hearth of Crediton Manor.

And as these two talked disconnectedly, as if they would fill the gap of any silence that might fall in the quiet house, there came the wail of a woman, desperate yet sunken.

'It is Mistress Crediton,' said Mathews with a downcast look.

'He ill uses her?'

'God help us, he will use buckles and straps to her, Sir Nicholas.'

A quivering shriek came brokenly down the stairs and seemed to form the word 'mercy'.

Sir Nicholas was an evil man who died unrepentant, but he was not of a temper to relish raw cruelty or crude brutalities to women; he would break their souls but never their bodies. So he went to the door and listened, and old Mathews had never liked him so well as now when he saw the look on the thin, dark face.

For the third time she shrieked and they marvelled that any human being could hold her breath so long; yet it was muffled as if someone held a hand over her mouth. The sweat stood on the old man's forehead. 'I've never before known her complain, sir,' he whispered. 'She is a very dog to her lord and takes her whip mutely – '

'I know, I know – she adores his hand when it caresses or when it strikes; but tonight, if I know anything of a woman's accents, that is a note of abhorrence – '

He ran up the stairs, the old man panting after him with the snatched-up lantern.

'Which is her chamber?'

'Here, Sir Nicholas.'

The young man struck on the heavy oak panels with the hilt of his sword.

'Madam – Madam Crediton, why are you so ill at ease?'

She moaned from within.

'Open to me. I'll call some of your women – come out – '

Their blood curdled to hear her wails.

'Damn you to hell,' cried Sir Nicholas in a fury. 'Come out, Ned Crediton, or I'll have the door down and run you through.'

The answer was a little break of maniac laughter.

'She has run mad or he,' cried Mathews, backing from the room. 'And surely there is another clamour at the door – '

Again the bell clanged and there were voices and tumult at the door; Mathews went and opened, and Sir Nicholas, looking down the stairs, saw in the moonlight a dirty farm cart, a sweating horse, and some of the patched and rusty crew who had been keeping vigil in Goody Boyle's cottage.

'We've brought Esquire Crediton home,' said one; and the others lifted a body from the cart and carried it through the murky moonlight.

Sir Nicholas came downstairs, for old Mathews could do nothing but cry for mercy.

'It was Edward Crediton,' repeated the eel-catcher, shuffling into the hall, 'clothed all but his coat and hat, and that was under the bed – there be his watches and chains, his seals and the papers in his pockets – and for his visage now, there is no mistaking it.'

They had laid the body on the table where it had so often sat and larked and ate and drunk and cursed; Sir Nicholas gazed, holding up the lantern.

Edward Crediton – never any doubt of that now, though his face was distorted as by the anguish of a sudden and ugly death.

'We never found Robert Horne,' muttered one of the mourners, trailing his foul muddy rags nearer the fire and thrusting his crooked hands to the blaze.

Mathews fell on his knees and tried to pray, but could think of no words.

'Who is upstairs?' demanded Sir Nicholas in a terrible voice. 'Who is with that wretched woman?'

And he stared at the body of her husband.

Mathews, who had loved her as a little child, began gibbering and moaning.

'Did he not say he'd have her? And did not yon fool change places with him? Oh God, oh God, and has he not come to take his place – '

'But Robert Horne was *dead*. I saw him dead,' stammered Sir Nicholas, and set the lantern down, for his hand shook so the flame waved in gusts.

'Eh,' shrieked old Mathews, grovelling on his hands and knees in his bed-gown. 'Might not the devil have lent his body back for his own pitchy purposes?'

They looked at him a little, seeing he was suddenly crazed; then Sir Nicholas ran up the stairs with the others at his heels and thundered with his sword, and kicked and shouted outside Anne Crediton's chamber door.

All the foul, muddy, earthy crew cowered on the stairs and chittered together, and in the parlour before the embers old Mathews crouched and huddled and whimpered.

The bedroom door opened and Robert Horne came out and stood and smiled at them, and the young man in his fury fell back and his sword rattled from his hand to the floor.

Robert Horne was a white death, nude to the waist and from there swathed in grave-clothes; under the tattered dark cloak he had ridden in was his shroud knotted round his neck; his naked chest gleamed with ghastly dews, and under the waxen polish of his sunken face the decayed blood showed in discoloured patches; he went down the stairs and they hid their faces while his foul whiteness passed.

Sir Nicholas stumbled into the bedchamber. The moonlight showed Anne Crediton tumbled on the bed, dead and staring, with the posy of kecksies on her bare breast and her mouth hung open and her hands clutching at the curtains.

The mourners rode back and picked up Robert Horne's body whence it had returned to the kecksie patch and buried it in unholy ground with great respect, *as one to whom the devil had given his great desire*.

Ann Mellor's Lover

I have always been interested in clairvoyance – after all, I hardly know anyone who isn't; but my interest has always been rather overwhelming – a kind of haunting preoccupation, wholly pleasant but teasing, like something you can't place or explain or reason about always must be.

I've never gone in for it scientifically, never had the time or the money – or perhaps, the courage.

But I've studied – well, all that kind of thing, half-furtively, and thought about it a great deal.

Of course, it hasn't helped really – I mean not in explaining the queer things that have happened to me.

This is one of them.

I feel bound to put it down while it is clear in my mind. I find that unless I put these things into words I lose them. They become faded, then confused, and finally disappear altogether. It's a great diversion to me, a great interest, and sometimes a queer sort of pain too.

I haven't very much else in my life. Just an old bookshop that I keep myself and that keeps me quite comfortably. My father kept the shop before me, and I've hardly ever left it – it was through the books that the clairvoyance began, when I was quite a youth.

I say clairvoyance, but that is merely because I don't know the right word or the exact word or a better word – I don't mean crystal-gazing or raising spirits or anything of that kind.

I mean my peculiar affinity with the past. It is like a kind of second sight; but instead of seeing into the future, I can see into the past. Only now and then, of course, and fitfully and not at will.

Little glimpses are offered me now and then – tantalising, some-times no use at all, sometimes startlingly complete, as this was.

I can't explain it. I've heard it called race memory and cited as proof of reincarnation. I don't know what to believe.

This is the tale.

One day I was undoing a parcel of secondhand books; they had lain in the shop some time, and I rather forgot where they had come from. I buy a great many books and from many strange places. There wasn't much in the parcel, though some of the bindings were good – calf and vellum.

I picked up one of these – a fat volume of an enticing brown colour faintly traced with gold – and was looking for the half-effaced title when a loose sheet fluttered from between the covers on to the floor.

I picked it up and found it was a rubbed pencil drawing of a girl's head. Nothing much in that, yet from that first second I set eyes on the thing I knew it was significant and vital. I knew that it was a clue that I was bound to follow through the labyrinth of the past. The feeling really was that I knew all about it – the whole story, but could not for the moment remember it.

Just a small pencil drawing on a neat square of yellowed paper; no signature or initials or date.

No help in the book, which was merely a volume of outrageously dull Nonconformist sermons printed a hundred and seventy years ago.

No help in the costume (I think I am an expert in that, and can place a period by a bow or ringlet), for the girl's hair flowed unconfined in a perfectly natural fashion, and the sketch stopped at the curve of the bare throat.

She was dark and lively, looked at once wild and weak, and her eyes sought mine with a direct appeal.

'Now who *are* you?' I asked myself. 'Who *are* you?'

I felt sure that I knew her and should soon know all about her – not at once and suddenly, but slowly, by the following up of small clues, as had happened to me before.

There was an old gilt frame in the shop among my lumber of fine old odds and ends, and I put the sketch into this, adjusting it carefully behind the glass, the frame being much too large, and then took it upstairs and hung it in my little parlour.

I was filled with the greatest curiosity and excitement. I felt that what I was going to find out affected me very closely and personally. I was entirely absorbed by this thought as I went about my business that day, and when evening came and the shop was shut I hastened upstairs to make myself comfortable in my old leather chair, fill my pipe, and stare at the pencilled head that hung above my mantelpiece.

I imagined that as I sat and gazed at her the whole thing would come back to me – as it sometimes did, a clear glimpse, a scene flashing out of the darkness of the past.

But this evening nothing came but two words that leapt into my mind and would not go – one was 'Norway' and the other 'Nightingale'.

I was very disappointed, for the words meant nothing to me – no possible clue whatever; I knew nothing of Norway and had never even been attracted to the country; and 'Nightingale' was a mere word to me also, devoid of every association.

Yet I knew they must be connected in some way with my pencil sketch – the first feeble beginnings, as it were, of my fumblings into the past.

For two days nothing happened. For two days that face looked at me – no pencil lines on a bit of yellow paper, but now a warm-coloured human face; she lived before my inner eye, a complete creature. Her hair was dark brown and it hung in rather fine curls; the carnation of her face was glowing and warm; her expression flashed from resentment to appeal, and was always, bewildered.

In my mind I could not quite see her dress – but I thought that she wore something white, frilled, and that her background had water in it; that is, that she moved or lived in some place where there was water.

On the third day after my discovery of the pencil sketch that had affected me so powerfully, I attended a sale at an old house in rather on out-of-the-way part of London.

There were some fine old books there that I bought very cheaply, and I was quite pleased with my afternoon's work. This satisfaction did not, however, interfere with my absorption in the unknown, dark, troubled creature about whom I felt such excitement. I discovered no further clues to her identity nor anything that explained the words, so persistently in my mind, of 'Norway' and 'Nightingale.'

I turned for home very briskly. It was late December and brightly cold. I took the shortest cut I could to the nearest Tube station, asking my direction as I went, for I was not sure of my way in this neighbourhood, which was one of those fallen from sub-stantial splendour into a kind of gloomy respectability. Heavy stone houses, built about fifty years ago, darkened the streets, and, hemmed in by these, I suddenly came upon an old church and churchyard, railed round neatly and divided by a paved path, which I knew to be my short cut through. I saw at a glance that the restored church was uninteresting and the rows of grey and white tombstones affected me with a sense of mere futile ugliness. I was hurrying on with a sense of the uncomfortable nip in the air and the grey dullness of my surroundings when *something* brought me to a sudden stop.

I found myself clinging to the railings of the churchyard, staring at a heavy square stone tomb, which was again surrounded by an iron railing, through which some patches of recent snow had drifted and now lay soiled and frozen.

There was one simple inscription on the flat side of the tomb:

ANN MELLOR
Who died in the 23rd year of her age, 1750

'A broken and contrite heart, O Lord,
Thou wilt not despise.'

There was nothing strange in this, save that no names of relationship or residence were given. The text I had seen before on gravestones, but not often; it had always seemed to me too obvious an appeal to sentiment to be taken quite seriously.

But now I trembled with excitement and curiosity. I knew and felt that this was *she*.

I managed with some difficulty to mount the railings and examine the tomb all round. There was no further inscription – nothing whatever.

Still, I now knew her name, her age, the year she died. Ann Mellor! It was so familiar that I wondered how it was I had not recalled it before. I made my way through the tombs and found a gate near the church door.

It took me very little time to get hold of the verger and receive permission to look at the registers – but there was little reward for my pains. The entry was there accurately enough: 'Ann Mellor, spinster, of this parish, aged twenty-two years.'

The date of the entry was December 24th, 1750.

So she had died in December and been buried on Christmas Eve.

I knew this much more about her, and I went on my way quite elated and shivering with a desperate kind of excitement.

In about another ten minutes in the colourless twilight I wandered round the neighbourhood, knowing quite well how useless it was. How could there be any relics of 1750 – a hundred and seventy years ago – among these massive Victorian houses, these wide modern streets?

'Why,' I reflected, 'the place must have been in the country then – that church stood among fields – *she* used to come here by coach –

yes, a small yellow-and-black coach. I can see her in it, with a wide hat and a black lace scarf tied under it, and – '

The picture was blurred again: I only knew that *she* used to come to this church by coach, a small black-and-yellow coach.

I remembered that the book from which the pencil sketch had fallen had borne the date 1749 – probably it had been in Ann Mellor's possession during the last year of her life.

The thought of this book allured me. I was about to decide to get home to scrutinise it further when I found myself almost running into a wooden hoarding, which in my absorption and the now encroaching darkness I had not noticed, stretched directly across the street, which was one of mean, drab, low-windowed villas that appeared to be mostly untenanted. I perceived that the fence enclosed a piece of waste ground; I placed my eye to a knot-hole in the wood and saw by the dismal white of the electric light given from the street lamp that the ground was covered with builders' rubbish and the skeletons of half-demolished houses.

The sight was very dreary, yet as had the churchyard, it gave me no effect of depression. I stood quite a long time, regardless of the cold, staring at the heaps of fallen masonry, the scaffolding poles, the patches of shadow, the splotches of bleached light from the electric standard.

At last I turned and retraced my steps down the cul-de-sac.

At the corner I glanced up at the name of the street – 'Palmyra Villas.' There was a policeman passing, and I asked him if this atrocious name was also that of the last portion of the street which was being demolished.

'No,' he said; 'they used to call that *Nightingale* Lane. A nice old slum it was, too. Condemned it, they did, and time too.'

'It wasn't always a slum,' I said.

'Not likely. Fine old houses some of them was; quite a lot of chaps came over here buying knockers and fanlights and other bits. All gone now, though,' he replied.

He evidently took me for a prowling and mercenary antique dealer. I fostered the idea and got from him the name of the firm doing the housebreaking.

Nightingale Lane – *she* had lived there – but not always, because she used to come to church by coach. 'Of this parish' – not *lived*, but *died* there. Nightingale Lane – perhaps the nightingales had sung near here in 1750 – one hundred and seventy years ago.

After that I went home and wrote neatly on the edge of my pencil sketch: 'Ann Mellor, who died in Nightingale Lane on Christmas Eve, 1750.'

Though I had found out so much, there seemed no opening for further investigation; yet I was not at all troubled – I knew that soon everything would be made clear to me.

It was not, of course, a question of coincidence (personally I do believe that there is such a thing), but of finding out, through this peculiar faculty of mine, the story of Ann Mellor.

I knew that this story had something to do with me; I felt such an extraordinary intimacy and interest, such an excitement, nay, palpitation at the thought of Ann Mellor.

I was not in the least distracted by the fact that I had looked at her tomb and read the entry of her death one hundred and seventy years ago. This death seemed to me a mere incident that we, she and I, had long left behind. A visit to the housebreakers of Nightingale Lane, a patient research among the purchasers of the oddments from the old tenements procured little result.

But there was a silver shoe-buckle found buried in the cellar of one of the houses. That I bought at once.

'Why, that was *her* house, the house at the corner,' I said. 'And I remember going down to the cellar, when . . . '

It was all blurred again – only just that glimpse when I recalled the house, and going down to the cellar, and losing a shoe-buckle in the dark, and searching a little for it, then giving it up impatiently. This connected me personally with Ann Mellor. I began to feel that we had been together in curious scenes – it was all blurred, dark, troubled, but I knew that I should understand very soon.

The haunting of the word 'Norway' puzzled me very much – it did not seem to fit into the story at all.

That evening I took the pencil sketch, the book from which it had fallen, the silver buckle, and holding all of them tightly in my hand, concentrated on an effort to find out more of the person or persons to whom they had belonged.

Usually when I did this my second sight, or clairvoyance or whatever you called the faculty I had, rewarded me with distinct visions or pictures.

This time there was nothing.

Instead, I felt there was somewhere I ought to go – impelled as it were, to get up and walk to some given point.

I put on my hat and coat, placed my treasures in my pocket, and hurried out. It was evening, wet and cold, and just at the hour when the theatres are full and the streets empty. Quite automatically and without knowing in the least where I was going, I walked rapidly to Oxford Street, then turned sharply to the left in the direction of the Marble Arch.

I was rather surprised and disappointed, for I thought I had been guided in the direction of Ann Mellor's tomb and the ruins of Nightingale Lane. This part of the world appeared to have no association whatever with the story I was trying to discover.

The great closed opulent shops with the expanses of shining glass looked blank and alien, as did the long glimmer of the polished road, along which the huge and gaudy motorbuses rolled through the murky night splashed with artificial light.

I crossed Park Lane to the Marble Arch, crossed again, and walked along by the Park railings.

'My God!' I said suddenly, 'I've been here before.' A sudden pang of rage and terror possessed me, and I had a distinct vision of *pine forests, mountains, and a large lake or bay* – flashed, like a photo picture on the screen, across the dark fronts of the heavy houses fronting me.

The road was empty, and I swung across impulsively. In the centre I stopped and put my hand to my throat. I knew that I had reached the end of my journey.

Under my feet was the metal triangle let into the pavement to mark the site of Tyburn gallows.

I turned away very quickly, shuddering under the drizzling rain.

How did this sinister place enter into the story of Ann Mellor? And what was the meaning of that clearcut little vision of pines and mountains and lake?

I fell into an extreme agitation, and the material objects about me became unreal; they seemed to wane and roll away as if they were painted on a curtain that was being pulled aside.

I thought of what I had heard and read of the fourth dimension.

That night when I went to bed I put the book, the buckle and the sketch under my pillow.

I knew what was going to happen and half dreaded it, yet deliberately prepared for it.

I was going to meet Ann Mellor. As I closed my eyes and lost all sensation of time and space, there seemed a second's black unconsciousness. When I opened my eyes, I was standing at a little window that looked down from some height on to the Thames. There were ice-floes on the grey water, and the air was chill. By looking up the river I could see a vast amount of shipping; great masted vessels crowding together in the broad reach of the river.

A few seagulls swooped and swerved in front of me – gleaming, yet white and grey, like the river and the ice-floes.

I turned to face the room, which was completely panelled in plain wood. The floor sloped a little and the door was low; a tea equipage stood on the table; the fireplace had Dutch tiles with little figures in blue.

The room affected me with a delicious sense of home, and yet – something poignant and heartsearching.

The low door opened. And *she* entered.

She wore a white muslin dress all frilled, and carried a calf-bound book.

'You like to keep me waiting,' I said, speaking English awkwardly.

Ann Mellor went to the tea-table.

'Mrs Briscoe says you come too often,' she said. 'Do you come too often, Eric – do you?'

I faced her. 'You are a hussy and lead me on. You will not let me stay away.'

She gave me a look, half smile, half frown, of wayward passion.

'Ay, bully me,' she said. 'That is my thanks and my reward. My aunt scolds because you come – and this is your gratitude.'

'You'll marry me, you pretty little wretch, and then there will be an end of these quarrels,' I said.

'God helping me, no,' she answered; 'I'll not marry you.'

'You will,' I swore.

I was close to her now, only the table between us, and her provoking face was a short space from mine.

The delicious magic of that moment seemed intolerable; when I held and kissed her, the joy of it seemed unbearable. It was supreme, but more a supreme pain than a supreme satisfaction. She had played fast and loose with me for so long – now yes, now no, denying, provoking – and I looked back on a life that had held very little denial or provocation.

'You have got to marry me,' I said. 'You are nothing but a girl, and I'll make you.'

'I'll not marry a foreigner,' she pouted.

'A penniless jade like you to choose! I am a rich man,' I boasted. 'I could put three thousand pounds into your English bank tomorrow.'

An elderly woman joined us and my chance was over. She looked on me with disfavour, and scolded Ann for trifles.

I was bored, but would not go for fear of missing another opportunity of talking to Ann alone. I picked up the book she had brought in and took it to the window. It was a dull volume of sermons, very new and stiff in the binding.

I yawned.

I took out my pocket-book and pencil and under cover of the open book made a pencil sketch of Ann as she sat at the tea-table bickering with Mrs Briscoe. When I had finished the sketch I idly shut it up in the book and put the book on the windowsill.For another half-hour I sat there listening to the women gossiping and scolding, then I rose.

I looked at Ann insolently, tormented by the thought of her crushed in my arms, angry with her for ignoring me.

'Will you come to church this Sunday, as usual, Ann?' I asked.

'Leave her at peace in church, do, Mr Ericson!' cried the aunt. 'And we will not go to the Nightingale Lane Church tomorrow – it is too far.'

'Yes, we will go,' said Ann. 'I like the preacher and the coach ride.'

She looked at me as she spoke, and I went straight up to her and took her by the shoulders, regardless of the other woman.

'My little love,' I said, 'do not deny me any more. Have you ever thought of death? We might be dead and cold – think how cold, these hearts of ours – before the spring is in flower – '

'Dead,' she laughed – 'dead!'

'Dead and love frustrate.'

Mrs Briscoe drew her away from me. 'God save us from these foreign manners,' she shrilled. 'You are nothing but a North Sea rover – '

I laughed very heartily at this, for I was one of the richest timber merchants in Kristiansund, and I swaggered away, fingering the sword on my hip.

As I walked through the streets of Wapping I was making plans to abduct the girl and marry her by force.

First I went to Nightingale Lane, looking for lodgings, and found them at the house of Mrs Porter. Then I went to the Black Bull in Holborn and picked up with some town bullies of my acquaintance, and arranged matters with them over a bottle of Tokay.

Two sham bailiffs were to arrest her for an imaginary debt on her way to church – to bring her to me at the Black Bull, where we should be married, I having my clergyman ready, and then I would take her to Nightingale Lane, near the church she so loved.

Here I cannot very well remember sequences – all is blurred, as by the haste and excitement of violent action.

I knew that for several hours I was moving about hastily in great agitation and temper from one place to another, chiefly between Wapping, the Black Bull, and Nightingale Lane.

Always was the cold, the rain, the scatters of snow, the iron-coloured river, the lead-coloured sky.

My schemes succeeded perfectly.

The sham bailiffs stopped the coach and forced out Ann Mellor, leaving Mrs Briscoe shrieking vainly in the grey silence of the wet Sunday morning, and brought her to me where I waited in the private room at the Black Bull.

My darling was brought in, not without indignity. I did not wish to spare her; I felt all the cruelty that passionate love will often show towards the beloved object.

'I knew that it was you,' she said.

'Of course you knew it was I,' I replied – what other man was there who would so dare to mishandle her?

I thought that she would appeal to my rascal clergyman or my ruffian witnesses, but she did not.

And we were married and left alone.

'Take me away from here,' she said; 'anywhere from this vile tavern.'

'I've lodgings,' I said, 'in Nightingale Lane.'

She turned her head away when I came near her, only repeating, 'Take me away.'

'You must watch your temper now, madam,' I smiled. 'You are my wife.'

At that she broke into violent weeping, like a little child, and gave me a deal of trouble to get her away into the coach.

When we reached our lodgings, which seemed the dearest place in the world to me, my wife fell from tears to abuse and railed incoherently. I tried to humour her.

'Why, Ann,' I said, 'you know this is the best manner in which to deal with your tiresome relatives – come, look up and kiss me. You know that you love me.'

'And if I do,' she answered, with the foolish inconsistency of women, 'does not that make it worse?'

So we quarrelled, she tragic, I smiling, till the landlady brought up the supper.

I asked her for some of the wine I had had sent in from the Black

Bull yesterday, and she, grumbling, said it was in the cellar and had no mind to go there in the dark. So I took the key and the candle and went myself.

One of the buckles was loose and slipped on my shoe. I smiled to see it, thinking of Ann sewing it on for me, and laughing over the thread.

I stood awhile in the cellar, forgetful of my errand, thinking that this was my wedding night and how I loved my darling.

I thought of my own home, and how I would take her there, and the great joy and contentment we should have together.

When I had selected my wine, I noticed, in stooping, that the loose buckle was lost. As I searched for it, a draught blew my candle out, and being in the dark I gave up the business and went upstairs.

I found the house full of strangers; Mrs Briscoe was there with two of my wife's uncles and four constables. I understood amid the noise and confusion (I could not understand the English so very well) that I was to be arrested on a charge of abduction.

I laughed in their faces. I was so sure of Ann. 'The lady will tell you herself,' I said, 'that she is very willingly my wife.'

'Swagger away, my fine young man,' sneered Mrs Briscoe; 'you are nowt but a foreign bully.'

'Ann will tell you what she thinks of me,' I answered.

We all went into the little room where she was. She must have heard us coming, for she stood ready, against the table. She still wore her hat with the black lace under it round her chin, and her dark cape over her white dress.

When she saw her relatives and the constables crowding in, she crossed instantly over to me and put her hand in mine.

I felt as if I should suffocate with the glad leap my heart gave. I placed my bottle of wine on the table.

'You see,' I said, 'my wife stands by me.'

Ann took her hand away. They asked her formally if she was a willing party to her elopement and marriage.

'Cannot you see,' she cried, 'by the way you find me that I am here by outrage and deceit?'

'Girl,' I asked aghast, 'do you deny your husband?'

'Had I had my will you would have been no husband of mine,' she said bitterly.

I could afford to laugh at this, knowing how she loved me, but the others seized on her statement and made her swear to it, which the passionate girl did.

'I'll hurt you as you hurt me,' she cried. 'This shall be a black day's work for you.'

I let them disarm and arrest me; I did not know much of the English laws, and I asked what my punishment would be.

One of the uncles answered me. 'The girl's an heiress. In stealing her you've stolen property.'

'Twenty pounds a year and a thousand in the Government!' I answered. 'What is that to me? I am a rich man.'

'No matter. You've committed a felony. We look after property in this country. If you are found guilty, it is the gallows.'

Ann and I looked at each other. 'See how you frustrate love,' I said.

'I did not mean what I said,' she stammered; 'I married him willingly – '

'The girl speaks in pity,' said Mrs Briscoe; 'I can prove how she was forced away – '

The girl tried to get at me now, but was forced back.

'This is a bitter marriage night,' I said. As they took me away, I heard her laughing like a maniac.

So I last saw her, down on her knees, holding them all at bay, laughing like a maniac.

I woke up in my little bedroom above the bookshop, and took from under the pillow the pencil sketch I had made so long ago, the book Ann was reading that day, and the buckle I had lost on my marriage day in the cellar in Nightingale Lane. It was all absolutely clear now; I remembered the trial, the walk to Tyburn, that devastating vision of my own land that had come upon me as I reached the fatal spot.

Two sentences of my dying speech stuck in my mind. I said, 'I die for transgressing a law I knew not of'; and again, 'I am so much in charity with my wife that I believe she had no hand in this.'

I was rather curious to see what history had said of my case, so, that day being a Saturday, I went to the British Museum as soon as the shop was shut and looked up the trials for the year 1750. I could not find any full report here, nor did I trouble to search for it. The brief record was sufficient.

At Tyburn, in December 1750, was hanged Eric Ericson, a wealthy young Norwegian of good family, for the abduction and marriage of Ann Mellor, heiress of the late William Mellor, a merchant, of Wapping. He pleaded the complicity of the girl, but she denied him at first, retracting too late. Her relatives obtained permission to annul the marriage and for the girl to retain the name of Mellor.

I felt very exultant and triumphant.

'She died of it,' I said, as I closed the book, 'in Christmas week my darling died. She went back to the lodgings I had taken for her. They could not do anything with her. She turned away from them all and died.'

I hurried home through the iron December twilight as I had hurried before to Nightingale Lane. At last I was going to be happy with Ann Mellor.